Striking a chord . . .

Joan backed up to head into the kitchen again, wondering if she should wait until Miriam had found solid evidence, wondering if she was an idiot for believing Miriam at all. Distracted, she bumped into the corner of the desk. The beautiful guitar propped against it went tumbling sideways to the floor.

DJOAAAANNNNN! jangled the guitar strings.

They both stared at the guitar a moment. Then Joan shook her head and picked up the instrument by the neck. "Oh, shit, I hope I didn't damage it."

"It said your name," Miriam whispered.

"Now stop it!" Joan said. "We're getting all weirded out over nothing."

"Strum it," Miriam said.

"What?"

"Joan, please! I think . . . maybe it tried to speak to us."

"Oh, God, this is ridiculous. Listen." Joan propped up her leg on the sofa and strummed the open strings.

Joooaaaannnn . . .

KARA DALKEY

CRYSTAL SAGE

A ROC BOOK

ROC
Published by the Penguin Group
Penguin Putnam Inc., 375 Hudson Street,
New York, New York 10014, U.S.A.
Penguin Books Ltd, 27 Wrights Lane,
London W8 5TZ, England
Penguin Books Australia Ltd,
Ringwood, Victoria, Australia
Penguin Books Canada Ltd, 10 Alcorn Avenue,
Toronto, Ontario, Canada M4V 3B2
Penguin Books (N.Z.) Ltd, 182–190 Wairau Road,
Auckland 10, New Zealand

Penguin Books Ltd, Registered Offices:
Harmondsworth, Middlesex, England

First published by Roc, an imprint of Dutton NAL, a member of Penguin
Putnam Inc.

First Printing, May, 1999
10   9   8   7   6   5   4   3   2   1

Chapter 1

Joan Dark pulled her truck into the parking lot of the Dawson Butte Condominiums and beeped the horn. And waited. Two bleary-eyed faces peered down from windows at her, neither of them Miriam's. The engine of the truck rumbled like a purring dragon between the stucco walls of the condo complex. Joan felt conspicuous, her Ford F150 parked amid the Mercedeses and Volvos. She leaned back and tapped the steering wheel. She stared at the transplanted foliage in the condo landscaping and wondered how much water they were wasting to keep the ferns and ivy green. Still no Miriam. Joan's new trainee had many good qualities, but promptness, it was becoming clear to Joan, was not one of them.

Joan poised her hand over the horn to beep again and then stopped. Any of the residents might someday become clients of her cleaning service, and there was no point in giving a bad impression. She considered hanging some flyers on doorknobs. The residents seemed to have the right demographics—too rich and too busy to deal themselves with the habitat they lived in. Joan mentally kicked herself for thinking in biz-speak and decided to forget the doorknobs. She was already late to her morning appointment at Gillian's place and didn't want to be any later than she had to.

Joan found it was getting warm in the truck cab, even though it was only 8:00 a.m. It was going to be a hot June day on the Front Range. She hopped out of the truck and leaned against the front fender, running her hand through her short blond hair in mild exasperation.

She glanced around, trying to remember what the land had looked like before the condos were built. It had once been the McClusky ranch. Joan hadn't known the McClusky family well, although her family had gone to a few cookouts and parties with them when she was a child. She seemed to recall the McCluskys owned a few too many sheep to be real popular. She couldn't remember now just where the barn had stood, the condo landscapers had done such a good job of changing the lay of the land. There was even a big artificial pond now where Joan was certain no body of water had been before. As if by magic, the landscapers had erased all the history, geological and human, of the area. Joan thought it sad to see the places she'd loved as a kid vanishing.

Joan wondered if the current condo residents ever thought about what lay beneath their foundations, what had been before. *Probably not. That's why they bought condos. Nice, anonymous places to hang your expensive prints and store your skis. Far as they're concerned, the only thing location provides is a pretty view out the window.*

Joan felt a familiar funk coming on and tried to stifle it. She stared at the door and steps leading out of the condo building and tried to will Miriam to appear. Miriam believed in all sorts of strange powers of the mind. *Only been working with her three weeks and already I'm starting to think like her.*

Joan noticed the paint was starting to peel on her business logo on the truck door. Under a rainbow of the words "Joan Dark Cleaning Service" was a cartoon figure of Joan of Arc in full armor, but bearing a broom instead of a sword. Joan had gotten flak from French ex-pats, Euro-trash, and feminists alike over it. Which was why she kept it—any logo people noticed was a good sign, so to speak.

She heard a door slam behind her and turned to see Miriam finally rushing down the concrete steps. Despite Joan's warnings to wear old and unloved clothes, Miriam was dressed in her usual New Age gypsy garb: long madras skirt, peasant blouse, sandals, and a bandanna tied around her long, wavy brown hair.

Joan managed a smile but no words in edgewise as Miriam rushed over to the passenger-side door. "Hi! G'morning! Sorry I kept you waiting, but I got caught up in today's reading and I just had to finish it and explore it a little further and like that. You won't believe what came up!" She flung herself breathlessly onto the bench seat.

"You're right," Joan said sardonically as she levered herself back into the truck cab. "I won't." She put the truck into reverse and added, "What was it this time? Tea leaves? Bible readings? Goat entrails?"

Miriam grinned, not at all embarrassed. "Goat entrails! Now there's the stuff—I'd try it, but do you have any idea how much goats cost these days?"

"Actually, I do. About a hundred and twenty dollars or so per goat, depending on the breed. But, hey, I could give you good tips for cleaning up afterward."

"Hmm. Pricey. I bet the neighbors would complain about the smell, too. You know how picky condo associations get."

"Actually, I don't. But I've heard stories."

"They're all true," Miriam said and then laughed.

Joan pulled out onto the frontage road that ran along I-25. She had to admit Miriam had a nice laugh. It wasn't phony, like some folks'. Miriam was strange, but it was genuine strangeness, if there could be such a thing, and Miriam was good-humored about it. "So?"

"So what?"

"So what was the reading you got so caught up in?"

"Oh! You know, just the good old tarot."

"Good ol' tarot? Is that a special deck with good ol' boys on it? Maybe with the suits of rifles, beer, trucks, and dogs?"

Miriam laughed again. "Now that would be something, wouldn't it? Kinda negative energy unless you played it for fun, like I guess the King of Beer would have to be holding a Budweiser. No, I use the Aquarian deck, usually. I try to do a reading every day, just to get focused in the morning, you know?"

"I find coffee does the trick for me." Joan turned right onto Devil's Head Road and noticed there was a new mini strip mall being built on the corner. "Man," she muttered, "I could swear that wasn't there last week. Those things are popping up like prairie dogs."

"Only the real prairie dogs don't get to live there anymore," sighed Miriam.

"Yeah, well, that's no great loss," said Joan. "They're just pests." Miriam gave her a disapproving raise of an eyebrow, so Joan quickly changed the subject. "Did you know Dawson Butte's got an expresso bar now?"

"Espresso. Really? Cool."

"Whatever. What's it doing here? We're miles and miles from the nearest ski resort!"

"Hey, it's a place where the hindigirls from the ashram and the boys from the Air Force Academy can get together."

"Oh, yeah, I'll bet that would lead to some Dates from Hell. But an expresso bar? No doubt about it. Dawson Butte is being Californicated. Ooops. Uh, no offense, Malibu girl."

Miriam shrugged. By now she was probably used to the slurs and "negative energy" Coloradans directed at Californians who moved into the state. At least, Joan hoped so.

"Anyway," Joan hurried on, "pretty soon this town will look just like Boulder. Here's a prediction for you—in ten, twenty years the Front Range will be all one megacity from the Springs to Fort Collins."

"Do you want to hear about the reading," Miriam said with a gently tolerant smile, "or do you just want to vent?"

"Oh. Sorry," Joan said. "I think I got out on the proverbial wrong side of the bed this morning."

Miriam nodded. "That would fit."

"Fit what?"

"The reading. It said there'd be an overturning of things."

"Come to think of it, I did knock a glass of water off the nightstand when I got up."

"Well, there you are. A portent. See, the final card, the one that's supposed to be a summation of the whole reading, was the Tower."

"Should I be hearing ominous music in the background?"

"Maybe."

"What's it look like, this Tower card?"

"It shows a stone tower being hit by lightning and two people falling from it."

"So . . . we should stay out of church steeples and high-rises?"

"No! You're not supposed to take it *literally*," Miriam said with mild exasperation. "It just means something will happen that changes completely the way we see our lives or the world. Profound transformation. Like they say on one of my dad's Firesign Theatre albums, 'Everything you know is wrong.' "

"Fireside what? Is that some Boomer rock group?"

Miriam sighed. "Never mind. Tell me about our job today. What dragons are Joan Dark and Company going to slay in our eternal battle against the forces of Entropy?"

"I think you're getting your mythology mixed up. It was Saint George who slew dragons. Saint Joan just killed Englishmen. Anyway, our *client* today is an old friend of mine from ninth grade. She's back in town for the summer, working on her master's thesis. She wanted cleaning help so she could just concentrate on her work."

"Cool. What's her thesis on?"

"How should I know? She was studying musicology, I think, up at CU Boulder. Look, just remember, our job is to clean her place, not to socialize. If she's home, we should be as unobtrusive as possible and not distract her with too much chitchat. If she isn't home we're not supposed to analyze the furnishings, okay?"

With a little mock salute, Miriam said, "Got it, Chief."

"Good." Joan doubted, however, that the mini-lecture would have any effect. Miriam was actually a good worker, once she concentrated on the job. But she also couldn't resist "reading" a room or handling objects and making guesses about the personality of the owner. Damnable thing was, she was right more often than she should have been. Joan figured Miriam was just a good observer, a budding Sherlock Holmes who should have gone into forensic science instead of the hoo-hah she dabbled in now. At least that was the most comforting explanation.

Joan hadn't really planned on taking a trainee so soon. She had as many clients as she could handle, but she wasn't overworked. And she was surprised that Miriam Sanderson, who was from a well-off family who'd made their money in real estate development, had chosen to apprentice herself to a house cleaner. Miriam could surely have gotten a job in a tourist gift shop or an entry-level position in any major corporation on the Front Range. It was true that Joan's and Miriam's fathers were friends. But despite what Miriam often claimed about cleaning being "honest work," Joan figured there was something odd going on. She hadn't had the nerve to pry, but she wondered if her dad had felt they owed Mr. Sanderson a favor since the Sanderson Development Company had gone and bought the Dark family ranch.

The truck jerked suddenly, and Joan realized she had unconsciously stomped on the brakes.

"What's wrong?" said Miriam, sitting up and looking around.

"Nothing, nothing." Joan shook her head, bewildered. "Just . . . uh, I thought I saw a critter starting to run across the road. Guess it was just dust or litter or something."

"That's okay. It's nice that you brake for animals."

"Um, yeah." Joan started up again, glad they were only a block from Gillian's place.

It was in an older, prairie style house that had been split into a triplex. Gillian's apartment was a converted attic. Joan's only complaint about this was that it meant she had to haul the vacuum cleaner up a couple of flights of outside stairs. She pulled into the shaded driveway and parked, then strapped on her utility belt (Miriam called it the "bat belt"), which held a couple of spray bottles, rags, sponges, rubber gloves, and rolled-up garbage bags. Suitably attired for battle with grease, dust, and grime, Joan ascended the wooden stairs. She made Miriam haul up the vacuum—it's what trainee sidekicks were for.

But at the top landing, Joan paused. Gillian's door was ajar. Gently, she pushed it further open. "Hello? Gillian? It's me, Joan. You home?" There was no answer.

"Anything wrong?" Miriam puffed as she came up behind.

"Probably not. She probably just went down to the store for something." Dawson Butte was a small enough town that some people still left their doors unlocked. Though these days, given the traffic between Denver and the Springs, it probably wasn't as safe as it used to be. Joan stepped into the apartment and glanced around.

It looked as it had the two times she had come to clean before, cluttered and untidy. If there were signs of an altercation she probably wouldn't have been able to spot them. The desk just ahead of her was scattered with paper, beneath which she could see part of an electronic keyboard. The computer was on, and the monitor was displaying a screen saver that looked like sheet music. To her right, what passed for a living room had cushions and throws strewn over the secondhand furniture. To her left, she could see the tiny alcove kitchen, which was stacked with dirty dishes. The futon on the floor in the closet bedroom beyond was piled with rumpled sheets and coverlet. Nothing unusual.

"Ooh, bad *feng shui*!" said Miriam, entering behind her.

"Bad what?"

"The, you know, the arrangement. Look, she's got her desk and her chair so that her back is to the door when she's working. And just past the desk is a big picture window, so the luck runs in the door, hits her in the back, and jumps right out the window, boom-boom-boom. See?"

Joan paused, wondering whether to be rude or diplomatic. Choosing the latter, she said, "No, but I'll take your word for it. After all, the old poker players of the West used to say you should never sit with your back to the door."

"Well, they knew a lot about luck, didn't they?"

"Yeah. Guess so. Okay, now—"

"Oooh, pretty guitar! Does she play?" Miriam had squatted down and was inspecting a shiny acoustic guitar of blond wood that leaned against the desk.

"I don't know! She's a musicologist, so probably she does."

"Yeah? Wow. Looks like she's got a MIDI rig on her

computer. You can shape sounds every which way with those."

"Shape sounds?"

"Yeah, I know. It seems a contradiction in terms, but you can. It's really cool. My brother used to do stuff like that for this studio he worked for. . . ." She trailed off, lost in memories.

Joan sighed. "Look, Miriam, remember what I said about paying attention to the job? Now, our instructions are that we are to tidy up the living area and the kitchen, but we are absolutely not to touch anything on the desk, and we can leave the bedroom alone. Got that?"

"What? Oh, yeah. Sure." Miriam slowly stood, staring again at the guitar.

"Okay. You can start straightening up this room. Feel free to use the vacuum whenever you're ready. I'll go tackle the kitchen. All right?"

Miriam took a deep breath and swung her arms like a child burning off energy, or warding off something. "Yeah. Sure. Sounds good."

"Okay." Joan went into the kitchen, shaking her head. She was beginning to wonder if Miriam might just be too distractible for this job. Or any job, other than detective or working for some psychic phone service. Joan glared at the stacks of dishes and glasses and wished that Gillian owned an automatic dishwasher. But at least she had a double sink. Joan put the stopper into one drain, poured in a little detergent, and began to run the hot water into the left tub of the sink. She gently placed the dishes in to soak, and then began to spray and wipe down the counter. One thing good about Gillian's place—it was so small it didn't take long to clean.

After a few minutes, Joan realized she wasn't hearing any movement from the other room. She wondered what Miriam had found to fascinate her now. *Hope it isn't the computer or the stuff on the desk.* Joan leaned over and glanced out the kitchen doorway.

Miriam was standing in the center of the living room, hugging a cushion and staring abstractedly at the wall. It looked like she had hardly begun to straighten up.

"Miriam?" Joan walked out of the kitchen, preparing another mini-lecture.

"Something's wrong," Miriam said, and the way she said it made Joan's skin prickle.

"What? What have you found?"

Miriam shook her head. "It's . . . it's just . . . a feeling. Something happened here."

Joan steeled herself to patience. "Miriam, I . . . respect your ability to notice things. But I'm not about to call 911 and tell the guys down at the station to come over just because you feel some bad vibrations or something."

"No, no. I understand."

"If you see anything tangible, like bloodstains, or ripped clothes, freshly broken furniture, or like that, then we'll stop everything and call the police, okay?"

"Yeah," Miriam said softly, glancing all around as if not wanting to look at anything for very long. "Okay."

Joan backed up to head into the kitchen again, wondering if she should wait until Miriam had found solid evidence, wondering if she was an idiot for believing Miriam at all. Distracted, she bumped into the corner of the desk. The beautiful guitar propped against it went tumbling sideways to the floor.

DJOAAAANNNNNN! jangled the guitar strings.

They both stared at the guitar a moment. Then Joan shook her head and picked up the instrument by the neck. "Oh, shit, I hope I didn't damage it."

"It said your name," Miriam whispered.

"Now stop it!" Joan said. "We're getting all weirded out over nothing."

"Strum it," Miriam said.

"What?"

"Joan, please! I think . . . maybe it tried to speak to us."

"Oh, God, this is ridiculous. Listen." Joan propped up her leg on the sofa and strummed the open strings.

Joooaaaannnn . . .

And in the diminishing harmonics she heard . . .

> *oh help, please help me help me*
> *ow ow ow ow ow ow ow ow ow*
> *I'm scared I'm scared I'm scared*
> *please help please help please help*

Joan nearly dropped the guitar.

"You hear that?" Miriam said.

Joan stared at the instrument and said, "I get it. This is some high-tech trick. Gillian set it up for us to find and she's either videotaping this or hiding somewhere laughing her head off. Very funny, Gillian! You can come out now."

The apartment was silent except for the hum of the computer.

"I don't think it's a trick," Miriam said. "Let me see the guitar."

"Sure." Joan gave it to her, glad to get it out of her hands. The wood had felt too warm beneath her fingers.

Miriam peered inside the sound hole and ran her hand around the sides and back. "There aren't any pickups inside or outside. It can't be an electronic effect."

"Maybe they're built right into the wood. You know how chips keep getting smaller these days. You said she had a special sound rig on her computer." Still unsettled, Joan conducted a search of the apartment, opening closets and peering under furniture. There were very few places a person could hide, and none of them held Gillian, nor did Joan see a conspicuous video camera.

When she returned to the living room, Miriam was sitting on the sofa with the guitar on her lap. "Gillian, is that you?" she said to the instrument. She plucked a string.

Meeeeee, sang the guitar.

Miriam plucked more notes and Joan heard,

> *no trick no trick*
> *please help please help*
> *it's me it's me*

Swallowing hard, Joan knelt down beside Miriam. "Gillian. If that is you, what happened to you?" She nodded at Miriam to play something.

Miriam began a fairly complex picking style, which produced such a cacophony of words and notes that Joan couldn't make sense of what the guitar was saying:

> *work on pa per*
> *don't   mis take   came   old*
> *   know   bal lad   some   how*
> *   dis turbed old   power lay of*
> *am a dan   made   me   gui tar help*
> *   ow   eep   that   tick les stop it*
> *   stop it   stop it!*

Joan reached up and grabbed the instrument's neck. She felt as though she were stopping someone's mouth. "Miriam, that isn't working. Just try playing one note over and over, okay?"

"Okay."

> *don't-know-don't-know-oh-God-the-man-in-gray-the-man-in-gray-did-this-said-my-work-dis-turbed-him-oh-please-help*

"I've heard of men in black, but a man in gray?" Joan asked.

"Aren't they the sort of space alien that abducts people?" Miriam asked.

Aliens Turned My Friend into a Guitar. Joan could imagine the headline on the tabloids. *Wonder if they'd pay big bucks for the story.* Getting back to reality, Joan said, "She mentioned her work. Gillian, is there some clue on your desk?"

Miriam plucked.

Noooo, sang the string, *don't touch stay a way from desk*

"She says stay away from it," Miriam said.

"I heard her." Joan went to the desk anyway and glanced over the scattered paper. A file folder labeled "Amadan Project" stuck out from the midst of the pile and Joan carefully tugged it out. She opened it and read the first page of hand-scrawled notes, but didn't understand the academese written there. "We need to have more information of some kind if we're going to do anything."

"So you believe it now?"

Joan rolled her eyes. "I don't know, but I don't have any other explanation yet. And I'm sure as hell not going to call 911 and tell them my friend's turned into a guitar." She turned her attention back to the file and grumbled, "Boy, when your cards said 'profound transformation' they weren't kidding."

"Yeah," sighed Miriam. "Can't get more profoundly transformed than this. Definitely a Fortean phenomenon."

"A what?"

"You know, Charles Fort, the guy who studied anything weird? He was a phenomenologist. Or maybe I'm getting it confused with pataphysics, the study of things that only happen once."

"Sounds crazy to me."

"No, that's right, it was invented by Jarry, and he only pretended to be mad."

"Will you stop babbling and let me concentrate? Maybe you could call this Fort guy and ask him about this."

"I'm not a medium, Joan. Fort is long dead. Besides, he never explained anything, just documented the appearance."

"Well, we'd sure have something to show him." Joan found toward the bottom of the file a piece of cream-colored stationery with a heraldic shield at the top depicting a green cross and harp. "Aha. I think I've found something." She read aloud:

"Dear Miss McKeagh,

"Please accept my apologies for this letter appearing "out of the blue," as it were, but we have only just come across your letter to Father O'Donnell among his effects. It is apparent that he never answered your correspondence, and on behalf of the rectory I should like to apologize. Father O'Donnell, I fear, was of wandering mind in his later years and although a dear soul, was not always to be relied upon. Now that he has passed away, God rest him, we are attempting to sort out some of his unfinished work.

"The manuscripts you cited are, indeed, in our collection, and I must congratulate you on your research, Miss McKeagh, for we ourselves were unaware of their existence until very recently. Father O'Donnell was very protective of the library, and since his departure we have discovered quite a few items which he had stored away for safekeeping, apparently unrecorded.

"Naturally we feel, as he did, that because of the delicate condition of these ancient musical works, they cannot be moved. But given your demonstrated scholarship, and your local relatives who speak proudly of your accomplishments, we would be pleased to allow you to view the documents you request, should you ever be in Ireland.

"Huh," Joan said. "The page ends there, and the next page of the letter is missing." Joan searched through the rest of the file in vain.

"Okay," said Miriam, "so she was looking up old Celtic manuscripts. We have the first clue."

"Not much of a clue," said Joan. "Here's part of Gillian's notes. Looks like she was doing a translation of something." Joan read:

"By the command of the holy fathers, I write this confession in the hope that it will bring the forgiveness of God, that He will lift from my kin the punishment now visited upon us for our great sin of consorting with the powers of darkness. From father to son has the Lay of the Amadan been taught, since before the holy cross was made known in our fair land. He who had the sweetest voice and most cunning hands was taught it. To play the seven'—word unreadable—'in the'—unreadable—'upon Midsummer Eve will bring forth the Amadan, the Gray Lord, Prince of the Fair Folk. So loves he the music that untold'—unclear—'blessings'? 'gifts'?—'are shown to the player. Long has our family thought him an angel, but the holy fathers have now made it known to us he is none but Lucifer, and the misfortunes that now befall us must prove that they are right. Let it be known that my father's lute, long prized as one of the Amadan's gifts, was cast into the flames and the unholy screams that issued from it as it burned showed to us the holy fathers' truth."

Joan's voice trailed off, and she turned to look at the guitar. The final sentence had made her shiver.

"A screaming lute," murmured Miriam, hugging the guitar protectively. "So maybe Gillian isn't the first person ever turned into a musical instrument."

"Assuming we believe all this."

"You know, Midsummer Eve *was* last night," Miriam added, eyebrows raised apologetically.

"Damn. This is weirder than *The X-Files*. Let's see what's on the computer."

"Joan, Gillian said—"

"I'll be careful." Joan hit the return key and the screen saver faded, revealing the typical PC desktop screen. Joan peered at it until she saw an icon labeled "Amadan Seq.1." Finding the mouse under another pile of paper, Joan ran the cursor over to the desktop icon and clicked.

Haunting, ethereal music swirled out of the speakers and seemed to hover around Joan like living spirits. Sounds that were not quite human voices and chimes that were not quite bells as well as violins combined with the sounds of wind in rustling leaves, birdsong, and the gurgle of a rushing brook. Joan felt transported, sensed the shade of ancient oaks around her, could almost smell the loam of virgin forest . . .

And then it stopped abruptly, the ensuing silence like being encased in lead. Joan looked down and saw Miriam sprawled on the floor, holding the plug of the computer cord that she had just pulled out of the surge protector power strip. "Sorry," Miriam said with a rueful smile. "The guitar told me to."

"You might have wrecked her computer doing that," Joan growled, annoyed that the beautiful music had stopped and annoyed with herself for being annoyed.

"Might have wrecked you if I let it go on," said Miriam. "It was pretty, wasn't it? Kind of reminded me of some of Kitaro's stuff."

Joan blinked. "You . . . you weren't . . . affected by it?"

"You were in the focus of the speakers, I wasn't. Maybe that made the difference."

There were footsteps coming up the outer stairs. Joan

froze in panic, then sighed with relief as she saw the middle-aged landlady push open the door.

"Hello? Oh, hello, Joan. Cleaning day today, huh?" Agnes was short, gruff, with a leathery face and reeking of cigarettes, but she always seemed happy to see Joan. Joan supposed that given the way Gillian kept house, Agnes was just glad somebody was taking care of the place.

"Hi, Agnes. Yep, we just came to clean. This is my new assistant, Miriam. We were just, uh, straightening up Gillian's stuff. The music didn't disturb you, did it? I hit one of her computer keys by accident."

"Oh, no. I just thought Gillian must be up here, and I came to talk to her. You seem a little nervous, dear. Anything the matter?"

"Well, when we got here, the door was open and Gillian . . . wasn't here, so we were a little concerned."

"Yeah," Miriam chimed in, as she stood up. "And we were looking around to see if everything was . . . all right . . . here." She raised her hands in an awkward gesture to indicate the room and the guitar slipped and fell onto the floor.

> Ow   hel lo   hel lo
> Ag nes   Ag nes
> sor ry   sor ry
> owwwwww

The landlady frowned at the guitar. "Did that thing just talk to me?"

"Uh, yeah," Joan quickly improvised, "it's a trick guitar. A little thing Gillian's been working on. Programmable and everything. She thinks it could be a popular gift item. So, anyway, we were trying it out and were waiting around to tell Gillian about what we thought of it when she gets back."

"Huh, imagine that," Agnes said, shaking her head. "The things they do with technology these days. Well, I expect that Mr. Amadan fellow found her, then, and she's out talking with him."

Joan and Miriam shared a look. "Amadan?" Joan asked. "You know who he is? That is, we've heard Gillian mention him, and it might be important. For us to know. About him. In case we have to reach her."

The landlady blinked and said, "Well, I've only seen him once, today when he came around asking for her. I think I still have his card. Let me see." She felt around in the pockets of her housedress and came up with a business card. "Yes, here it is." She handed it to Joan.

It was silvery and shone when angled toward the light. All it said was "Brian Amadan," and beneath that in smaller letters, "Development Specialist."

"Damn," said Joan. "There's no address or phone. What did he look like?"

"A very handsome gentleman. Foreign, I think. Wore a beautiful gray suit. Armani, I bet. He had gray hair but doesn't look that old, tied back in a ponytail, you know, Hollywood-style. Very gracious. Made me blush like a schoolgirl."

"Do you know what he wanted to see Gillian about?" Joan asked.

The landlady frowned. "I don't remember now. It was something connected with her studies, that's all."

"Uh-huh."

The landlady peered around the room, noting the clutter in vague disapproval. "Well, dear, if you see her, tell her she still owes me this month's rent. I gave her a few weeks leeway just this once because I know she's on a student's budget, but I have bills to pay too."

"Sure, Agnes. I'll tell her."

"Thank you, dear." With a nod to Miriam, the landlady left.

As soon as the footsteps had gone some way down the stairs, Joan went back over to Miriam and the guitar.

"Good cover," Miriam said.

Joan wasn't sure if she was being sarcastic. "Uh, thanks." Joan held up the business card in front of the guitar's tuning pegs. "This is the guy, right, Gillian?"

Yessss, sang the string Miriam picked.

"He turned you into a guitar?"

Yesssss

"He can change you back?"

Don't know watch out bad guy

"Okay, okay. We'll be careful. Do you know where we can find him?"

Nooooo

"Well, shit, that's a big help."

"Here, let me see the card," said Miriam, holding out her hand.

"Sure." Joan put the card in her palm. Miriam's hand jerked violently as if the card burned her, and it fell to the floor.

"What's the matter?"

"I don't know," Miriam said, frowning. She bent over and picked up the card carefully with just her fingertips.

"Can you . . . you know, read something off of that?"

Miriam winced. "I'd rather not."

"I don't suppose your . . . talents can tell us where he is right now?"

"I'm not real good at psychic location. I only get those kinds of impressions when I'm not trying to." Miriam placed the card gently onto her left palm and gasped.

"What is it?"

"Wow. I get the sense of something old. And cold. And powerful. Shit, I don't like this, Joan." She handed the card back.

Joan took it and turned it over and over. She couldn't "feel" anything from it, other than that it had probably been very expensive to make. "I don't like it any better than you do. But what are we gonna do? It says 'Development Specialist,' whatever that means. If it's real estate, maybe your dad knows him."

"Maybe. Worth a shot. I'll give Dad a call." Miriam gently set the guitar down on the couch and went to the phone on the desk. She dialed. "Hello? Oh, hi, Mom. Is Dad in? Well, maybe you can help us. I was wondering if he knew another developer by the name of Brian Amadan." She spelled it out, then waited. "He isn't? Okay, thanks for trying." Hanging up, Miriam said, "That name isn't in Dad's Rolodex."

"Oh, well. We could try the phone book."

"He's not from around here," Miriam said.

"How do you know?"

Miriam frowned and fluttered her hands in a frustrated gesture. "I just . . . it just felt . . . foreign."

"Like Europe?"

Miriam shook her head. "Like Elsewhere."

"Some sort of elfland, you mean?"

Miriam folded her arms tightly across her chest. "Yeah, but not the warm, friendly Tolkien kind."

Joan sighed. "This is crazy. If you're right, what in the Sam Hill are *we* supposed to do about it? Unless you have some *really* magical powers you haven't told me about."

" 'Fraid I don't," Miriam said. "But we have to try to help her. If you'd been turned into a guitar, how would you feel?"

Joan rested her hand on one warm curve of the guitar. "Pretty scared, I guess. But . . . how? Where do we even start?"

Miriam sat on the edge of the disheveled sofa. "Knowledge is power. We've got to learn more about this Amadan guy."

"Right. And then what? March right into the big bad guy's hideout so he can tie us up and tell us all about his evil plot to take over the world by turning everyone into accordions and banjos until the good guy comes along and rescues us?"

"Oh, chill *out*, Joan. This isn't a TV movie-of-the-week. Besides, you left out the two car chases and the mandatory love interest."

"How could I forget? Maybe Pinky and the Brain are behind it all and all we'll need is a couple of mousetraps."

"If only it could be that easy," said Miriam. She crossed her eyes and said, "*Narf!*"

They both laughed awkwardly, then stared at the floor in silence for a long moment.

"This is real, isn't it?" Joan asked softly.

"Yeah," said Miriam. "Guess so."

"Damn." Joan felt a sickening heaviness in her gut, same as when her dad told her he was selling the ranch; a feeling that meant her life was about to change irreversibly, and not for the better. "Well, we don't have any more jobs lined up for today. So I guess we can spend this afternoon doing research. After that . . . we'll see. If this Amadan guy is in business anywhere, he will have left a trail. He has to, if he's going to get money out of anyone. We just have to find out what business he's in or pretending to be in."

"If it's money he's after." Miriam thought a moment. " 'Development specialist' could mean lots of things. If not property . . . maybe he teaches women how to get bigger boobs."

"Miriam!"

"Sorry, just thinking out loud. It's possible, you know. Development could also be psychological, or spiritual. . . . If I were a real sorcerer . . ." Her words trailed away, and she stared off into space.

"What is it?"

"There's a New Age shop in town. If this guy has any connections in the Front Range spiritual communities, that's a place to start."

"Angels and crystals and junk, oh my."

Miriam sighed. "This isn't the time to be judgmental. Remember what you've got on your lap there."

"Oh, yeah, sorry," Joan said, looking down at the beautiful guitar. "You're right, it's a place to start. Let's finish up here and go."

"What? You want to keep cleaning after all this?"

"The landlady will get suspicious if we don't. And we might come across some more clues. And Gillian already paid me for the month. I owe her the job."

Chapter 2

The New Age place Miriam had in mind was in a nondescript storefront that, Joan recalled, used to be a Laundromat. The sign above the door read THE ANGEL'S WING, painted in pink, purple, and silver. It was situated on a shaded avenue off Main Street, and Joan instinctively parked the truck under a tree so that the cab wouldn't get too warm.

Joan left Gillian-the-guitar wrapped in a blanket in the space behind the truck seats. She hoped the landlady hadn't seen them leaving with the guitar, and hoped she could come up with a good story if accused of stealing it. Now she felt guilty leaving the truck windows shut, as if Gillian were a puppy that might overheat. *God, I don't even know what sort of care and feeding she needs in her current form*, Joan thought. *If any.*

Miriam didn't wait for Joan, but hopped out of the truck and ran up the sidewalk and into the store. Joan envied Miriam's casual acceptance of the situation. Joan had long ago ceased to believe in miracles or the supernatural and had stopped attending the Lutheran church her family went to as soon as her parents would let her. Having to think again about the possibility of powers beyond her understanding didn't sit well with her. Joan stood on the sidewalk halfway from the truck to the shop and found herself wishing desperately that she could again be out on the ranch, riding her horse, Misty. That had always been good for troubled times—letting Misty amble beneath the pines and cotton-woods over the buttes, seeing the high plains stretching away for miles to the east, the Rockies rising in the west, smelling the scent of the sage and prairie grasses. That was the balm to soothe her soul.

But the horse was dead these five years now, and the ranch was sold, and Joan had to face her new troubles without them. She turned and went into the shop, wind chimes tinkling as the front door opened and closed.

Miriam was already at the counter, chatting with a young guy. Joan glanced around the shop. There were the usual bookshelves, knickknacks, statuary, clothing, jewelry, monotonous music, and faint scent of incense. Still, Joan noticed the effect was rather soothing. There was a sort of naive optimism in the lavender crystals, pewter dragons, embroidered affirmations, feathered dream-catchers, CDs of whale songs, and T-shirts with wolves and dolphins on them. A Disneyland of the Spirit. It wasn't Joan's sort of thing, but she could understand the appeal. And she guessed she'd rather be stuck in an elevator with ten New Agers than with some fungidelicals she knew of.

"Joan!" Miriam was motioning for her to come join her.

Joan walked over and noticed that the guy Miriam had been talking to looked familiar. "Ted? Hey, I didn't know you were back in town. How's college life?" The slender, dark-haired young man had grown since Joan had baby-sat him years ago. He had grown up handsome, too. Joan felt a twinge of regret, since she didn't believe in robbing cradles.

"Hi, Joan," he said, a little awkward. "CSU's okay. I'm back just for the summer. I'm doing some mountain biking up at Roxborough and over at Manitou Park. Hey, I heard your family sold your ranch."

Joan felt something clamp down inside. "Yeah. That's old news. It was a while ago."

"Sorry to interrupt old home week," Miriam said, "but about this person we're trying to find . . ."

"Oh, yeah," said Joan, grateful to Miriam for the change of subject. She pulled the silvery business card out of her jeans pocket and placed it on the counter. "This guy Brian Amadan. You know anything about him?"

Ted picked up the card and frowned at it. "Name's kind of familiar. Let me ask Frank—he's the owner here. Just a sec." Ted went through a doorway curtained with some imported Indian cloth.

"Told you," said Miriam, with a smug grin.

"You win," said Joan.

The curtain was opened by a taller, thin man with a weathered face, beaked nose, and the expression of a disgruntled hawk. His gray hair was pulled back into a ponytail, and for a moment Joan wondered if this "Frank" might also be Mr. Amadan. But he was scowling at the card and put it down on the counter with a loud snap. "You lookin' for this guy?"

"Yeah!" said Joan and Miriam in chorus.

"Don't," he said.

"What do you mean?" Joan asked.

He put his forefinger down on the card as if stabbing it with a knife. "This guy's bad juju."

Joan couldn't quite believe what she'd heard. "Bad what?"

Frank put his elbows on the counter and leaned forward. "Some people in this racket, they're fakes but they mean well. Or they're fakes, but just want your money. This guy, he's the real thing. And he don't mean well. And he don't just want money. If I were you, I'd stay clear of him." He pushed off the counter and started back through the curtain.

"Wait!" Joan said. "What if I told you that we had a really good reason to find this Brian Amadan?"

Frank paused and looked back at them. "I'd say I'm sorry to hear that." Then he continued on through the curtain.

Ted shrugged, embarrassed. "Sorry. That's just the way he is. Wish I could be of more help."

"That's okay. You tried. Call me if you remember anything else. Let's go," Joan said to Miriam. As they were walking back to the truck, Joan said sarcastically, "Well, that told us a lot."

"Actually, it did," Miriam said. "Mr. Amadan has a rep. That means others will know about him. So we'll find someone willing to tell us who he is, what he does, and how to find him."

"Yeah, but who? Where?"

"Joan, wait up!" Ted called from behind them.

Joan turned and saw Ted running down the sidewalk toward them. He pulled a folded-up piece of purple paper out of his pocket and looked back at the shop as if afraid he was being watched. In a conspiratorial hush he said, "Here. I knew I'd seen the name before. I found this in a stack of flyers next to the counter." He quickly handed the paper to Joan.

She unfolded it.

"What's it say?" Miriam asked, reading over her shoulder.

"Well, well, well. Our friend Mr. Amadan is giving a seminar called 'Open Spaces/Open Minds' in several places. He was up in Denver last month, down in Colorado Springs a week ago. He's going to be at Summit Rock on . . . shit, that's the day after tomorrow!"

"Gotta go," Ted said suddenly. "Good luck." He dashed back to the store.

"But that's great!" Miriam said. "We'll be able to catch up with him."

"Miriam, Summit Rock is over in the San Luis Valley. That's at least a four- or five-hour drive, over winding mountain roads, if you don't stop for meals."

"So? We've got a whole day to get there. You got something against long drives?"

"I've got something against dropping everything for a wild goose chase after some bad-juju guy. We've got clients to clean for, remember? Real-life stuff. Cleaning people have to be dependable. It's part of our job."

"So what you're saying is, cleaning up rich people's dust bunnies is more important than helping Gillian. Is that it?"

Joan sighed heavily, putting the heel of her hand against her forehead. "No! I just . . . Okay. It's just that . . . I mean, we can't ignore the real world just because weird stuff is happening. And we don't even know if it's weird stuff. Or even what we can do about it. And meanwhile, losing clients means I may be having a hard time paying bills next month."

"Meanwhile Gillian can't pay her bills at all."

"Yeah, well, she must have known the job was dangerous when she took it. She knew something about this Amadan guy, yet she went and, I dunno, summoned him anyway."

"What *is* this? Are we playing Blame the Victim now? If she's part of that family that passed down his song, she expected him to be friendlier. What *is* your issue here?"

"I don't know," Joan said, staring down at her feet. "Spending a couple of hours asking around is one thing. But to take a couple of days . . ." She rubbed the back of her neck, feeling a headache coming on.

"So take a couple of sick days."

"Self-employed people don't get sick days."

"Bullshit. My dad takes them whenever he wants to."

"Yeah, but your dad . . ." Joan paused to keep herself from saying ". . . is a Californian." Instead she finished with, ". . . doesn't need the income as much."

Miriam sighed, her hands balling into fists. "Look, if you want to cut down on time, we could fly up, I guess. Then rent a car."

"No, thanks. I've ridden the Vomit Comet up to Gunnison before. Puddle jumpers over the mountains are no fun."

"All right, then. If it's a real hassle for you, I could take her up to Summit Rock by myself," Miriam offered.

Joan looked at Miriam, who was only two or three years younger. Joan couldn't see herself sending sweet, sensitive Miriam alone up against someone who was supposed to be "bad juju." Two days off wouldn't be that great a loss. *Would I give up two days' wages to save a life?* Joan thought. *Of course I would. If that's what we're doing.* "No, no. We'd better both go. More hands make lighter work, as my grandpa used to say."

Miriam grinned. "All right! Girl power on the case!"

Joan rolled her eyes and got into the truck, as Miriam hopped in the passenger side. "I live only a few blocks from here," Joan said. "Let's stop at my place and I'll pack a bag and leave messages for my clients."

"Okay." Miriam turned and spoke to the guitar behind the seat. "How are you doing, Gillian?"

The guitar, of course, said nothing. Miriam reached over the seat and under the blanket and plucked a string.

Fine, Gillian plaintively sang.

Nervous and antsy, Joan tapped the steering wheel of her truck as she drove. "This truck is old, you know. Eats a lot of gas."

"I'll pay for gas," Miriam chirped. "Or we can take my Subaru. It's in good shape. I take it on long drives all the time."

"Yeah. Yeah, maybe that's a good idea. We'll take your car. We don't want to run the risk of this old beastie breaking down halfway."

Actually, Joan was pretty sure the truck had the heart to make it over the mountains. She just didn't want to put it at risk. Lots of nutty tourists and drunk kids roared over the winding mountain roads every day. One or two died every weekend, going off the pavement, sometimes taking innocent motorists with them. The truck was Joan's investment—heck, it nearly *was* the business. It had served her dad for many long years on the ranch, and its cab still smelled of cattle, mud, and old hay. It was her friend. She couldn't ask it to charge over the mountains for her on some stupid, crazy search for someone who might be a nasty sorcerer.

"Does your truck have a name?" Miriam asked.

"What? No, I don't name cars. My family never has."

"My family always does. My Subaru is named Sheila, because that's the Australian slang for girl. You know, because of what's-his-face from the movies who's in those ads?"

"Okay, sure." Joan had no idea what Miriam was talking about, but that was nothing new.

"What was Joan of Arc's horse's name?"

"I don't know. I don't think she had a special horse."

"I was just thinking that if she did, you could name your truck that. Or maybe you could name it after the prince she did all her fighting for, what's-his-name, the Dolphin."

"The Dauphin? Nah, he was a wimp. I'd never name a truck after him."

Miriam laughed. "Too bad. Are you related to the real Joan?"

"Well, that depends on which side of the family you talk to. My paternal grandmother used to like to claim we were related. Distantly, of course, since Saint Joan herself didn't have any children. Grandma told me all the stories. My granddad, though, once said that the family name used to be longer and more Germanic but got shortened at Ellis Island, like so many other immigrants' names."

"Huh. Which do you believe?"

Joan shrugged. "Depends on who's asking and on what day." She pulled up in front of her house, a little one-story, one-bedroom place built in the 1920s. Her folks had bought it for her out of the proceeds from the ranch. Joan liked the place because it was cozy and easy to take care of. She hated it because it was cramped and to her it felt like it had been bought with blood money.

As she parked and walked up the sidewalk, Joan felt a growing anxiety. It only got worse as she unlocked the front door and went in. She stopped just inside the front room, realizing what it was. *I should have asked Miriam to stay in the truck.*

Joan glanced over the sparse furniture, hand-me-downs from her folks again, old and worn and covered with brown throws. No frills or knickknacks except the little second- and third-prize gymkhana trophies from so long ago, and the portraits on the wall. She suddenly saw it all as a stranger might see it and felt embarrassed. Worse, she knew Miriam would "read" her house and feared what she might see.

"Oh. Homey," Miriam said as she walked in.

"Yeah, well, interior decorating isn't my line. Besides, I spend so much time cleaning other people's places I don't like to clutter up my own nest."

"I can understand that," Miriam said, staring around at the walls.

Feeling extremely self-conscious, almost naked, Joan hurried over to the answering machine. There were no messages, which was both a relief and a disappointment. Joan checked her Day-timer and called the three clients she had for the rest of the week, telling them that she had to go out of town on an emergency and would be back the next week. It all went very quickly, and too soon Joan had no more calls to make and had to go back and see what Miriam was looking at.

Miriam was gazing wistfully at the large portrait of twelve-year-old Joan. The child was wearing a big smile, and her arms were clasped fondly around a horse's neck. "That your horse?" Miriam asked.

"He was, yeah. That was Misty. Named after a children's book. He was a great guy, smart—I won those trophies on him. He died at a ripe old age five years ago. Just as well, I guess. Don't know what I would have done with him with the ranch . . . gone."

Miriam turned and faced her. "You really miss that place, don't you?"

Joan felt something like fury catch in her throat, and she kneaded the hem of her T-shirt in her fists. "What makes you think that?"

"This place. It's so somber. It's like . . . you're in mourning."

Joan felt her jaw tighten and her teeth clench. She growled, "Yeah. Well, all I can say is, I hope your daddy makes some good money off of that land." Joan stomped into her bedroom and pulled the overnight case down from the top of her tiny closet. She flung it onto the bed with enough force to make it bounce twice and yanked open her dresser drawers. She tossed clothes into the case, not really even noticing what she was packing. A part of her mind knew she was acting crazy, but somehow she just couldn't stop.

"Hey," Miriam said, coming into the bedroom. "Hey, I'm sorry. I didn't mean to get you upset."

"Yeah. Sure you didn't."

"Look, it's not like my dad's some sort of Snidely Whiplash, twirling his mustache and demanding people's deeds. Your folks wanted to sell. If you didn't like it, why didn't you talk them out of it?"

Joan jammed her fists into the mass of clothes in the suitcase. "Because that land sucked up years of their lives. Almost completely wrung them out, too, toward the end. But your dad's company came along and offered them more money than they'd ever seen at once in their whole lives. And now they've retired and are tootling around the country in an RV that's bigger than this whole house, and they're happy, goddammit! I wasn't gonna talk them out of their chance at happiness." Joan sat heavily on the bed and felt tears leak out of her eyes.

Miriam came over and sat beside her, putting an arm around her shoulders.

"I'm sorry," Joan said between sobs. "I don't know what's come over me. Why I'm acting this way. I shouldn't have blown up all of a sudden like that."

"It's the Tower," Miriam said gently. "The whole world's turned around for you. Sometimes when you turn over a new leaf, you find some ants and worms underneath that you didn't realize were there."

"Oh, right," Joan said, gently sarcastic. "It's all in the cards. I forgot. How come you aren't . . . so upset then?"

Miriam shrugged. "I've had my world turned upside down before. It's not new to me. These days I'm always expecting it."

"Like people changing into guitars?"

"Like people changing all sorts of ways. I hope you're ready to keep an open mind about all this, because . . . I think we can expect more strangeness over the next few days."

"Oh, great. Was that in your cards this morning too?"

"Yesterday's astrological chart, actually." Miriam smiled sheepishly. "Mercury's in retrograde, and . . .

well, I'd explain more, but you'd think it was just mumbo jumbo."

"Yeah. I guess I would." Joan took a deep breath and gathered her thoughts. "Well, we'd better get a move on if we're going to help Gillian. I could use a hand getting some of the equipment in from the truck."

Miriam saluted. "Your faithful sidekick is ready and willing to help."

They brought in the vacuum cleaner, "bat belt," and other cleaning gear and stowed it in Joan's laundry alcove. Then they drove back across town to Miriam's condo. As Joan pulled into a parking slot, she said, "Are you sure I won't get towed if I leave the truck here? It doesn't exactly blend into the environment—kind of like an elephant in a lion herd."

"Pride," said Miriam.

"What?" asked Joan, wondering what philosophical point her faithful sidekick was trying to make now.

"Pride of lions. Not herd. You lived among cattle too long, girl. Don't worry. I'll call and leave a message with the condo association manager. It'll be okay. C'mon up."

Joan started to get out of the truck when Miriam added, "Aren't you going to bring Gillian?"

"Hmmm? You don't think anybody would steal her here, do you?"

"I meant she might be more, you know, comfortable, upstairs with us."

"Oh. Yeah. Okay." Joan had no idea how a sentient guitar might feel, and was still having a hard time wrapping her brain around the fact that the guitar *was* Gillian and felt anything. But her parents had brought her up to be considerate, and Joan figured it was better to err in the right direction. She pulled the blanket-wrapped guitar out from behind the seat and carried it—her—along.

Joan followed Miriam up the steps and down a narrow hallway to the apartment door. She had imagined Miriam's place would look like the New Age shop, filled with fantasy gewgaws and exotic smells. Joan was almost disappointed when they walked in.

Decor was by Pier 1, with a simple rattan chair and couch, and a couple of Asian prints on the wall. There wasn't much of the mystical to the place, other than the amethyst geode on a pedestal by the door. And the lump wrapped in purple silk on the Turkish inlaid-wood coffee table, which Joan presumed was the tarot deck and which she had no intention of touching. Joan tried to "read" the place as Miriam might, but the only impressions she got were Simple Tastes and Money.

"Have a seat," Miriam said, "while I pack and make some calls. Want anything? I've got some great Lapsang souchong tea I bought the other day."

"No, thanks."

"Okay. I think I have an old guitar case lying around. We can try it on Gillian and see if it fits." Miriam went off into another room, and soon Joan could hear her talking on the phone to someone.

Joan sat on the couch and unwrapped the guitar. The wood felt warm again beneath her hands, though she wondered if that was just from its having been left in a hot truck cab. "You were a smart woman," she said to it, feeling silly. "How could something like this possibly happen to you?"

Joan began to play notes at random.

I know yes I was smart too smart God I feel stu pid

"*You* feel stupid. Here I am talking to a guitar."

ha ha ha ha ha ha ha I'm sor ry

"It's okay. It's not your fault," Joan said, as sooth-ingly as she could. She ran her hand over the curves of the guitar. It felt amazingly alive in her arms, a sensa-tion both intriguing and disturbing. "Boy, what some musicians wouldn't give to have an ax like you."

Joan remembered a Patsy Cline song she had tried to learn on guitar, long ago. She used to love listening to the old Patsy Cline records her folks would play late at night, when she was a child. Songs like "Crazy" and "Walking After Midnight." Better than lullabies. And sometimes she would sneak out of her bedroom and catch a glimpse of them dancing together in the living room, by candlelight.

She began strumming the guitar and singing "Crazy." Gillian's strings began singing along, in harmony. After a few bars, Joan stopped. "Wow. So you know that song too?"

Miriam bustled in, carrying a stuffed backpack on one shoulder and a battered guitar case under one arm. "All set. I told the manager about your truck, and she says it's fine if we leave it for a couple of days. Was that you singing just now? You've got a nice voice."

"Oh. Thanks."

"Ever sing professionally?"

"No, I'm strictly a shower singer. Only time I sang in public was glee club in elementary school. I won't even go near karaoke bars."

"Huh. Well, maybe you should consider it. Anyway, here's the guitar case. Kinda old, and not in the best shape. Let's try her out."

Joan handed Gillian to Miriam, who placed it—her—gently into the cardboard case. "Looks like she'll rattle around a bit in there."

"I can fill the extra space with towels. That should make it more comfy. Just a sec." Miriam ran off and returned with a handful of bath towels, which she carefully placed over the guitar's sides, plus one beneath it and one over the strings. "That should do it."

Joan was going to protest, thinking Gillian might feel stifled, but then thought better of it. It was better that Gillian have some sort of protection. What if a string broke? Would it hurt? What if her wood got dented? When they changed her back, would part of her be broken? If the guitar's neck snapped, would she die?

"What's wrong?" Miriam asked.

"Oh, it's just that there's so much we don't know. About taking care of her and stuff. I'm worried we might do something wrong."

"Guess we'll have to learn it as we go along," said Miriam, closing up the guitar case. It was like watching a coffin lid fall into place. "Ready to go?"

"Ready as I'll ever be."

They loaded up the Subaru, and Joan folded herself into the passenger seat, feeling cramped and uncomfortable. As they pulled out of the parking slot, she gazed wistfully at her truck, silently apologizing to it, feeling as if she were saying good-bye to an old friend. *I'll be back soon. I promise.*

Joan stared out at the landscape as they headed south on I-25, drinking in the sight as if it might be a long time before she saw home again. The town of Dawson Butte was nestled in a long north-south valley lined by pine-garbed hills and buttes, including the one the town was named for, as well as more colorfully named Raspberry Butte and Monkey Face. To the east rose the very easternmost line of foothills to the Rockies. Beyond those, the great plains rolled away. To the west, the hills marched up to the mountains. The valley itself still had prosperous ranches and farms, though more and more of them were giving way to suburban developments and shopping malls to serve the two major cities that sandwiched it. Joan remembered how empty and uncluttered the valley had been when she was a little girl. She had nothing against civilization and its amenities, but she didn't want to be smothered in it.

All too soon, they were in the outermost suburbs of Colorado Springs, spreading out over the hillsides. Then they could see the city itself nestled up against the Rampart Range. Unlike Denver, where the mountains are a distant line of purple and white against the horizon, at Colorado Springs the mountains are Right There, jutting up from the high plains floor and towering over the city. To the south was the low hulk of Cheyenne Mountain, of NORAD and Cold War fame, its summit bristling with TV, radio, and microwave antennae as if it were a gigantic porcupine. To the west rose the majestic, world-famous Pikes Peak.

They stopped for lunch in the Springs at a yuppie fern-bar type of place, but it had a nice view of Pikes Peak and it served semivegetarian food, which was what Miriam preferred. Joan ordered the buffalo burger and ignored Miriam's raised eyebrows. To forestall a possible lecture, Joan asked, "So what do you think of this place?"

"This restaurant?"

"If you want, but I meant the Springs in general."

"Oh." Miriam gazed out the window beside their table. "Could be a nice city," she mused. "Has some of the right things . . . mountains at its back . . . not much of a river in front, though. Too much tortoise, not enough phoenix."

"What are you talking about?"

Miriam laughed. "It sounds weird, I know, but it's really just shorthand with symbols. By tortoise, I mean the need to defend itself from any perceived outside threats. The Springs screams DEFENSE, what with the Air Force Academy and Cheyenne Mountain. Trouble is, it wants to hold fast against all aspects of change too. Maybe that's why it's such a conservative place."

"Hunh. Maybe. What's the phoenix stand for?"

"A soaring spirit. Inspiration, sensuality, an openness to the world around."

"I see."

"It's much more complicated than that, really. Like I said, it's shorthand and all elements of a place have to be weighed in relation to one another, as well as their position in time."

"In *time*?"

"Everything is changing, constantly flowing into a new state of being. You can't think of it as a static thing, like a still photograph. It all . . . flows, you know?"

Joan shook her head. "I'm afraid you've lost me."

"Oh, you'd get it eventually. It's not that hard a concept, it's just thinking in different terms. Anyway, I'll feel better when we get up into the mountains. More dragon and phoenix there."

Joan stared out the window at Pikes Peak, but she could not agree with Miriam. For Joan, mountains were fine at a distance, as part of the view, but she mistrusted them. It was out of the mountains that storms came howling down onto the plains, bringing wind, lightning, and flash floods. Whenever she'd had to travel through them, she'd always had the acute sense that mountains were not mankind's friend. They might let you pass by them, ignoring you with grand hauteur. Or they might, on a whim, send down a storm, or a rockfall, or an avalanche, to kill you. Joan had lost a couple of friends to the White Death—they were snowboarding too near a cornice on fresh powder when one unwise exuberant shout had brought the mountainside of snow rumbling down the slope to sweep them away. The mountains gave Joan no inspiration or joy, only the urge to tread carefully and watch her back at all times.

Joan finished her burger and plunked down the exact change for the bill and tip. "You can pay for dinner," she told Miriam.

"I get the more expensive meal, huh?" she asked.

"Depends on what you eat."

"Right." Miriam picked up three dimes from the tip and idly tossed them back onto the table. She did this several times in a row.

"Seen *Rosencrantz and Guildenstern* too often?" Joan asked.

"What? Oh, the coin-tossing. No. It's just that so much of what's going on has to do with transformation. My I Ching is out in the car, but I remember enough to get the gist."

"I Ching, now? Miriam, why not just let events happen? Why do you have to be peering into every crystal ball to try to second-guess what's coming?"

Miriam paused and stared down at her hands before answering. "I . . . I like to feel prepared, that's all. Remember you talked about missing a spiritual sense? Well, I don't like to feel as though I'm stumbling into the future blind."

"Don't you like surprises?"

"Not certain kinds of surprises."

"So all this fortune-telling is a psychological crutch, in other words."

"Crutches are useful when you're feeling lame."

Joan put her cheek on her hand and sighed in resignation. "Okay, okay, what do the coins say?"

"Oh. They don't say anything. They represent lines, which are assembled into trigrams—"

"Cut to the chase, Miriam. What did you see?"

"Oh. Well, it's good news. We will be successful. The changing lines show that things will open up for us."

"Changing lines?"

"Don't ask. It's complicated. Just take my word for it that most hexagrams give two messages. Trouble is, our first message is the I Ching passage 'Taming Power of the Great.' That's too bad. I was hoping for 'Taming Power of the Small.' "

Joan got up to take the bill to the counter. "What difference does it make?"

"Well, 'Taming Power of the Small' means that to overcome your difficulties you need only be your soft, gentle, caring self. 'Taming Power of the Great' means you have to have skills or knowledge."

"To be hot shit at something."

"Yeah," Miriam said sadly.

"Well, who's to say we aren't? You've got some pretty . . . unique skills. Maybe I do, too, and just don't know it yet. See, that's what I don't trust about these divination systems. What if your crutch is made of rubber and makes you discouraged or leads you to make the wrong choice?"

"That's where you have to trust your guts," Miriam said.

"Yeah?" said Joan. "My guts are telling me I'd better use the bathroom before we hit the road again. I'll meet you out at the car."

Chapter 3

They took US 24 out of Colorado Springs, with Joan driving. As the road rose steeply through Fountain Creek Canyon, Joan felt acute disquiet at the hulks of the mountains pressing close, and discomfort at being squeezed into too small a car. So she vented on something else. "Look at all those tourist signs—Garden of the Gods! Seven Falls! Cave of the Winds! Manitou Cliff Dwellings! I feel like I'm being shouted at by highway robbers. 'Give Me Your Money!' "

"Well, it's not like tourists aren't willing to spend money, and they want to be able to find the neat things they're looking for. It's a sort of symbiosis."

"Sounds like a disease. Which I guess is kinda accurate."

Miriam made a rude noise. "Why do people always put down tourists? What's wrong with traveling and looking at things?"

"Because it's seeing without understanding."

"So? Isn't that better than not seeing at all?"

"Hmm. Have to get back to you on that."

"Haven't you traveled much?"

Joan thought about it. "Through the southwest, sure.

I've been east only a couple of times, to visit relatives. Nope, guess I haven't."

"Oh. You said your parents seem to be having fun traveling around now."

"I just figure they're going through second childhood."

Miriam opened her mouth, then shut it again. Finally, she said, "I'm sorry. I shouldn't be arguing with you so much. I'll shut up now." She opened her backpack and pulled out a battered copy of the I Ching.

"Never apologize for arguing," said Joan. "Besides, it's helping me keep my mind off of what we're doing and why."

"If you'll pardon me," Miriam said, opening up the book, "I'm going to try to think more clearly on exactly that."

The region of rustic exurbs and tourist traps gave way to more miles of rocky canyon. Eventually they went through the small town of Woodland Park and entered into a broad, high valley. Miriam said, "Stop the car. Please?"

"Why? What's wrong?"

"Nothing. I just spotted a photo opportunity."

Joan rolled her eyes, but she spotted a widening in the shoulder and she pulled over. Miriam pulled a small Nikon camera out of her backpack and got out. Not knowing how long Miriam would be out admiring the view, Joan got out too and sauntered along behind her.

Miriam was headed for a small cluster of red-and-white cattle grazing behind a barbed-wire fence. The animals glanced up and their ears flicked forward, alert. "Look," she said, "there are cows all the way up here!"

"Sure," said Joan. "This is probably BLM land. They lease rights for ranchers to graze their cattle up here during summer months. Nothing special about it."

"How do the ranchers find them again?"

Smirking, Joan said, "You see those markings on the hindquarters? Those are called brands. Time comes to move them, the ranchers come up and find every steer that has their brand on it."

"Seems cruel to me."

"What?"

"Branding."

"Did getting your ears pierced hurt?"

"Well, yeah, but I chose to do it. I didn't have people roping me and tying me down."

"Would you rather the cattle get lost and starve?"

Miriam didn't answer but walked closer and closer to a group of three cattle, which raised their heads and watched her warily. Alarmed, Joan saw Miriam go right up to the fence and reach out to one cow, talking to it.

"Miriam! What are you doing! This isn't a petting zoo."

"I just wanted to see if they were friendly."

"If they're well bred, they'll steer clear of you as if you were a possible predator. Get too close, they might knock you over—they've got calves to defend. Miriam, don't mess with them. They aren't pets, they're somebody's investment. Leave them alone."

Miriam sighed and looked back at her. "I see beautiful, living, breathing animals and all you see is an investment? Like they were . . . bars of soap? Aren't you being just a little materialistic?"

"I'd say I'm being realistic."

"Oh. So, when you look at a pretty view like this, all you see is rocks, plants, and somebody's money. Right?"

Joan gazed out over the mountain meadow for a few moments. "I see that it's been a dry year in this region. There's barely enough forage for any size herd of cattle, when you add in deer and elk grazing. This rancher may have to spend money on extra feed, and that will cut into his profit margin. The cattle appear to be a Hereford/Charolais mix. Expensive. This rancher is taking some economic risks. From the youth of those calves, he's letting the cows bear late, April probably, which is safer for the animals, but they may not bulk up enough by fall to give much profit, and they don't look like they're thriving that well. This guy has a lot of work ahead of him to keep his ranch in the black. I wish him luck." Joan looked back at Miriam, who was staring at her open-mouthed. "What?"

"Okay. I apologize. You can see a lot. It's just a . . . really different perspective."

"There's nothing magical about it, Miriam. It's just experience. If you'd grown up on a ranch, you'd see and know the same things."

As Miriam snapped a couple of pictures, she muttered, "Kind of glad I didn't. It's an unromantic way of looking at the world."

"Believe me, no matter what the cowboy poets say, there's nothing romantic about cattle. They're stupid and smelly and die a lot. People like you all seem to think that life is this magical, glowing force that flourishes all by itself. Anyone who works the land knows better. It's not that ranchers don't care—we try to do our best by the animals, that's only smart husbandry.

But maintaining life is hard work. There isn't any way around that."

"Maybe because a ranch isn't a natural habitat for animals," Miriam grumbled.

"Oh, bullshit!" Joan said.

As if in horror at her expletive, the cattle rolled their eyes and began to amble away, with cautious glances back over their shoulders.

"Miriam, more buffalo ran through Colorado before white men moved in than the number of cattle raised here now."

"Look, just . . . forget it," Miriam said. "Let's get back on the road."

As they got back in the Subaru, Miriam stuck her hand toward Joan, offering to shake. "Agree to disagree?"

With a rueful grin, Joan took it. "Guess we'd better."

"Good. 'Cause it turns out the changing lines in that I Ching hexagram I threw said that we would only achieve success through teamwork. 'Progress with another of strong character,' the book said."

"Heh. We're a couple of characters, all right," Joan said, starting up the car.

As they headed on over Ute Pass, past signs indicating Florissant Fossil Beds, Miriam said, "You know, if you miss your ranch so much, couldn't you have just taken a job as a cowhand on some other ranch?"

"Sure. I had offers from neighbors, even. But . . . it just wouldn't have been the same. Every rancher does things different, and we're independent cusses. I'd probably squawk and complain about anything any other rancher did. No one wants a cowhand like that."

"I understand. I guess."

"And it's not just the life I miss. You know, it's the land itself, its smell, and the way it looks at sunrise. The way I figure it, it's something biochemical. You live so many years on one piece of land, eating and breathing its dust and plant spores and what-have-you, it gets ahold of you. You become part of it. I spent almost my whole life on those acres. Noplace else will feel the same."

They wound on down US 24 through the lower part of South Park—an enormous high valley ringed with ancient cinder cones and snowcapped peaks. Miriam lauded the scenery as spectacular, and Joan merely thought of how bleak and treacherous the land would be in winter. At the valley's western edge, US 24 joined with 285, and before long they entered a narrow, bouldery canyon. A sign on their right read, ENTERING CHAFFEE COUNTY, and below that the county slogan, NOW *THIS* IS COLORADO. A couple of miles of twists and turns later, they saw what the slogan referred to. The view opened up onto the Arkansas River Valley, across which a row of majestic blue-and-white mountains rose up to meet the sky.

"Wow!" said Miriam. "Now here's a place that lives up to its advertising."

"Um," said Joan.

"According to the map, those are the Collegiate Peaks—the mountains are named after colleges and universities. Most of them are over fourteen thousand feet high, too," Miriam burbled. "I know a guy who's climbed almost all the fourteeners in the state."

"Why?"

"Why do I know such a guy?"

"No, why does he climb them?"

51

Miriam gave her an odd sidewise look. "Because they're *there*. It's an accomplishment. It builds self-esteem."

"I learned that you get self-esteem by doing your job and getting things done. Things you can see the results of. Not by climbing slippery rockpiles that aren't fit for human habitation."

"This state is really wasted on you, isn't it?"

"Hey! East of the Front Range, Colorado's beautiful. Lots of open sky, land you can farm or ranch on. My granddad once said that in his day, wilderness meant useless land, a place where people couldn't do anything worthwhile."

"Oh, that's real anthropocentric."

"Real *what*?"

"Human-centered."

"Well, yeah. I'm a human. Most of human progress has been to keep Nature from killing people."

"You shouldn't look at it like that."

"Whose side are you on, anyway?"

Miriam sighed loudly. "Never mind."

Past the truck stop and diners at Johnson Village, they turned south on 285 and by three-thirty had made it down to Poncha Springs. Miriam suggested a quick detour down US 50 to Salida for some early dinner.

"Why Salida?"

"It's the last stop for a long while with cool places to eat. I stayed there last year when I went skiing at Monarch. There's a café there you've just gotta see."

"Uh-oh."

"No, really. No matter what you believe, it's really fun. Has good food, too. And serves breakfast all day."

"You sold me."

They puttered down US 50 into a small town of un-assuming one-story houses and single-wide trailers. Miriam pointed out a long, low brick-faced building with wide shingled eaves. The red-and-yellow sign on a pole next to it read, FRONT PORCH FLAPJACKS.

"Doesn't look like much," said Joan.

"Some of the best restaurants don't," said Miriam.

They went into the vestibule, and Joan blindly walked past the glassed-in frame on the right-hand wall.

"Joan, you've gotta look at this."

Joan did. And coughed out a laugh. "Salida UFO videotapes?"

"Yeah! There's this local guy who says he's taped lots of flyovers of extraterrestrial craft."

Joan peered at the sample still photo from the tape. "That doesn't look like any spaceship. Just lights in the sky. Could be a weather phenomenon."

"Well, maybe it looks different in motion."

"I'm not buying a tape."

"I'm not telling you to. Just have a little imagination. If Gilly could become a guitar, lights could be an alien ship."

Joan frowned at her. "They're completely unrelated!"

"Not philosophically."

"I stay away from philosophy. That way madness lies. Let's go in."

Inside, Front Porch Flapjacks was your typical western diner: valance over venetian blinds on the windows, country-style wallpaper, glass-front counter displaying candy for sale, to the right of which was a wood shelf unit of Colorado-related books and a metal rack of postcards. But behind the glass counter were more advertisements for the UFO videotape and photo-copies of local newspaper articles about the "sightings." Joan and Miriam sat at a typical vinyl-upholstered booth. In a little wood crate stood a cheap humor book titled *You, Too, Might Be a Country Person.*

"If a waitress comes up and tells us she's an ab-ductee, I'm leaving," muttered Joan.

"It's not that sort of place," said Miriam.

In fact, the young waitress was quite pleasant and efficient, and Joan's omelet and Miriam's salad were both good.

As she was mopping up salad dressing with a dinner roll, Miriam asked out of nowhere, "Do you find it hard to meet guys in Dawson Butte?"

Joan thought a moment. "Depends," she said cau-tiously. "If you're not picky, there's guys everywhere."

"Yeah, well, there's the rub, isn't it? Being picky."

"Guess so. Um, what sort are you looking for?"

Miriam stared off at nothing. "Good question."

When she didn't elaborate, Joan went on, "I expect if you want someone of your, um, philosophy, you might do better up in Boulder."

Miriam did an odd shrug and tuck of her chin. "Those of my 'philosophy,' as you put it, aren't such a promising bunch. A lot of them act sensitive and spiri-tual because they know it will help them get laid. The sincere ones are either nice and already married with kids, or they . . . can be genuinely crazy. And want you to be just as fanatic as they are." She shuddered, clearly at some awful memory. "Or maybe I'm just unlucky in love."

"Well, there's plenty of that bad luck going around," Joan said. "You're not alone."

"Don't you have anybody special?"

"Not at the moment."

"Let me guess," Miriam said with a grin. "Cowboys are your weakness."

Joan grinned back. "Well, some of them are damn fine to look at. And a smile from them can really light up your day. But—"

"But?"

"But they're gone for long periods of time, just like truckers. And some of them aren't too bright. And some of them have an attitude. The last guy I dated was all right until he started telling me how to run my business. I had to dump him before I experienced what you might call a hostile takeover."

"Hunh." Miriam shook her head. "Why do they do that?"

"Oh, mostly they can't help themselves. Usually they even mean well. Men just like to fix things, even if they aren't broke."

"Think we can get this Mr. Amadan to fix Gillian?"

Joan stared at Miriam a moment, then sighed. "I don't know what to think, Miriam. For all we know, maybe he thought he was fixing something when he changed her."

"That's a scary thought."

"Yeah. There's lots of scary stuff about this. Mr. Amadan might not take too kindly to our asking him to undo his work."

"If it was his work," cautioned Miriam. "Besides, the landlady said he was nice to her."

"And the shop owner, Frank, said he was bad juju."

"Maybe Frank had pissed Mr. Amadan off somehow."

"Maybe Gillian pissed Mr. Amadan off somehow."

"Well, Frank didn't get turned into a guitar."

Joan stared down at the table, shaking her head. "This all just seems so crazy. There's so much we don't know."

"That's why we're here," said Miriam. "To learn things."

Uncertain whether Miriam was talking about the trip or the meaning of life in general, Joan went and asked the waitress for the check.

It had gotten dark by the time they were through with dinner. Miriam took over driving, which suited Joan fine. At least at night one didn't have to see the mountains. But the apron of light cast by the car's high beams on the road ahead did little to keep the emptiness of the land beyond at bay.

"They sure keep a lot of dark up here," Joan muttered.

"Yeah, this is where the Colorado dark mines are," Miriam said. "We export dark to all over the country. Didn't you know that?"

Joan found herself resenting something in Miriam's joking but couldn't put her finger on it. "That must explain why there's getting to be less dark on the Front Range. Denver and the Springs are shipping theirs out."

"Gives you a *Twilight Zone* feel up here, though, doesn't it?" asked Miriam. "We could be driving into another universe, or time, and not know it. Anything could be out there in the dark."

"Yeah, and it could jump out of the bushes at us," Joan grumbled, "looking remarkably like a deer or an elk. Aren't you driving a little fast for these turns?"

"Take it easy. I used to do Topanga Canyon in my dad's Miata all the time. I love twisty roads. You really think we might see some deer?"

"Sure, up close and personal if you're not careful."

"Oh, all right." Miriam eased up on the gas.

Joan hunkered down in the car seat and closed her eyes, not wanting to watch the darkness anymore. In time, she dozed off, and she didn't awaken until Miriam shook her shoulder.

"We're in Summit Rock. I found us a nice bed-and-breakfast. I hope that's okay."

Joan yawned and stretched. Through the windshield she saw a sign that said THE WELL OF LIFE LODGE, over the doors to a large gingerbread-Victorian house. "Won't it be a bit expensive?"

"Don't worry. I put it on a credit card. Might as well pamper ourselves, given what we're going through. Better than some depressing motel."

"If you say so." Joan got her suitcase out of the back of the car and followed Miriam into the house and up a couple of flights of stairs. Their room had a ceiling of odd angles, and the beds had frilly, flowered designer coverlets with matching pillowcases. Incongruous Hindu paintings hung on the walls beside wildlife art prints of Beverly Doolittle. Joan's road-weary mind didn't want to deal with the juxtaposition, so she stretched out on the bed and instantly went back to sleep.

She woke up again to Miriam shaking her. "Hi. I thought you might want to sleep in, so I brought you some breakfast."

Joan sat up, rubbing her eyes. "What time is it?"

"Eight-thirty or so. They stop serving breakfast at ten, so I figured I'd better nab you some."

Joan looked at what Miriam had brought. Two oat-bran muffins, a banana, and an orange. "Miriam, this is so healthy my arteries will seize up from shock."

"I'm sorry. I didn't know what you'd want, and—"

"That's okay. Thanks for being so . . . thoughtful. Is there any coffee?"

"Yep," said Miriam, proffering her a mug. "I didn't know what you wanted in it, though, so I brought these." She spilled a handful of creamer and sugar packets onto the bed.

"Black will be fine," Joan said, gratefully taking the mug. The first sip proved the coffee was very good, too. "God, I don't know why I'm so tired."

"Altitude, probably," Miriam said. "We're at about eight thousand feet here, I'd guess. My mom and dad always get sluggish for a day or so whenever we get up in the mountains. It's never seemed to affect me much, though."

"Lucky you. I knew there was a reason not to like the mountains."

"Oh, you'll perk up. Just take it easy for a while."

"I don't think I'm going to have a choice."

After breakfast, shower, and a change of clothes, Joan let Miriam drag her out for a walk on Main Street. Which was followed shortly by a detour into the nearest place resembling a drugstore for sunglasses and sunscreen lotion.

"Yeah, it is bright up here, isn't it?" said Miriam. "Isn't it wonderful, all this sunshine and clear air?"

Joan blinked through her new Ray Bans, relieved that her eyes no longer hurt. "Yeah. It's a wonder the pioneer miners didn't go blind and burn up like vampires."

"Oh, you'll get used to it."

"Yeah, sure, like some people get used to having arthritis." Joan glanced up and down Main Street and saw that Summit Rock seemed a town at odds with it-self. Old West tourist shops stood beside New Age kitsch shops, along with buildings from the original mining town it must once have been.

"If you feel up to it," Miriam said, "I got the address of Mr. Amadan's office from the B-and-B owner. It's just up the street a couple of blocks."

"Good work, faithful sidekick. Let's get Gillian out of the car and go find our wicked sorcerer. Before I lose my nerve as well as my eyesight."

The walk took them uphill to a new-looking two-story log building with stained-glass bay windows and a steeply sloping green metal roof. Before they went in, Joan had to sit on a bench, artfully made from weath-ered wood and chrome auto fenders, to catch her breath.

"This isn't fair," Joan said, nearly gasping. "I won't be able to think straight enough to face this guy."

"Just relax. We won't go in until you're ready."

"You're being awfully calm about this."

"I just figure there's no sense worrying about what I don't know. If we both end up as guitars too, that's life. Maybe we can all be in a band together."

"Well, thank you, Ms. Optimism. With my luck, he'd make me into a tuba. A good thing I don't believe in most of this stuff or I'd run away screaming."

"C'mon. You're named after a brave warrior woman."

"Who quite likely was schizophrenic and crazy as a bedbug."

"If you've got enough breath to say that, you've got enough to go inside."

"You're right." Joan stood and picked up the guitar case. "Let's get it over with."

They entered through carved oak doors, and a discreet notice board indicated that Mr. Amadan's office was up another flight of stairs.

"Figures," Joan grumbled as she trudged up the wood staircase, holding on to the banister the whole way. At the top, she swayed, blinked, and wondered if she was having a hallucination brought on by oxygen deprivation.

The log walls of the long room before her were lined with trees—pines, blue spruce, and aspens. Joan could not tell if they were real or fake, but there was a near-overwhelming scent of pine. Taxidermed mule deer peered out from the branches as if they were alive and startled at the arrival of newcomers. She heard rushing water, birdsong, and wind. Joan had the curious, dizzying impression that she was inside and outside at the same time.

At the far end of the long room was a reception desk, behind which sat a young Amerind man. He wore his long black hair in two braids, and a necklace with a round pectoral of black and white beads hung over his chamois shirt. Behind him on the wall was an enormous portrait of a gray wolf that stared out of the painting with feral green eyes.

"Wow," said Miriam, nearly twirling around in a dance. "Isn't this cool?"

"I feel like I've taken a wrong turn into a natural history museum. Don't the stuffed animals bother you?"

"Well, I suppose they should. But they seem to fit here. It's like he's brought a chunk of forest inside."

"I'm surprised this place feels good to you. You hated the feel of his business card."

"It's . . . different. Maybe he didn't design this room. It doesn't feel at all the same. This is, I dunno, inviting Nature inside. It's wildness, life, potentiality. There's a magic here."

"If Gillian's condition is any indication, it may not be good magic."

"You think it's not good because it's not centered around people."

"Let's not get into that again. C'mon. Let's inquire if his lordship is in." They walked up to the Amerind receptionist, who turned a superior, vaguely disapproving gaze on them.

"May I help you?" he said blandly.

"We would like to speak with Mr. Amadan," Joan said.

"Do you have an appointment?"

"Um, no. But it's very important." Joan shifted the guitar case to her other hand.

The young man glanced down at the guitar case disdainfully. "What might I tell him is the reason for your visit?"

"It concerns music, and a certain friend of ours by the name of Gillian McKeagh."

The slightest hint of a smile appeared on the young man's lips. "Despite what some people think, Mr. Amadan does not run a musicians' agency."

Joan felt herself getting angry. "That is not why we

are here. We . . . have come to see that a wrong is redressed. Just tell him. He'll know what we are talking about."

The young man sighed and pulled over a pen and paper. "I can leave him a note, but he is not here at present."

"Why didn't you tell us that in the first place?"

"You did not ask."

Some very unkind and politically incorrect rejoinders popped into Joan's mind, but she heroically held them back from her tongue. "When do you think he will be returning?"

"Not today. He is preparing for this evening's seminar. Possibly tomorrow, unless he decides to leave town early for his next appearance."

"Where is his next appearance?" Miriam asked.

The young man glanced at a desk calendar. "Grand Junction."

"We can't go chasing him all over Colorado, Miriam."

"I guess we'll have to catch him at the seminar, then." Miriam turned to the receptionist. "Are there tickets still available for his seminar this evening?"

The young man's face split into a beaming plastic smile. "Why, yes, there are! Although you may want to arrive early—his talks are very popular and you may find yourself standing."

"That's fine," said Miriam. "We'll take two tickets, please."

"Excellent! That will be one hundred and fifty dollars apiece, please. Three hundred total."

"A hundred and fifty dollars!" Joan protested. "That's outrageous!"

The receptionist's dour scowl returned. "Mr. Amadan feels that what is dearly paid for is truly learned. You don't expect him to travel hundreds of miles and share his knowledge for several hours for free, do you?"

"And I suppose he needs to pay rent on posh digs like this wherever he goes," Joan grumbled, eyeing the decor.

"You could put it that way," said the receptionist.

"I guess we'll have to catch him after his show, then."

"No," Miriam said, pulling her wallet out of her skirt pocket. "We can't take the chance we'd miss him." She pulled out a credit card and tossed it lightly onto the desk. "Do you take Visa?"

"Of course!" beamed the receptionist, his false smile returning.

"Miriam!"

"It's okay. I've put so much on this card already, it hardly matters. I'll tell my dad I spent it on clothes. He wouldn't mind that so much."

The receptionist handled the card and receipt business expertly and handed Miriam two silvery-gray tickets. "It starts promptly at seven. Don't be late—he won't allow in stragglers."

"Thanks," said Joan sourly.

"My pleasure," said the receptionist. "May you find the enlightenment you seek."

As they left the office, Miriam said, "He was kinda cute, wasn't he?"

"Miriam, he was dissing us and loving every minute of it!"

"Well, I guess he's entitled, isn't he?"

"If being a minority entitles you to be a jerk."

"Joan! Have some understanding."

63

"Sorry. It must be another blind spot in my character. Speaking of blindness, let's go sit down somewhere out of this sun. Even with these sunglasses, I'm getting a headache."

They found a little watering hole just off Main Street called the Blue Moon and went in and sat at the bar. It had a bit of the Old West and the New West mixed together, cowboy prints hanging above white-linen tables. This time of day, it was empty except for the staff.

"Afternoon, ladies," said the tanned, blond bartender. To Joan's eyes, he was another work-to-play jock, taking whatever job was available to support his sport, whichever that might be. But with his friendly, guileless grin, he was more welcoming than the last guy they'd spoken to. "What can I get you?"

Miriam ordered a glass of the house white wine. Joan ordered coffee. When the bartender returned with their drinks, Joan showed him Amadan's seminar flyer. "You know anything about this Brian Amadan?"

"Oh, yeah. He's doing a big seminar here tonight."

"Yeah, we're going to it. But we don't know much about him. A . . . friend recommended that we go."

"He's real popular. Draws quite a crowd every time he comes to town."

"So he's been here before?" Miriam prompted.

"A few times in the past couple of years. Heh. I hear tell he came through town in the fall with some of his hunting buddies. They even brought hounds with them—some sort of rottweiler-wolf mix, my pals said— and hunted on horseback through the Sangre de Cristos. At night even. Man, that must have been wild, hearing those hounds baying."

"That explains the stuffed ex-wildlife in his office," Joan said.

"Yeah. Some of the locals were upset with the noise, but I guess he greased a few of the right palms to make it all right. He's not lacking for money, that guy," he added, a bit enviously.

"Given what he charges for seminar tickets, I'm not surprised," Joan said. "But what's he like? Personally, I mean."

"Heck if I know. I've never met him, myself," said the bartender.

"Have you heard other people talk about him?"

"Sure. Plenty. But it's kinda contradictory. Apparently if he likes you, he's smooth as silk. If he doesn't like you, he's colder than a block of ice. A good tipper, they say. Hope he comes in here sometime."

"What's his seminar about?" Miriam asked.

The bartender gave her an odd look. "Beats me. Something about taking care of the wilderness, making it fit for all creatures, et cetera. That's all I know. What brought you up here to hear him?"

"Curiosity," Joan hastily put in. "We heard about him from some friends over in Dawson Butte. Apparently he's a real . . . powerful speaker."

"Yeah, that's what I hear too," said the bartender. "People seem to come from all over for his seminars."

"He isn't, like, running a cult, is he?" asked Miriam.

The bartender went back to wiping the counter. "Not that I can tell, but I wouldn't know. You're asking the wrong person, really. Why don't you ask the lady who just came in? She looks like the type that goes to his seminars." He tilted his chin toward a woman who sat at a booth across the room.

She had shoulder-length pale blond hair, with heavy bangs, and although she was pale for a Coloradan, everything about her screamed wealthy Aspenite, from her white leather faux moccasins to her gold-appliquéd white leather top and silver squash-blossom jewelry.

"Okay," said Miriam, and she hopped off the barstool and walked over to the booth. "Excuse me," she said to the woman in white. "Um, are you going to the 'Open Spaces/Open Minds' seminar this evening?"

Joan wanted to dive under the bar in embarrassment and scream, "I'm not with her!"

"Why, yes," said the woman, raising her elegant, well-plucked brows. "I am." Her voice was low and musical, and Joan wondered if the woman was an actress.

"Oh, good, because my friend and I are really curious about this Brian Amadan guy. Do you know much about him?"

Joan covered her face with her hands.

"I . . . do not know him personally. I am sorry," the woman said.

Joan just knew the woman was seeing Miriam's neo-hippy garb and thinking she was a wannabe groupie.

"Oh, that's all right," Miriam said. "It's just that, well, my dad's a real estate developer and he sent me up here to check out what Mr. Amadan is saying. He's thinking of buying some land in this area."

"Ah. I see."

There was an awkward pause, and Joan peeked between her fingers. The woman was looking at Miriam with a wide-eyed, accommodating expression, except that her half-smile seemed coldly amused.

"So . . . can you tell me, like, what to expect? At his seminar, I mean?"

"I fear you may be disappointed," the woman said, with an ever so slightly condescending tilt of her head. "Unless your father is also in the landscaping business."

"Um, he works with landscapers. So I might learn something useful about . . . landscaping?"

"Since you have said you are going to the seminar, I suggest that you wait and discover for yourself what the Amadan may teach you." Her voice had the unmistakable tone of dismissal.

"Oh. Well. Okay. Thanks." Miriam practically scurried back to her barstool.

"No offense, and I mean this in the nicest way," Joan murmured, "but that has got to be the lamest interrogation I have ever heard."

"I know," Miriam whimpered, putting her head down on her arms.

"I want you never, ever to do that again while we are on this little trip, all right?"

"Okay."

"Because I just might become too embarrassed to be seen with you, and that wouldn't help Gillian any, would it?"

"I feel stupid enough, okay? Don't rub it in."

The bartender came up and refilled Miriam's glass with a rueful grin. "Sorry I steered you wrong," he said to Miriam. "This refill's on me." He reached over and patted her arm, then walked away.

Miriam stared thoughtfully into her glass a moment, then murmured, "Maybe I was just distracted by her glamour."

Joan clicked her tongue. "Glamour. You Californians.

You're all infected with Hollywooditis. You go gaga over anyone who looks like a movie star."

"That's not what I meant," said Miriam sulkily. "Not what I meant at all. Something about her . . . felt the same way as Mr. Amadan's card."

Joan frowned and glanced over her shoulder. But the Aspenite lady was gone.

Chapter 4

They went for late lunch/early dinner, and since Joan insisted on buying they ended up at a little bus-your-own bistro where Miriam could get tabouli salad and Joan had a bowl of chili. Miriam was uncharacteristically silent, still dying of shame, Joan figured. So Joan regaled her with Tales from the Dark Ranch. Like the time the whole family plus hands had to go out in a driving rain to rescue some cattle that were too stupid to get out of a ravine while the water from a flash flood was rising around them. Or the time seven-year-old Joan brought home a baby skunk she'd found out in the pasture, much to her parents' consternation. And the day her horse, Misty, figured out how to unlatch the corral gate. All to let Miriam know she was, in fact, forgiven.

Since they had been warned by Amadan's receptionist that the seminar would be full, Joan and Miriam headed over early to the Mountain Spirit Theater. And it was fortunate they did, for already a crowd was gathering outside it.

"Boy, he wasn't kidding we should get here early," Joan said, craning her neck to see if there was a line anywhere or if the theater doors were open.

"Yeah," said Miriam. "I hope we can get seats."

"Hmmm. Maybe I shouldn't have brought Gillian along." Joan was finding it hard to keep from bumping into other people with the guitar case.

"There's little point in being here without her," Miriam said.

Joan was prepared to feel out of place, given how much they'd paid for the tickets, but she noted that the other people in the crowd were dressed in a range of clothes from shorts and T-shirts to business suits and dresses.

While the crowd slowly shuffled in, Joan saw a sign on the side of the building declaring the theater a historical landmark. It had once been an opera house when Summit Rock was a booming mining town. In its seedier days it became a venue for melodramas and the upstairs was used as a bawdy house. In the eighties it had been lovingly restored and renamed. But as the sign praised the up-to-date theater tech installed, Joan wondered just how "restored" one could call the place.

As they squeezed through the tiny lobby, thick brochures printed on fake parchment paper were pressed into their hands by ushers. Joan tried to glance at hers, but she had no room to lift her arm, what with trying to handle the guitar case.

By the time Joan and Miriam got in, there were few seats left, and there didn't seem to be two together. And there were none down front.

"Oh, drat," said Miriam. "Where should we sit?"

"We'd better choose fast. You just go find a seat. I'll be nearby."

Miriam snagged one of the last ones, on the far-left aisle toward the back. Joan had to content herself with leaning against the wall a little closer to the stage. Joan had hoped to have a seat down front so that she could blatantly hold Gillian in front of her, and thus "catch the conscience of the king," as Hamlet put it. However, she doubted she would be noticed at her distance from the stage, so she kept Gillian in the guitar case.

Soon the walls were lined with people, and ushers closed the entry doors. The ushers were fair-haired young men, but too pale of skin and pretty-faced to be Rockies jocks. Joan assumed they must have been hired from Hollywood or the East Coast, or possibly they were Euro-trash. After finding everyone a place to stand or sit, the ushers stood at attention at the back.

The lights dimmed slowly until the theater was in total darkness. Nature sounds—frogs chirruping, birds singing, the soft susurration of wind and water—played over the PA. Music began, again similar to that Gillian's MIDI had played, but even more haunting; sweet, high notes trilled, and Joan imagined wood nymphs in deep forest blowing on panpipes, or lutes plucked by satyrs and fauns. Faint but clear voices could be heard in the sighing of the wind, ethereal harmonies. Closing her eyes, Joan truly felt transported.

A male voice, smooth and low, with a slight British accent, spoke in the darkness. "Long, long ago, there was a time when trees were the giants and guardians of the earth. A time when wildlife and water were plentiful, when only the wind played the tune to which all the earth's denizens danced."

Joan could see clearly in her mind's eye towering trees, sequoias perhaps, sunlight slanting through them onto meadows and lakes at which fantastical animals, large and small, gathered to drink. The vision was so strong she could smell the forest and the creatures, and she found herself hungering to be there.

"Then," the voice continued, "the earth turned in its sleep, and volcanoes spewed, continents moved, mountains thrust upward, and, in time, the earth became infected with a virus called Man."

As if in amazing fast-forward video, Joan saw the forest blown down in a cataclysmic explosion, its mighty trees subjected to mudflows, fire, and ice, the land uplifted and then overrun by tiny creatures that were people scurrying like ants to build cities like anthills where forest had been.

"It would be easy to believe," the voice went on, "that the paradise that was earth has been forever lost. That we shall never again know that Eden for which we were born."

What is he talking about? Joan wondered. *Surely that forest existed long before humans evolved. Why should it mean anything to us?*

"But we must not lose heart. The potential for that world exists, even here in the Colorado wilderness, deep in its bones, beneath your feet. Some of you can feel this. Some of you know. And I have come to give you what help I can to see that the world we so long for is . . . reborn."

At his last word, the lights came up, slowly. And Joan saw the very forest she had visualized at the back of the theater stage. As though it were a window on another world, a man dressed in a gray suit stepped out of that forest onto the stage. He was exactly as Gillian's landlady had described him—tall, lean, elegant, graceful, his gray hair tied back in a queue. But as he paced the stage, Joan noticed his eyes—they were pale and feral, like the eyes in the portrait of the wolf that hung over his receptionist's desk.

"Welcome to my seminar, 'Open Spaces/Open Minds,' in which I will reveal to you those methods of managing your property that will help bring about this rebirth of the land. Of course, you already know the simple things that must be done," he said, and Joan had the impression there were specific people in the audience he was speaking to. She wasn't one of them. "You must not let the water that sustains this land be sucked away by that . . . growth that infests the Front Range."

A few cries of "Hear hear!" and "Yeah!" erupted from the audience.

"You must discourage any landowner here in the San Luis Valley or elsewhere from making such a deal with the devil. But this is an obvious step. There are so many smaller, less dramatic things you can do to help awaken the potential paradise that lies below."

He crossed to the right-hand side of the stage to a large, thronelike carved wooden chair and sat in it, steepling his hands. He began to speak quickly, spitting out his words rapid-fire, and Joan saw members of the audience hastily scribbling in notebooks. Mr. Amadan spoke of planting oak: "Oak is the most important, most vital—it is the king and father of the forest." He mentioned other trees, such as apple and hazel, hawthorn and elder, Scotch pine and birch. "Shun the willow," he said, "for its mind is dark and it keeps to itself. Do not plant ash or rowan, for their powers turn against us."

He then went on to advocate certain herbs and shrubs, describing a method of planting each that involved phases of the moon and ritualistic phrases and gestures. He claimed that this would bring the "spirits of the earth" to one's aid in reforming the landscape. "Do all this," he said, "and in time you may find proof that you have successfully prepared the land—your herds and flocks will prosper, mushroom rings of power may appear in your groves, and you might even hear music on the midsummer wind."

It was the sheerest woo-woo, Joan decided, and yet many of the people standing and sitting around her were avidly nodding, writing, soaking it in. *It's no wonder he's speaking in Summit Rock,* she thought. *This is the place to find suckers for his philosophy. But won't they figure out pretty quickly that his approach is worthless? Half of the stuff he mentioned won't even grow here.*

The lights were dimming again and the music returned. But this time the special effects were heightened. A great forest appeared around them, as if the audience were sitting in a sun-dappled glade. Birds flew overhead and perched on branches nearby. Animals with large, bright eyes scurried under bushes and chittered. A breeze heavy with the scent of growing things wafted by. Despite knowing it was all tech-trickery, Joan almost wept with longing to be in that forest, to run freely with the deer, drink from crystal-clear streams, and spend her life exploring the forest's mysteries. Sighs flowed through the audience and then scattered applause that grew into a standing ovation.

The house lights came up full and the illusion vanished. Apparently so had Mr. Amadan—the stage was empty. No, Joan realized, there he was by the right-hand exit, near where she stood. He bowed, smiling, and said, "You all have powers you have been unaware of.

Go forth and work wonders upon the world." Then he turned to leave.

Joan rushed toward him. "Mr. Amadan! I need to speak to you!"

But she was not alone, and was quickly caught in a crush of people shouting much the same thing. The pretty-boy ushers blocked their way as Mr. Amadan left through the double doors.

"I need to speak to him!" Joan said to one of the ushers.

"You and many others," the usher said.

"It's very important!"

"Without doubt, but the Amadan speaks to no one without an appointment."

"But—" Joan was pushed back by others surging forward, and she gave it up as a lost cause. She managed to extricate herself from the crowd, and she caught up with Miriam in the theater lobby.

"Wasn't that amazing?" Miriam said, wide-eyed, as Joan approached.

"What? Oh, the show. Sure, good special effects, very pretty, but his message was pure bunk. You couldn't support any size community in an environment like that unless we all went back to being hunters and gatherers, and even then—"

"Joan, you're being materialistic again," Miriam chided.

"It may be bunk," said a pudgy guy standing next to them wearing glasses and a gimme cap, "but it works for me."

"It works? You mean you actually grow that stuff?" Joan asked.

"Heck, no. I sell real estate around here, and this guy

Amadan makes people want to buy land, just to try what he's telling them. Business has been booming ever since he started coming to town. Call me if you're interested. I've still got some homesites available out by San Isabel Creek. Some good deals left, but they're going fast." He handed her his card.

"Um, thanks," Joan said. As he turned away to give a sales pitch to other attendees, Joan handed the card to Miriam. "Here, your dad can put it in his Rolodex. C'mon, let's go."

They stepped out onto Main Street, into the cool mountain night air. Joan looked up, and even with the streetlights nearby, the stars were incredibly bright.

"I'll just bet that real estate guy gets business," Miriam said. "Maybe I'll have my dad call this guy and buy some acreage up here for me."

"Miriam! Have you forgotten why we came here? This guy turned Gillian into a guitar, remember?"

"Exactly! And if he could transform Gillian . . . well, maybe we're looking at this all wrong." There was a strange glint in Miriam's eyes that Joan found unsettling. "Maybe there is something bigger, more important, going on here than we thought. A way to transform the whole world. Wouldn't it be interesting if some of what Mr. Amadan said would work? How do you know it wouldn't? You should have a more open mind about this. That's probably what his seminar title, 'Open Spaces/Open Minds,' means."

"I think it refers to the open space you have to have between your ears *instead* of your mind to believe this stuff. Look, I may not have your feel for spiritual matters, but I've learned enough about business to know a scam when I see one. Some people in that audience were in on it and the rest of us were marks. If Mr. Amadan has got a racket going, mystical or monetary, it's *not* a good thing. Miriam, this is the guy Frank at the New Age store called 'bad juju.' You didn't like the way his business card felt, remember?"

Miriam looked away. "That's . . . that's true. But that forest . . . I really wanted to be there."

"So did I," Joan admitted. "So he's got a good line and a good lighting designer. It doesn't mean he's telling the truth."

Miriam wrapped her arms around herself, as if suddenly cold. "You're right. You're right, of course. I guess I . . . wasn't thinking."

"S'okay. Right now we have to think about how to talk to Mr. Amadan, since we missed him at the seminar. C'mon, I think better when my feet are moving." *He doesn't just want people's money,* Joan thought. *He wants people to grow things for him. But why?*

As they strolled down Main Street, Miriam said, "I guess we'll just have to follow him out to Grand Junction." Somehow she didn't sound unhappy about the prospect.

"Unless we can get his attention someway sooner." Joan saw some of the seminar attendees go into a coffeehouse that was still open. A hand-lettered sign on the window said, OPEN MIKE NITE. BRING YOUR POEMS AND MUSIC AND SHARE.

"I think I've got an idea," Joan said. "You play pretty good guitar, right?"

"Yeah, I'm okay. But what—"

"C'mon."

Joan pushed open the door, and the quiet roar of conversation spilled out. The place was packed. She went up to the guy at the counter with the buzz-cut hair and pierced nose. "When does the open mike start?"

"Any time we get a volunteer," the guy said. "We've had two poets already. They were pretty bad. You want to get on the list? Or you can go right on up if you want. Nobody else seems too eager to perform right now."

Joan blinked and tried to make sense of the young man's rambling response. "Uh, give me a minute or two to confer with my accompanist and we'll just go onstage. We only want to do one song."

The young man shrugged. " 'Sall good. Whatever you wanna do."

"Okay." Joan pulled Miriam aside into what passed for an empty corner of the place.

"Joan, you want us to go up and sing? Why?"

"Hey, you said I should consider performing. Now's my chance. But seriously, these people know Mr. Amadan. Better than we do, anyway. I think I see one of his usher/bodyguards here."

"Yeah, so?"

"So we're going to get Gillian to sing for them. You know Patsy Cline's 'Crazy'?"

"Uh, that hasn't got the easiest chord progression in the world, you know."

"Doesn't matter. Fake it. Gillian knows it, and she can sing along. It'll just get the audience's attention more if you flub a chord or two."

Miriam took Gillian out of the guitar case, and Joan went through the song quietly once with her. As soon as Joan figured Miriam knew roughly what she was doing, Joan bounded up on the stage and adjusted the mike.

"Hi there," she said nervously to the crowd. A couple of people said hi back.

"Um, my name is Joan Dark and I wanted to sing one of my favorite songs for you. This is my friend Miriam, and I want you to notice the guitar she's carrying—it's very special. One of a kind, in fact. It was made by our very own Mr. Brian Amadan, whom I know some of you heard speak earlier tonight."

That caught their interest. A few of the better-dressed people sat up and turned their heads.

"That's right," Joan said, nodding to them. "Mr. Amadan made this with . . . his own hands. Quite a talented guy, huh? Well, it turns out this is kind of a magical guitar. She can sing, and she's going to sing along with me. So listen up, 'cause this is going to be a, uh, unique experience."

Joan nodded to Miriam, who looked as though she'd rather be somewhere else. Miriam sat on the one folding chair onstage and curled herself around the guitar. Joan waited while Miriam made her way through the opening chords. Pretending she was in the shower, Joan began to sing. "I'm crazy . . ."

Miriam's timing wasn't the best, so the song limped along. Joan didn't much care, for she was noticing how certain members of the audience were staring at the guitar. Joan deliberately gave Miriam a chance to do an instrumental bridge early, and as Miriam gamely made her way through the progression, Joan held the mike close to Gillian's sound hole.

The voices the strings produced were a strangely harmonic cacophony—

I'm cra-zy . . .
help me help me help me
I'm scared scared scared
Am-a-dan did this to me . . .

When the verse came around again, Joan did only one more plus a chorus and then finished the song.

The applause was loud, and there were appreciative whistles, hoots, and stomps. The guy Joan had pegged as Amadan's usher stared at her a moment, then got up and left. *Aha,* thought Joan. *Maybe now we'll get his attention.*

Joan followed Miriam off the stage, and immediately a couple of people came up asking to see the guitar. "I'm sorry," Joan said, "but we don't let anyone else play her. She's almost like a friend to us, and we don't want to see her damaged." After conversing the minimum amount so as not to seem rude, and buying a café mocha to go, they left the coffeehouse and walked back to the Well of Life Lodge.

The middle-aged man at the front desk smiled at them as they walked in. "Hey, are you Joan and Miriam?"

They looked at each other before Joan said, "That's us."

The man reached into the cubbyhole boxes behind him. "Got a message for you."

"Already?" Joan took the silvery note card and read it aloud to Miriam. "Mr. Brian Amadan requests the honor of meeting with you tomorrow morning at ten a.m. at his Summit Rock office."

"Yes!" Miriam said. She jumped up and down and high-fived Joan.

"Okay, okay, down, girl. We have to go and plan our strategy."

They argued long into the night but could come up with no better approach than the direct one. After Miriam's fiasco with the woman at the Blue Moon, Joan figured the cagey detective scenario was out. Better just to say what they wanted and hope for Mr. Amadan's goodwill. But Joan went so far as to suggest the good cop/bad cop game, with Miriam acting the fervent admirer of Mr. Amadan's philosophy, which she could clearly pull off with enthusiasm, and Joan playing the firm, hard-nosed bitch.

The next morning, Joan again slept late, so Miriam again brought her a breakfast that was entirely too healthy.

"You don't understand, Miriam," Joan tried to say around a dry mouthful of oat-bran muffin. "If it doesn't have protein, fat, or sugar, it isn't breakfast."

"I guess they had some of that down in the dining room. I didn't notice it."

"Mmph. Never mind. I'll make up for it at lunch."

Though she tried to get her brain focused on the problem at hand while showering and dressing, Joan felt no better prepared as she followed Miriam back into Mr. Amadan's forest-primeval-style waiting room.

She couldn't put her finger on it, but something felt different about the room, as if something more alive and unfriendly than taxidermed squirrels was watching them from the pine and aspen boughs. Glancing at the portrait of the wolf over the receptionist's desk, Joan confirmed her impression from the seminar. The resemblance to Brian Amadan was uncanny.

The Amerind receptionist glanced up as if he had never seen them before. "May I help you?"

"Good morning," said Joan, with an equally plastic smile. "This time we do have an appointment." She handed him the silvery card.

"Oh, of course. He's expecting you. Please go right in." He indicated the set of double doors to his right.

"Thank you." With a slight, sardonic bow, Joan walked through the double doors, Miriam right behind her.

Out of the corner of her eye she saw Miriam jump, startled, as they entered.

At first it seemed like an ordinary enough office—green carpeting, two wood-and-canvas chairs facing a broad cherrywood desk. Behind the desk sat Mr. Amadan, no less imposing up close, his gray eyes no less daunting. He wore the same gray suit, and gray silk gloves adorned his long, lean hands.

But behind him, the large picture windows that took up most of the wall did not show the Sangre de Cristo Mountains or Summit Rock's Main Street. Instead it was a nightscape of a forest meadow. What appeared to be fireflies glimmered here and there—moving, and the branches of the trees were swaying in a silent wind.

A video window, Joan thought. *He must be damn rich to afford such a big one of those.* It disconcerted her, however, that the fireflies, when they flew close, were more human in form than insect—

"Welcome, Ms. Dark, Ms. Sanderson. Please, have a seat, if you like. I am so glad you could come." Mr. Amadan's voice was even more resonant than it had been in the theater, and Joan wondered if he had ever been an actor.

Miriam was about to take one of the chairs when she

blinked at it and stepped back. She seemed uncomfortable and jumpy. Mr. Amadan watched her a moment, and Joan hoped she wasn't going to blow it again. Miriam wasn't yet exuding the charm Joan had told her to.

"Care for a mint?" Mr. Amadan said, pushing a crystal bowl with little green squares in it toward her.

"Oh. Thank you," Miriam said, taking one and popping it into her mouth. She sat cautiously on the chair and smiled politely.

"Would you—" Mr. Amadan began, proffering the bowl toward Joan.

"No, thanks," Joan said. "This isn't really a social call."

"I believe it was I who invited you here," Mr. Amadan said. "Therefore I believe I may set the tone of the meeting."

"That was a great seminar you did last night," Miriam said, finally easing into her role. "*Wonderful* special effects."

"Thank you," said Mr. Amadan. "I learned some things from a young performance artist in Pittsburgh."

"As I told Joan, it almost made me want to buy land here myself."

"I am very pleased to hear it," said Mr. Amadan. "I hope you will do so."

"Excuse me," said Joan, "but we would like to talk about our friend." She swiftly opened the guitar case and held up Gillian.

"Ah, yes," said Mr. Amadan, turning to her. "I understand you were bandying my name about at a bar last night. I should like you to understand that despite my public appearances, I am a rather private person and do not like my name taken in vain."

Who does he think he is, God? "It was the only way we could think of to get your attention. As you can see, it worked. Now about this guitar—"

"Yes, I see you discovered the little project Miss McKeagh asked for my help with. She was working on electronic music, and I gave her advice on how to install a microchip to give the impression the instrument was speaking. If you look carefully through the sound hole, you can just barely see it. She used the same technology I use for the special effects in my seminars. Her project turned out rather well, wouldn't you say?"

Suspicious, Joan held Gillian up and glanced down the sound hole. In the back, she could discern a silvery glimmer and what appeared to be wires leading to the support slats on the guitar's body. For a moment, Joan was nonplussed. She lowered the guitar, feeling like an idiot and preparing to eat crow. Her hands slipped and the guitar fell to the floor.

> *liar!*   LIAR!
>   *liar!*   *liar!*   LIAR!
> Liar!   LIAR!
>   I'm   real   REAL
> Real   me   me   me

Mr. Amadan scowled at the guitar as Joan picked it up. Joan looked inside the guitar again, and the silvery chip and wires were gone. She slipped her hand beneath the strings and as far down the sound hole as she could, feeling nothing but wood.

"Sorry, Mr. Amadan," Joan growled, "but I don't quite believe you."

"Believe what you like," he said coldly. "What do you want me to do?"

"Change her back!" Joan demanded. "You did this to her because she was involved with research that you didn't like. Was she about to discover some secret of yours? Change her back!"

"By what Right or Rule do you compel me thus?" said Mr. Amadan.

Joan could hear in his question some ancient echo of rite and custom. If she could just find the right reason, the right thing to say, he would do as she asked. *Damn, I don't know enough about him. I'm in over my head.* "In the name of God?" she said, wincing at the weakness in her tone.

Mr. Amadan paused, then half of his mouth tilted up in a smile. "I am not of that faith," he said, "and I suspect neither are you to any great extent."

"In the name of fairness, then!" said Miriam, jumping up from her chair. "Here you are, a more powerful . . . person, and here we are with no other weapon than a wish for justice. Surely whatever Gillian did could not have been bad enough to deserve this. Surely she ought to be forgiven. She was Joan's friend, and Joan has come to beg for her life back. We can't hold a gun to your head. We can't even threaten you. An evil man would take advantage of us, but a great man, a noble man, would consider our request and be magnanimous, because his power permits him to be. Surely Gillian has learned her lesson and will not give you cause for anger again."

Mr. Amadan leaned back in his chair and raised his eyebrows. "You speak eloquently on your friend's behalf." He stood and approached Miriam, reached out one gray-gloved hand, and ran his fingers ever so lightly beneath her chin.

Joan saw Miriam shudder, but whether from fear or revulsion or . . . something else she wasn't sure.

"You have Talent," said Mr. Amadan, with the seductive purr of a tiger. "My . . . company appreciates people with Talents. Would you like to come work for me? I can assure you, the benefits are . . . comprehensive."

Joan saw Miriam waver, lean closer to him, as if she would fall into his arms. *What is he doing to her?* Joan felt a mixture of worry, anger, and even, inexplicably, jealousy. "What about Gillian?" Joan shouted.

That seemed to break the spell. Miriam blinked and stepped back quickly. "I'm sorry," said Miriam, "but she's right. We have to think about our friend first."

Mr. Amadan sighed. "Very well. You have compelled me in the name of fair play. Therefore, custom begs that I give you a chance. I will retransform your benighted friend, if you can tell me where I might find crystal sage, and tell me of its nature. Bring me proof you have found it and she shall once again be human. Do reconsider my offer, Miss Sanderson. It will remain open to you, for a time. Good morning to you both."

"But wait!" Joan began. "What is—"

"This interview is at an end," said Mr. Amadan. He waved a hand and the office was plunged into darkness. Near-darkness, that is, for Joan could see moonlight filtering down through a dense forest canopy around her. She heard chittering that might have been chipmunks . . . or laughter . . . from the shadows. The double doors to the office shone like a beacon, and Joan and Miriam grabbed each other and Gillian and headed through them as fast as they could go.

The receptionist glanced up at them curiously as they burst out into the waiting area, but Joan ignored him. "Him and his damn special effects!" she snarled at Miriam. "Bring me proof of crystal sage, he says. Yeah, like bring me the broom of the Wicked Witch of the West. He's just trying to scare us and get us out of his hair."

"Joan," Miriam said softly, her face pale, "he isn't faking it. When we were in his office, we weren't . . . here, you know? We were someplace else. And those chairs and his desk, they weren't what they seemed. They were . . . alive."

"Oh, stop it!" Joan said. "C'mon, let's go back in while the effects are off." She stormed back through the double doors—

—into an empty room. It was completely bare of furniture, and the picture window on the far wall now showed only mountains and the town below.

"You see?" Miriam hissed.

"I believe he told you that your interview was over," said the receptionist smoothly behind them.

Joan stomped out, then turned on the Amerind. "How can you work for that guy?" she snarled at him. "He's more full of tricks than David Copperfield."

The receptionist smiled a genuine but cold smile. "We share . . . similar values."

"But he's got all the humanity of that . . . that wolf there." She pointed up at the portrait.

"Sometimes it is worthwhile to have the wolf as one's ally."

"Even though a wolf can turn right around and bite you?"

The receptionist shrugged. "That is the nature of wolves."

This is hopeless, thought Joan. "C'mon, Miriam. Let's get out of this madhouse."

Chapter 5

As they trudged back out onto Main Street and into the bright mountain sunlight, Miriam said softly, "Thank you."

"Hmm? For what?"

"For shouting when you did, when Mr. Amadan was making his . . . offer to me. I swear, I would have taken it. What I saw in that window, in his eyes, was so . . . beautiful. It was everything I had ever dreamed of."

"Well, you know, you pulled the plug on Gilly's computer when I needed it. I was just returning the favor."

"Yeah." Miriam's face was creased with a frown, and she looked more somber than Joan had ever seen her.

"What's the matter?"

"Ever feel like your soul's been tried, and you didn't like the verdict?"

"Sure. Lots of times, when I was a kid in church. Maybe that's why I stopped going."

"I would have done anything for him. It's like having a taste of a drug so wonderful that you know once you give in to it, you're doomed. And you know you wouldn't care."

"Hey." Joan put a hand on her shoulder. "You're

okay now. At least we got away still in our own bodies, and our minds still intact."

"I hope so," Miriam said doubtfully. She took a deep breath and added, "Anyway, let's talk about how to find this crystal sage."

Joan rolled her eyes. "Miriam . . ."

"Joan." Miriam faced her with dark fire in her eyes. "You've got to trust me on this. It's important, whether it's ritual or riddle. While Mr. Amadan looked at me, I suddenly understood. The bargain he has made with us is binding—he has to honor it. But it's also sort of a test. For us. What he asked for *is* meaningful, somehow. But it's up to us to prove ourselves worthy by figuring out what he means."

"You saw all that by staring into his little gray squinties?" asked Joan. "Why? Why should he want to test us? Why should he care whether we prove ourselves? So he can hire us into his so-called company? What does he get out of it?"

Miriam jammed her hands into her hair. "Amusement. Maybe. But maybe something deeper. Honor and oaths mean more to his kind. Joan, listen to me. He's not like normal people."

"I'll say."

"No, really."

"So what kind of people is he?"

Miriam glanced up and down the street. "I'll tell you later. Anyway, if we don't do as he asks, there's no way he'll help us retransform Gillian."

"Suppose we find someone else to do it? You happen to know any powerful sorcerers in Colorado?"

Miriam shook her head.

"What if we take her into a church and have a priest bless her?"

"It would probably hurt her. Real bad."

"Hmm. Guess we're stuck chasing down plants for Brian Amadan, then." Joan ran her hand through her hair and sighed. "I wonder if he needs this crystal sage for part of his big replantation scheme. Well, I guess it won't hurt to spend one more day puzzling at this."

"What if it takes longer than a day?" Miriam asked. "It might take a lot longer, you know."

Joan feared Miriam might be right. "Shit. Bad enough what he did to Gillian. Now this Amadan guy might make me lose clients, too."

"The trials of the hero always involve sacrifice."

"You been reading too much Joseph Campbell, girl. Where should we start?"

They noticed a small National Forest Service office and went in. A young red-haired woman was organizing pamphlets on the shelf, and a young man lounged behind the counter reading a *Sandman* comic book.

"Hi, can I help you?" said the young woman.

"We're looking for information on a plant that maybe grows in the area," said Joan. "Ever hear of crystal sage?"

The guy behind the counter snorted. "Sounds like a character in a western soap opera."

"Don't mind Justin," said the redhead. "Too much partying has rotted his brain. Crystal sage, huh? I haven't heard of it. Let me check and see if it's a folk name for something." She pulled down from the shelves a couple of books on Rocky Mountain flora and flipped through the indexes. "Nope, I don't see it here."

"I suppose it could be the name of a mineral," Joan

offered. "We don't really know. Mr. Brian Amadan suggested we look for it."

"Oooh," Justin said. "Mr. Woo-woo himself. Did he want you to plant it on your lawn to bring the good-luck spirits?"

Joan scowled at him. "We don't know what he wants it for. Or if it even exists. But we thought it worth checking."

Miriam leaned over the counter and looked at the comic in Justin's hands. "Ooh, you like *Sandman*? Good taste."

Justin grinned back. "Thanks. Keeps me from falling asleep on the job."

"Your job is boring? I think it'd be great to work for the Forest Service."

"Sure," said Justin, "if you're lucky enough to get one of the rare outside jobs. Don't I feel lucky that I got a master's in ecological studies just so I could work a glorified tourist booth."

"Justin, don't make me give you more demerits for attitude," chided the redhead.

"Oh, sorry. A tourist booth run by the Boy Scouts."

"Uh, pardon us," said Joan, stepping toward the door, "but we'll just move along before we get caught in the crossfire."

"Sorry I couldn't be of more help," said the redhead. "You could try calling the bio department at Western State over in Gunnison, or Adams College down in Alamosa."

"Thanks," said Joan.

"Or you could try asking Buck Jones," said Justin.

"Who's Buck Jones?" asked Miriam.

"Justin, don't tease."

"Hey! If Mr. Amadan sent them, they might wanna know, right? Buck Jones is a little guy who hangs out at Molly's Peak—that's a bar over on Taylor. They say he shows up around midnight."

"He's a ghost," the redhead said, with a deprecating tilt of her head.

"A ghost," Joan said.

"Maybe, maybe not," said Justin. "He's a local legend, anyway. They say he's a leftover from the old mining days. If anybody knows about minerals, it'd be Buck Jones. Just show up at Molly's around midnight and maybe you'll see him."

"Er, thanks," said Joan. "Maybe we will."

They spent the afternoon wandering into gift shops and bookstores, inquiring after crystal sage. No one seemed to know anything helpful, though people tried to sell Joan and Miriam all sorts of unlikely things. They even tried a fortune-teller with a crystal ball, for the heck of it—a pleasant, plump young woman with more piercings of ears, eyebrows, and nose than Joan could count. She told them happily that they would achieve success in the music business (she had noted the guitar), they'd meet a handsome stranger who would bring romance, and their dearest wishes would come true. Miriam politely crossed her palm with silver while Joan firmly kept her mouth shut, and they left.

It was Miriam's turn to pay for dinner, so they ate at one of Summit Rock's better restaurants, a nice Italian place, but while Joan scarfed down a plateful of spaghetti, Miriam only picked at her fettucini primavera. Joan's inquiries of what was the matter only met with Miriam's sad shrug and smile.

By 11:45 p.m., Summit Rock was quiet as a tomb,

except for the occasional roar of a car barreling down Main Street. A cold wind was blowing down from the Sangre de Cristos, and Joan pulled her light jacket tighter around her, wishing she'd packed a parka. Miriam wore only a knit shawl over her usual clothes, and Joan wondered why she didn't seem to be freezing.

They turned onto a side street and strolled past old log homes, little wood shacks, and ornate Victorian confections of houses until they reached Taylor. The signboard for Molly's was the only thing lit on the street.

The bar was long, narrow, and tiny, and clearly hadn't been redecorated for the New Age crowd—probably not renovated for decades, Joan figured. It had a scuffed and worn bare wood floor and a ceiling of tarnished patterned tin. The bar itself had a traditional brass rail, and on the wall behind it was a faded portrait of a plump woman holding a stein of beer. On the far wall was a dartboard whose markings were nearly totally obscured by years' worth of dart holes. The place smelled of tobacco and ale and old sweat.

A pair of old men in straw cowboy hats sat mumbling to each other at one of the few tables. Another ancient fellow was wiping down the bar.

"Not what you'd call a good pickup joint," Joan murmured.

"But it looks like a good place to find ghosts," Miriam said. "It reeks with atmosphere."

"I'd say it just reeks." Joan walked up to the bar.

The old bartender didn't even look up. "Near closing time, ladies."

"We'd like to stick around to meet Buck Jones," Joan said.

The old man stopped and slowly turned his head. "Who told you about Buck Jones?"

"Justin down at the Forest Service office."

"Stupid kids," muttered the old man, as he draped the damp cloth over a spigot handle. "No respect. What do you want to see 'im for?"

"We want to ask him about a mineral," Miriam put in.

"Hunh. Don't want nobody chasing ol' Buck off. He's brought good luck to this place these many years. He don't take nonsense from nobody. He don't like the cut of your jib, he vanishes on you. Yep. Seen it many a time. He don't go for none of that spiri-chull stuff. He just is what he is."

"We just want to ask him one question," Joan persisted. "Then we'll leave him alone."

"Hunh. You gals go and sit at that table over there. I'll let you know when he shows up."

"Thanks!" said Miriam. They squeezed into a tiny booth whose table was scarred and worn. Joan thought she discerned a name with the date 1894 carved into the wood, but it might have just been fatigue and the flickering of the old light fixture overhead.

The old bartender brought them mugs of beer without their having ordered any. The other elderly gentlemen in the bar got up and curtly nodded good night to the barkeep before plodding out the door. Joan stared at the foam in her beer mug and wondered if she and Miriam had fallen prey to a local practical joke.

For long minutes they silently sipped their beer and listened to the drone of machinery from a back room. Joan nearly jumped when the barkeep walked up to their table and said, "He's here."

Joan and Miriam turned. At the table farthest in the back, under the dartboard, sat a little man. His white-and-gray beard flowed down to his knees and his leathery face was dominated by great bushy brows and a bulbous nose. He sipped at the beer in his mug as if it were ambrosia, gripping the glass with smudged, callused hands.

Joan stood, too suddenly, and his eyes opened wide. She approached with more caution. "If you please, Mr. Jones, we'd like to talk to you."

The little old man leaned back warily in his chair.

"We'd just like to ask you a question," Miriam said, beside her. Miriam placed two dimes on top of Mr. Amadan's business card and slid it across the table.

The fellow frowned and picked up one of the dimes and bit on it. He gave it a dubious look. "What's this fer?" His voice was gravelly and lower than Joan would have expected for his size.

"Um," said Miriam, "they told us you were . . . a ghost."

Oh, no, not again! Joan stifled the urge to pound Miriam with the guitar.

"Heh. These coins wouldn't hold down a gnat's eyes," Jones grumbled, "and no self-respecting ferryman would take 'em." Nonetheless, he put both dimes in his pocket. "Whatcha want?"

Breathing a sigh of relief and hope, Joan slid into one of the other chairs at the table. "We need to know where to find something. . . . It might be a plant or a mineral."

"Just a little diff'rence 'tween the two," grumbled Mr. Jones.

"It's called crystal sage," said Miriam.

"Haugh!" It could have been either a cough or a laugh. "Never heard of it."

"This guy," Joan said, tapping the business card, "says we need to find it for him."

Mr. Jones picked up the card and his lips moved, sounding out the name. His eyebrows suddenly shot up to his hairline. "Amadan!"

"You know him?" asked Joan.

"Know of him."

"He's in Colorado trying to get people to buy up land and plant special things on it."

Mr. Jones blew air out his lips and rolled his eyes. "The great fool. Hegh. You'd better just keep outta his way."

"Too late," said Joan. "We'd been warned, but he harmed a friend of ours, so we had to find him to set things right. We had a meeting with him this morning, but it didn't go too well."

Buck Jones shook his head and clicked his tongue. "Shoulda listened."

"We had to! He turned my friend into a guitar." Joan took Gillian out of the guitar case and held her up.

"Hegh. 'Zat all? She's lucky."

"She doesn't think so," Joan said as she gently put the guitar back in the case. "We told Mr. Amadan to change her back, and he said he needed us to find crystal sage and bring him proof. Does he mean it or was he just pulling our legs to get us out of his hair?"

"With him, hard to say," grumbled Mr. Jones, rubbing his bushy mustache.

"So, does crystal sage exist?" asked Miriam.

Mr. Jones leaned back in his chair and closed his eyes

"Crystals grow in caverns below sometimes shaped like little plants."

"Is that what Mr. Amadan meant?" asked Joan.

"Sometimes, over a long time, plants turn into stone," Mr. Jones went on, ignoring her question.

"You mean, like, fossils?" Miriam prompted.

"Sometimes these here jooky stores sell things made outta crystals."

"Yeah, we saw them. I don't think he wants some amethyst souvenir," said Joan.

"Then again," said Mr. Jones with a curious smile, "maybe he don't mean the plant kind of sage atall."

"So it could be sage as in wise person," Miriam said.

"Well, which is it?" said Joan, losing her patience.

Mr. Jones shrugged. "Beats me." He picked up his mug and took another long pull on his beer.

"I don't suppose you could ask him for us," said Miriam meekly.

Mr. Jones stared at her wide-eyed over his mug for a moment. "I don't get involved in politics," he said at last.

"Politics?" asked Joan, now thoroughly bewildered.

"Forget I asked, then," said Miriam. "We wouldn't want any trouble."

" 'F yer in with the Amadan, you're already in trouble." Mr. Jones tipped back his mug to drain the last of his beer. He smacked his lips and wiped his mustache with his sleeve as he set down the mug. He put his miner's cap back on, tipping it to them once. Then he said, "Good night, ladies. Good luck," and vanished. Like smoke.

"Wow," said Miriam.

"Wow," Joan agreed, nodding.

"Sorry I almost blew it there, with the dimes."

"S'okay. No hurt, no foul. Did you understand what he was telling us?"

"Not anything we didn't know already. Mr. Amadan's a bad dude, and crystal sage could be anything."

"Closing time, ladies," said the old bartender behind them.

"Oh, sure. Sorry." Joan left a generous tip on the table and hurried with Miriam out the door.

"So why did you give him twenty cents, anyway?" Joan asked when they were out of earshot of the bar.

"What? Oh, the two dimes. Well, it wasn't the amount that mattered. See, if he were a ghost, which I don't think he is now, then he would need two silver coins. Spirits need them to pay for their passage across the River Styx. But he was able to drink beer, so I don't think he's a ghost. I'm glad he thought the dimes were a sufficient tip, anyway."

"Where do you learn this stuff?"

"It's folklore! It's everywhere! How do you *not* learn it?"

"By reading books about the real world instead," Joan grumbled.

"After what we've been through, can you really say what the real world is?"

Joan paused, then said, "You've got a point. So if he isn't a ghost, what do you think he is?"

"I've got a hunch, but I'll tell you back at the hotel." She glanced around suspiciously. "You never know what might be listening."

"Oh, great," said Joan. "Now we're not only delusional, we're paranoid."

They hurried back to the bed-and-breakfast and

changed into nightshirts, but Joan was too wired to be sleepy. She sat up on one bed and Miriam sat on the floor with her back against the mattress side.

"Okay, so give," Joan said at last. "You said you had a hunch what Jonesy is."

"Well, there are legends about gnomes or dwarves called tommyknockers, who lived in the mines. They were said to be friendly and helpful to miners, as long as the miners didn't try to cheat them."

"Tommyknockers. Wasn't that a horror novel a while back? Never mind. So Jonesy said he'd seen something like crystal sage in a cave, or plants that turn into stone, like you said, fossils. Or wise guys. Dammit, why couldn't he just answer us straight rather than feed us more riddles?"

"Honor among thieves," Miriam murmured, pinching the bridge of her nose in thought.

"Huh? You know, I was just thinking, glancing at this brochure of Amadan's again, of a book my dad has. It's all about the colonization of America. Only it's not just about the pilgrims—it's all the plants and animals they brought with them. And then, as more people got here, they brought more and more of the old country with them, trees and flowers and stuff. Just to make the New World seem more familiar. Even for silly reasons. Rich guys would import every bird mentioned in the works of Shakespeare, for instance. Eventually so many plants and animals that never grew naturally here were here that the whole ecology became more like Europe, giving the local wildlife a hard time. That's what it feels like this Amadan is doing. Colonization. Trying to make Colorado more comfortable for . . . what? Who?"

"I bet I know," said Miriam.

"If you give me another riddle, I'll throw a pillow at you."

"It's not a riddle, but I'll bet you throw the pillow anyway."

"Nonsense. I'd never harm a perfectly good pillow without a reason. Spill the beans, girl."

Slowly, Miriam said, "I would bet . . . apples to acorns . . . that our Mr. Amadan is . . . a sidhe."

"A she? A woman in disguise?"

"S-I-D-H-E. One of the high faerie."

"You're not making sense, Miriam. Are you trying to say he's gay?"

"No! No! No!" Miriam pounded the edge of the mattress with her fist. "He's one of the Fair Folk. He's an elf!"

"An elf." Joan stared at Miriam. "Isn't he a little tall to be the Tinkerbell type? And, frankly, I just can't see him making chocolate chip cookies in a tree house. Miriam, this doesn't make sense."

Miriam covered her face with her hands and shook her head. "The real . . . I mean, the elves of ancient folklore were supposed to be tall and beautiful and powerful. I guess you never read Tolkien either. Maybe just as well. I read *Lord of the Rings* as a little girl and I always dreamed I would meet elves. Trouble is, when you read some of the older tales of the Fair Folk, they aren't nice at all. The more beautiful they are the nastier they are. They think of mortals as toys and play cruel games with us." She suddenly looked at the guitar case. "Isn't that right, Gilly?" She lunged across the floor, flung open the case, and pulled out the guitar. Miriam set Gillian on her lap and picked lightly on the strings.

bad sidhe bad sidhe bad sidhe
that's right that's right
watch out watch out watch out
so sor ry so sor ry

"You knew this all along," Joan said angrily to the guitar. "All this time you've been holding out on us."

I know I know I know
but you but you but you
would not would not would not
have be lieved
meeeeeee

"Okay, you're probably right," Joan admitted.

"I would have," Miriam said.

"So now the cat's out of the bag, Gillian," Joan said. "We've met your bad dude and he wouldn't help you. If you know anything else we ought to know, you'd better fess up, or you might be looking at being a guitar the rest of your life."

don't know don't know don't know

"You sure? C'mon, if you have any idea what crystal sage is, you'd better tell us if you want to have arms and legs again."

please help please help
i'm scared i'm scared
don't know don't know don't know
don't know don't know don't know

"Joan, go easy on her," said Miriam. "She's scared. Sorry, Gillian. You rest now. We'll keep working on it." She put Gillian back in the guitar case and closed the lid.

"Well, shit," Joan said, flopping back onto the bed. "That was singularly useless."

"Shhh! She can still hear us, you know," Miriam chided. "Besides, she did confirm what Mr. Amadan is."

"So let me guess. That window we saw in Mr. Amadan's office was showing us a view of—fairyland?"

"Yeah, essentially."

"I like my special effects theory better," Joan said, feeling weariness catching up to her. "It's less bizarre."

"I understand." After a long pause, Miriam said softly, "You know, we have to stop him somehow."

Joan rolled over on the bed, flopping her arms and head over the side. "Did you just say what I think I heard you say?"

"Well, we do, don't we? Someone's got to! You didn't feel what his . . . mind control was like. I did. We can't let him succeed, Joan. How many more Gillians might there be?"

"Oh. Sure. Right. A housekeeper and her apprentice are going to . . . meddle in the affairs of a guy older and way more powerful than they are? And stop him how? Sweep him away with a broom? Spray him with 409, or Black Flag for Fairies? Hey, he's an out-of-state land developer—surely no Colorado court would convict us if we just offed him with a gun."

"Joan, I'm serious!"

"So am I, actually. You've been reading too many fantasies, girl. If you think Mr. Amadan is breaking the law, which I'll bet he isn't, maybe we could call the sheriff, or the FBI. Or, since he's messing with the environment, we could alert the EPA. Since he's not from around here, maybe we should call in La Migra. . . . I'll bet he doesn't have a green card."

"He could probably conjure one on the spot."

"Well, there you are. Even if he decides not to flaunt his magic, he can flaunt his money—he could probably buy the best lawyers in the state. Heck, we couldn't even talk him into changing Gillian back. If he thinks we're really after him, you know, we could end up guitars too. Or worse, if we can believe Mr. Jones."

"It's not that hopeless," Miriam said. "We won something when Mr. Amadan said he was giving us a chance. He said we compelled him in the name of fair play."

"Okay, so he has some strange, twisted sense of nobility. We still don't know if we can trust him."

"The old folktales say the faerie tend to live by all sorts of rules. Clever people can outwit them by using those rules against them."

"Assuming the real kind are anything like the fairy tales, and assuming you know what the rules are."

"Well, yeah. There is that."

Joan shook her head. "I tell you, Miriam, I just don't see what more we can do."

"So you're saying you want to give up?" Miriam asked.

Hearing the dejection in her voice, Joan replied, "Not exactly, but—aw, heck. You're tired, I'm tired, we're both babbling. Let's get some sleep. Maybe we'll have better ideas in the morning. Okay?"

"Yeah," Miriam sighed. "Okay."

Chapter 6

When Joan woke up the next morning, Miriam was already dressed. Her skin was pale and her long wavy hair was even wilder than usual. Her eyes were red and puffy as if she had been crying.

"Are you all right?" Joan asked, throwing her own clothes on quickly.

"Yeah," Miriam said softly. "I guess I am, now. I hardly slept last night."

"Looks it. I mean, if you don't mind my saying so, you look terrible."

"Thanks," Miriam said, laughing a little. She had thrown a knit shawl across her shoulders and held it close as if she were cold.

"No, really, what's wrong? You caught the flu or something? Should I see if Summit Rock has a doctor? Even a witch doctor?"

Miriam shook her head, brown hair falling in front of her face. "No, I just . . . I couldn't sleep. And when I did sleep, I had these *dreams*."

"Nightmares?"

She shook her head again and picked at the yarn fringe of her shawl. "Sort of. But not . . . I dreamed I was in that place we saw in Mr. Amadan's window."

"Oh."

"And it was so . . . *beautiful* I felt like I couldn't possibly belong there. And then I'd wake up and I'd stare out the window at the stars, wishing with all my heart to go back there, and then I'd fall asleep and it'd start all over again."

"Oh, God." Joan sat on the bed beside her and put an arm around her. "He really played with your head, didn't he?"

"I guess."

"Feel up to some breakfast?"

"Sure. Anything normal."

This time, Joan got down to the dining room in time to see the whole range of "continental" breakfast that the B&B offered. She happily snagged several pigs-in-a-blanket while Miriam had a heaping bowl of hot oatmeal.

"Now this is what I call breakfast," Joan said, wiping her mouth with her napkin. Glancing around to make sure no other tourists were close enough to eavesdrop, she asked softly, "So, still feel like you want to take on Mr. Big?"

"I feel like I shouldn't be allowed a vote," Miriam said. "Unhealthy bias or something."

"I'm sorry. I shouldn't have brought it up. I think maybe we should just get you home."

"No, no, but Joan—"

"But nothing. I've lost one friend to this guy already. I don't want to lose another."

"You haven't lost Gillian. Not yet," Miriam murmured, staring into her coffee cup. "Are you ready to tell her family she's gone forever? And why?"

Joan put her elbows on the table and jammed her

hands into her hair. "Okay, okay, I know. Stop it. I've been thinking about this. Look, we saw Florissant Fossil Beds and Wind Cave on the way out. We can stop at them and see if we get any inspiration on this crystal sage stuff. When we get home, maybe I can do some research up at one of the colleges in Denver or the Springs, if I get some free time. Maybe you could ask among your . . . spiritual friends. Maybe there's some occult-chasing outfit we could turn this problem over to."

"Elf Busters? I don't know of any," Miriam said. "I'm afraid that's probably wishful thinking."

"Probably. Anyway, I might think more clearly when I get home. You ready to go?"

"Yeah," Miriam said thoughtfully. Then she added, "You'd better drive."

Joan drove down the mountain back to US 285 and headed north. Miriam was silent for much of the morning until they were over Poncha Pass and had made it to the crossroads that was Poncha Springs.

Miriam began craning her neck, peering out the windshield at the mountains as they passed the junction with US 50.

"What are you looking at?" Joan asked, surprised by this sudden enthusiasm.

"Mount Shavano. I think that's it over there. I'm looking for the Shavano Angel."

"The what?"

"I saw this postcard back in Summit Rock. It showed a picture of a snowfield on a mountainside that looked kind of like a stick figure with wings. Anyway, there's a story about her that's kind of charming."

Joan took a quick glance to the side but saw nothing

on the rocky slopes of the jagged mountain that resembled an angel. "What story?"

"I don't remember exactly. But it was like Zeus transformed one of the Olympean goddesses into an ice angel, punishing her for something, until she was moved by tears of pity for mortals' sorrows. She was banished to Mount Shavano and stayed there for centuries while the Indians came and the Europeans and so on. Then there was some big drought in this valley, and the angel felt so sorry for the people starving and dying that she melted, giving water to the people of the valley. So now she shows up every spring and then melts."

"Miriam," Joan said as patiently as she could, "I'm no expert in mythology, but Zeus is Greek and the Greeks didn't have angels, and they wouldn't have cared about Colorado anyway, and who makes up this tripe?"

Miriam sighed. "I just thought it was a nice story."

"Would've been better if it made sense."

Miriam leaned back glumly in her seat. "I guess she's melted and gone away already."

"Sorry to be a grouch," Joan said. "I've got nothing against legends and stuff, I just think they ought to grow naturally out of the lives of the people who live there, not be slapped on like a Gucci label on a saddlebag."

"I understand."

Joan glanced sidelong at Miriam, wondering if she did understand, or if she perceived life as a progression of stories and one merely had to decide which myth one was in at any given time. Joan was afraid that anytime now, Miriam would be expecting her to live up to her name and play the conquering hero. Joan wasn't feeling very heroic. Just the day-to-day running of her own business had been challenge enough.

They stopped for lunch at the Gunsmoke Truckstop Café in Johnson Village and parked past the gas pumps. A nondescript building on the outside, the café held a large convenience store, some video games, and a small restaurant. The service was slow, but the food was pretty decent, and Miriam seemed to perk up considerably.

"I'll take the next leg driving," Miriam said around a mouthful of salad.

"Well, okay, if you're sure you're up to it."

"Yeah, I'll be all right. I think the farther I am from Summit Rock the clearer my head gets."

"That's not surprising. I'd believe that of anybody. How's the *feng shui* of this place?"

"Hmm? Oh. Don't ask." She waved a hand in dismissal. "Energy flow real confused, but I expect the truckers don't mind. Probably keeps them awake."

Joan grinned. "Glad to see you're still you."

Miriam smiled back, but winced as well. "I hope so."

The sky had become overcast when they returned to the car, making the mountain scenery dull and drab. Neither Joan nor Miriam spoke much until they saw the first sign for Florissant Fossil Beds.

"Whaddaya think?" asked Miriam. "Shall we go in for a peek?"

Joan sighed. "Might as well, though I feel pretty silly about it. Remember, we don't have much time to play tourist."

"What does time matter?"

Joan paused a moment, wondering if Miriam's

question was practical or philosophical. Joan answered the practical one. "I wanted to get home before dark."

"Shouldn't be a problem," said Miriam. "We don't have to stay long. Oh, look!" She pointed out the DIG YOUR OWN FOSSILS sign as they turned onto Cripple Creek–Florissant Road.

"I'll bet the paleontologists just love that," Joan grumbled. "Fossils disappearing into tourists' pockets without any study of what they are or where they came from."

"What do you mean?" Miriam asked. "Wouldn't you like to hold a piece of the ancient past in your hand?"

"Not if it means some knowledge is lost forever. Let's just head up to the visitor center and see if there's anything to be learned there."

Miriam sighed and continued driving up the road. They came over a rise and entered a small, high valley. The valley floor had no trees—only grasses and very small bushes, making it all one enormous meadow— yet the surrounding hillsides were carpeted with pine. They could see the purple crest of Pikes Peak in the distance to the southeast.

To the right was a sign marking the Hornbeck Homestead. Joan saw a small log structure not much different from many ranch houses she was familiar with. Except the yard was too tidy and bare of machinery for it to be a working farm.

Not much farther up the road they turned off to the right and pulled into the visitor center parking lot. As Joan stepped out of the car, she could smell ponderosa pine and sage on the warm mountain air, and memories of childhood summer camps, and the attendant homesickness, assailed her. She pushed the thoughts away and joined Miriam walking up to the visitor center.

They put their two-dollar entry fee into the little envelope at the kiosk and then went into the small house that served as the Florissant Fossil Beds visitor center. Miriam turned left and went to a wall-sized glass case where a variety of fossils were displayed. Joan went straight ahead to the information counter, where she picked up a brochure and perused it.

"Mommy, where are the dinosaurs?" whined a petulant sun-blonded boy of about six.

"I don't think they have any dinosaurs here, honey," said his T-shirted tourist mom.

"She's right," said the short brunette in the National Park Service shirt behind the counter. "Our fossils here are mostly from the late Eocene Epoch, long after the dinosaurs were gone. But we have some nice big fossil sequoia stumps out back if you'd like to see those."

The little boy did not seem mollified, but something tickled at the back of Joan's brain.

Miriam came up behind her and asked the woman behind the counter, "I notice you have some lovely plant fossils in your display case. This may sound like a stupid question, but do you have any fossilized sage?"

"There are no stupid questions," said the young woman, "but, no, this area was an entirely different ecosystem at the time of the volcanic eruptions that made our fossils. It was much lower and wetter, almost subtropical. That valley you see out there was once a big lake, surrounded by redwoods and cedars, elm and linden trees, oaks and willows, not to mention many plants that are now extinct. Here, I'll show you an artist's rendition of what it looked like." She pulled out another brochure from behind the counter and spread it out for Joan and Miriam to see.

Joan froze where she stood. "Do you see what I see, Miriam?"

"Yeah. We've seen this before, haven't we?"

"You've seen this painting?" the Park Service woman asked, confused.

"Um . . . something very like it. Thank you for your help. Excuse us, please." Joan took Miriam's elbow and pulled her out of the visitor center.

"Is this what Mr. Amadan meant by returning Colorado to 'the way it was'?"

"Could be," said Miriam.

"But these fossils are from . . ." Joan consulted the brochure. "Thirty-five million years ago! Humanity is only, what, a couple of million years old at most? Just how old can he be?"

Miriam shook her head. "The sidhe aren't . . . human, not really. They take our shape, but they're as much spirit as flesh. All the tales say they're far older than we are, and that they're immortal."

Joan rubbed her forehead. "My brain hurts. This isn't making any sense."

"That's because it doesn't fit into the world we think we know."

"If they're so old and so powerful and aren't really human, why do they even bother with us?"

"Joan, you're acting like I'm some sort of expert on this! I don't know! Maybe the next time we see Mr. Amadan we can ask him."

"Why do I get the feeling there isn't going to be a next time?" Joan muttered. "Well, there's no crystal sage here, so we might as well move on. Want me to drive?"

"No. I'm enjoying the driving, actually. It keeps my mind off . . . things."

"I know just how you feel." Joan followed Miriam back to the Subaru. Joan took a last long gaze at the mountain valley and thought about what it must have looked like so many millennia ago—and an image of the tall, deep primeval forests of Mr. Amadan's desire superimposed itself upon her view. She blinked and shook her head, and the image vanished. Hoping she was just suffering from road-weariness, Joan got in the car.

They got back on US 24 and headed east toward Colorado Springs. The high valleys they passed through were not so unnerving for Joan—the more forbidding mountains stayed hidden behind rolling, piney hills. Still, she could not enjoy the view, and even the knowledge that they were headed home was not soothing. Though the skies outside were clear, a leaden pall of guilt lay over her.

The nice thing about being a cleaning lady was that when you saw dirt or a stain, nine times out of ten you could do something about it. Or tell the owner they'd have to buy a new rug or whatever. But there was no way Joan could see to clean up the mess Gillian had gotten herself into. And Joan felt it was her own fault that now Miriam had been messed up. And if she tried . . . well, she'd feel more like Don Quixote than Joan of Arc—attacking things bigger than she was, misunderstanding what they were.

Joan was so lost in her doldrums of self-doubt that she

only idly noticed the young hitchhiker with shoulder-length ash-brown hair walking alongside the road. His bare, well-muscled back was to them, and a gray T-shirt hung from his belt, swaying behind like a tail. He turned just as their car passed him and flashed them a handsome, loopy grin.

A few yards later, Miriam slowed down and pulled over.

"What are you doing?" asked Joan, fearing she knew what Miriam was doing.

"I'm going to pick him up."

"Miriam, we don't have time for this."

"Didn't you see it? That glow around him?"

"Glow? No, why? Is he radioactive or pregnant?"

"No, he's got the most powerful aura I've seen in ages."

"Aura? You see auras now?"

"Well, I always could, but I . . . don't usually tell anybody because . . . well, you know. But it seems to have gotten stronger since meeting Mr. Amadan. Anyway, doncha think he's cute? The hitchhiker, I mean?"

"Remember what happened in *Thelma and Louise* when they picked up a really cute guy?"

"Yeah. Geena Davis got to make love to Brad Pitt."

"*And* his character stole their big wad of money."

"We don't have a big wad of money."

"You've got credit cards."

"Joan, I just feel *right* about this, okay?"

Before Joan could argue more, the guy had caught up with them and opened the right rear door.

"Awooo, thank you, thank you!" he said as he bounced into the backseat.

Joan pegged him as one of those adolescent males

who have more energy than they know what to do with, so he'd spend it in unnecessary noise and movement.

"You're welcome," Miriam fairly gushed. "Where are you headed?"

"Anywhere you're going," the hitchhiker said, flashing his grin again with wide, golden-brown eyes.

Miriam blushed and said, "Okay."

Joan stared at Miriam. *What is going on with you?* She thought at her. She turned and asked the young man, "So, what's your name?"

He tilted his head and seemed to be studying the car dome light. Finally he said, "Cain. Cain Eslatranz." And then he grinned again as if he had made some big private joke.

"Oh?" Joan said with dubious interest. "Is that a Hispanic name?"

"Nope. Just a name."

"Uh-huh." *Probably not your real one either*, Joan thought.

"I'm Miriam and she's Joan," Miriam said as she pulled back out onto the road.

"Pleased to meetcha," said Cain.

"You from around here?" Joan asked.

"Yep." Cain leaned forward so that his head was between their headrests. Conspiratorially, he said, "A little man told me you ladies might be needing my help."

Miriam glanced at Joan with alarm and wonder. "A little man? Who? What's his name? Was it Buck Jones?"

"Dunno. Didn't tell me his name," Cain said, flopping back into the backseat. Gillian jangled as he accidentally kicked her case. "Awooo! Gee-tar!" Cain exclaimed, and he reached down to open it up.

"Be careful with her!" Joan yelled, turning around to

glare at him. "She's a friend. I mean, the guitar belongs to a friend of mine and, well, it's like a friend, too. You know what I mean."

Cain pouted, slightly hurt. "I'll be nice to her." He plucked Gillian out of her case and placed her on his lap. He began to pick gently on the strings, humming a strange tune.

Joan listened nervously as Gillian made uncertain noises—

> *what . . . what . . . what . . .*
> *who is . . . who is . . . this . . . what . . .*
> *where . . . um . . . ah . . .*

"Poor lady needs some consoling, she does," said Cain.

"Yeah, well, she's been through a lot lately," said Joan, wondering just what the guy was up to and how much he knew.

Cain began again to sing, if you could call it that, for the noises he made were closer to the tuneful whimpering of a puppy craving attention. Gillian continued to make uncertain noises. But after a while, as Joan listened, the sounds behind her became more like those of a couple making out in the backseat.

She glanced back and saw Cain crooning to the guitar cradled almost lovingly in his lap. Joan looked at Miriam, who seemed to be about to explode with suppressed laughter. Joan faced forward again with a disgusted sigh and tried to tune out the distraction.

But she got so tense and annoyed over the next several miles that when Miriam pointed out the sign for Cave of the Winds, Joan said, "Sure. Let's check it out. I could use a stretch, anyway." *Anything to get Cain out of the car and away from Gillian.*

Miriam turned left onto the road that led to the caves—a road so narrow, steep, and winding that Joan was glad they were in a Subaru. They glimpsed the building that was the cave entrance above a deep, narrow, rather impressive canyon. Signs by the road implied that some sort of laser show was performed there in the evening.

"Figures," Miriam said. "Why do these tourist places always have to gild the lily? It's such a cool canyon. Why junk it up?"

"Damn straight!" Cain said from the backseat.

"It's for the almighty tourist dollar," Joan said. "You should see what they've done to Royal Gorge. Better yet, you shouldn't. The world's highest suspension bridge wasn't enough. They had to build an amusement park next to it. With clowns running around in prairie dog and moose suits. It would make your gorge rise. Get it? Never mind."

"I get it," Miriam said. "I'm glad we're not going there." She pulled into the parking lot at the top of the road, which was about half full with cars and families. She said, "Well, Cain, we'll be stopping here for a while."

"S'okay!" Cain said. "Caves are cool. Good places to hang out. Me 'n' the lady, we'll wait."

As Joan and Miriam got out of the car, Cain did too, still holding Gillian. Joan scowled at him.

Cain stared back and then flashed an uncertain grin. "You don't trust me."

"Well, let's just say we don't know you very well."

"Don't worry! We'll be here. You go on and have fun. I'll keep the lady company."

Joan looked at Miriam. Miriam shrugged. "We'd better hurry," she said. "It's getting late, if we want a tour."

"Okay," Joan said dubiously. As they walked down the graveled road to the main building, Joan heard a car door slam behind her. She turned and looked back, stopped, and exclaimed, "That *asshole*!"

"Joan!"

"But he's pissing on your car!"

"Lots of guys piss beside cars," Miriam said in an embarrassed whine. "Will you keep your voice down and stop being so judgmental? Come *on*." She grabbed Joan's arm and tugged her along.

With one last glare at Cain, Joan turned and allowed herself to be pulled by Miriam toward the main entrance.

"I swear, I've never seen you so rude and testy," Miriam said. "What have you got against this guy?"

"Call me paranoid, but I just don't trust him. I'm surprised you like him so well, considering our 'Brad Pitt' has been making love to Gillian, not you."

This time Miriam did burst into laughter. "I think it's . . . nice. She deserves some attention."

"Yeah? You gonna think it's nice when we get back and both he and Gillian are gone? Just think what kind of money he could make selling her to some—who-knows-what?—musician. Imagine her working in a punk band, or a thrash metal group. I bet she'd scream for them real good."

"Now it's you who's got an overactive imagination. He said they'd be here. I do trust him."

Joan sighed heavily and shook her head. "For once I

really hope your intuition is on the mark. 'Cause if it isn't . . ." Joan couldn't think of how to end that sentence, so she didn't.

They passed a set of high metal risers on the canyon's rim and entered the main building. Joan was immediately aware of an unfinished feel to the place. There was a small snack counter (closed), a couple of pinball machines and toddler rides (unused), and a lot of open space. Through another door was the gift shop, which had the curious feature of having no books, brochures, or literature about the cave itself. Tickets had to be purchased at the gift shop counter. Out of the three possible tours, only the short tour was available, and Joan and Miriam managed to have caught places on the last tour of the day.

"Too bad," Miriam said, pointing out that the "Lantern Tour" had been blanked out. "That would be a good way to see a cave."

"Yeah, good way to trip and bump into things."

"Will you chill out?"

"Maybe when we get into the cave. I hear it's cooler down there. Even Cain said so."

It was, indeed, cooler when their tour group finally was allowed past the turnstile into the cave entrance. But Joan's temper wasn't eased any as they suffered through the typical banal banter of the perky college-student guide and the required photograph in the first cavern room, a photo that would clearly be offered to them at an exorbitant price at the end of the tour.

Cave of the Winds itself was not bad, as caves go, Joan decided. There were many winding, branching passageways whose walls had been carved by water into rippling, banded shapes. Still, Joan had seen Carlsbad when she was a child, and nothing could compare to that. Stalactites and stalagmites in Cave of the Winds were few and far between, with the usual silly names based on what they resembled. There was the usual "Fat Man's Misery" tight spot to annoy the heavier tourists and mysterious pools of still water that somebody had thought a garish colored spotlight would augment.

Every now and then, Miriam would jump a little as they passed a dark passageway.

"What is it?" Joan asked when Miriam backed into her.

"N-nothing. I just get the feeling . . . we're being watched."

"Well, hey, the brochure said that fairies and gnomes were once said to live in here."

"Yeah? Maybe that's more than hype."

Joan peered around herself when the tour group was stopped for the guide's spiel, but saw nothing but darkness in the deep recesses.

Joan was beginning to consider their time seriously wasted when the perky guide pointed out some tiny formations on the ceiling of a low passage, protected by chicken wire.

"These crystalline, plantlike formations are called white beaded anthemite. They are very pretty, but very delicate. And I hope everyone saw the sign back at the entrance that said there's a five-hundred-dollar fine for any theft or destruction of the cave formations."

Desultory agreement came from the tour group as they peered up at the ceiling. Miriam grabbed Joan's arm. "Do you think?" she whispered. They stared at the formations as the tour group drifted on ahead of them.

The anthemite was indeed pretty—white, glistening branching formations only a few inches high that resembled tiny bushes, just possibly resembling sage.

"No," Joan growled firmly. "Even if it is what Mr. Amadan had in mind, I'm not going to let him turn us into criminals just for his whims."

"Even if it's what would save Gillian?"

"*Stop* it. Maybe he just wants to get us into trouble so we won't bother him anymore."

"Or maybe it is the right thing." Miriam began to reach her hand up.

Joan pulled her arm down quickly. "No, I said. I won't let you. If it is the right thing, we'll find another way. If the Amadan's going to play dirty, we don't have to join in."

"Helloo?" the guide's voice echoed back through the chambers. "Did we leave someone behind?"

"Come on," Joan said to Miriam. "Blame me if you want, if we fail because of this. But I won't be talked into stupid vandalism by some inhuman, immortal creature that doesn't give a shit about humanity."

"I guess it all comes down to the same choices, doesn't it?" Miriam asked softly and angrily. "Whether you choose to do the right thing by society or the right thing for a friend." She snatched her arm out of Joan's grasp and hurried ahead to rejoin the tour group.

"I don't want that kind of choice," Joan said to herself, following after. "I want them to be the same thing."

Chapter 7

As expected, at the exit to the cave Miriam and Joan were offered their photograph for eight bucks. Miriam was willing to buy it, but Joan said, "Don't. It'll only encourage them."

The late-afternoon sky was dark with storm clouds when they left the gift shop. "Mmm. Dramatic," said Miriam.

"Monsoon season already," Joan murmured. "Starting a bit early this year." She was trying to keep herself from running to the parking lot to see what further atrocities Cain might have committed on the Subaru, or if he was still there.

The lot was mostly empty, only a few cars remaining. Joan finally let herself stare at the Subaru. It was empty. No sign of Cain. "Son of a bitch—"

"No, Joan, there he is!"

Joan looked where Miriam was pointing. Cain was sitting by the canyon rim, still holding Gillian in his arms. The guitar case was set out before him. He was talking amiably with a couple of tourists.

Joan let out her breath in a long whoosh, hoping the adrenaline would go back where it came from quickly.

"I don't like to say I told you so," said Miriam, "but I told you so."

"Yeah, okay. Ten points for the psychic. Let's go see what our hunky boy's been up to."

They strolled over as the tourists wandered off, and Cain smiled at them.

"Hi," Miriam said.

"Have a nice time in the cave?" he asked.

"It was all right," Joan said. She glanced down at the guitar case and saw a few quarters and dollar bills. "Looks like you've been earning your supper."

Cain shrugged and lifted the neck of the guitar. "She's much better now."

"I'm . . . glad to hear it. Can I have her back?"

"Oh. Sure!" Cain held Gillian out, and Joan carefully took the guitar from him. She knelt down to put Gillian into the guitar case, then paused. "Here, you ought to keep the cash. You earned it, after all." Shifting the guitar to one hand, she scooped up the bills and held them out to Cain.

He shrugged again and winced, looking at the money. "Don't need it."

"C'mon. Buy a steak and ice cream and put some meat on those bones."

"Hmm. Steak." Cain snatched the bills from her hand and stuffed them into his jeans pocket. Joan scooped up the quarters and gave those to him too. Cain examined one of the quarters as if he'd never seen one close up. "Is this real silver?"

"Not entirely, anymore," Joan said as she laid Gillian in the case and closed it up. "It's some alloy mostly. I forget what."

"Heh. Not much use, then." Cain dropped it on the ground.

"Hey!" Joan snatched it up again. "Just because they aren't pure doesn't mean they aren't handy. These are the coin of the realm for parking meters, Coke machines, pinball, Laundromats, pay phones, all that good civilized stuff."

Cain shrugged again. "I don't use those."

"A real live-off-the-land type," Miriam suggested.

"Yeah!" Cain agreed. "You could say that."

"Or a Luddite," Joan said sardonically as she stood. "Bet you really got something out of the Unabomber's Manifesto."

"Who?" asked Cain.

"Doesn't watch TV either, apparently," said Miriam.

"Or read a newspaper," Joan added.

Cain looked back and forth between the two of them with an embarrassed and worried grin. "Hey—"

A loud crack of thunder made them all jump. A patter of rain began to fall around them.

"Better get back to the car," Joan said.

Miriam pulled the keys out of her pocket and dashed to the Subaru, Joan following. To her dismay, Joan heard Cain padding along behind her. It began to pour as Miriam flung herself into the car and unlocked the passenger doors.

Joan got in and set the guitar case in front of her feet. Cain jumped in the back and slammed the door shut. Joan could swear she caught a whiff of eau de wet dog.

The rain came down in streaming curtains, cutting visibility around them to zero.

"I guess we aren't going anywhere for a while," said

Miriam. "Not until this blows over. I wonder if we're going to get hail."

The rain became so heavy that it was like sitting in a car wash. Joan began to feel unsettled in her guts. "Damn. We're going to have to watch for flash floods. Whatever you do, when we start driving, don't go down into the canyon."

"I don't plan to go *anywhere* for a while."

Cain began to make sounds that were between a growl and a whimper.

"You all right back there?" asked Joan, turning around to look at him.

Cain was staring intently at the windshield, teeth bared.

Miriam screamed.

Joan whipped around and saw two faces pressed against the windshield. Inhuman faces, narrow and greenish-yellow, with a phosphorescent glow from within. Their eyes were large and blue, with no whites, their mouths small with pointed teeth. The creatures slid over so that one was directly in front of Miriam, one in front of Joan, their delicate clawed hands grasping at the glass, eyes staring in joyful malevolence. Joan could see all too clearly the veins beneath the luminescent skin, and she knew these were not kids with masks.

Joan checked to make sure her door was locked and locked the door behind her as well.

Miriam screamed again.

"Stop that!" Joan said, desperately fighting down her own urge to scream.

"I saw these!" Miriam wailed. "They were in my dreams last night!"

Cain growled and rocked the car from the backseat. "Lemmeout!" he barked. "I'll get 'em!"

"Cain, no!" Joan said.

"Lemmeout!" His hands scrabbled at the door. "You go. I'll chase 'em off."

"Cain, don't," whined Miriam.

But he found the door lock and flung the door open into the rain. "Go!" he said and charged out, slamming the door shut behind him.

"Cain!" Miriam called.

The creature nearer Joan looked surprised for a moment, turned its face, and then disappeared into the sheeting water. The creature in front of Miriam blinked and then vanished too. Joan thought she heard strange cries but could not be sure through the thunder of rain on the car roof.

"Oh, God, where is he?" Miriam said, peering through the windshield.

"Turn on your headlights!" Joan said. "Maybe we'll see something."

Miriam fumbled at the dashboard and the lights came on, showing nothing but a wall of glistening rain ahead of them. They both watched, but saw no sign of Cain or the strange creatures.

"Drive," Joan commanded. "Let's get out of here."

"What? I'm not leaving Cain behind!"

"He told us to go."

"That doesn't mean we should."

They heard a distant, piercing "Awwwooooo" behind them. There came a slap-thud against the rear of the Subaru. Joan turned and saw one of the creatures plastered against the back window. She heard the hatch latch click. "It's trying to get in! Drive!"

Miriam started up the car, engaging the clutch so abruptly that the car jerked forward. The creature on the back slid off. Miriam crawled forward and bumped against the wood block at the front of the parking space.

"Can this car go over that?"

"I think so."

"Do it."

Miriam gunned the engine. The wheels spun for a moment, and then the Subaru gamely climbed over the block, only lightly scraping the underside.

"Thank God for high clearance," Joan muttered.

The car surged forward, out of the parking lot and across the entrance road. Miriam stomped on the brakes just in time to keep the front wheels from going over the sheer drop into the canyon beyond the narrow shoulder. "Now what?" Miriam whimpered.

"It's okay," Joan said as soothingly as she could, her hand on Miriam's shoulder. "Take it easy. Just back up slow and turn the wheels to the left. That should put us going the right way on the road out of here."

Miriam did as she was told, and as they rolled slowly down the road, Joan was gratified to see a cut hillside coming up on the right-hand side of the road.

"Great, okay, we're going the right way. Just keep close to this cut side here and go real slow and we should be all right."

"Okay," Miriam breathed, grimly clutching the steering wheel.

The car crawled down the steep, winding road, and Joan was glad there were no other cars. And then she was worried that there were no other cars. There had been a few tourists in the parking lot when the rain started. Where were they?

The Subaru held the road well, and they both breathed a sigh of relief when they reached the stoplight at the bottom, where the road connected to US 24. The red light gleamed balefully at them through the rain, like a demon's eye. There were still no other cars.

"I don't like this," Joan muttered.

"Which way do we go when the light turns?" Miriam asked, her voice still shaky. "I've forgotten."

Joan thought a moment, grateful that she had always been blessed with a good sense of direction. "Left."

"Okay."

Another minute and the light ahead did not change.

"Go," Joan decided.

"But the light—"

"Go anyway. I don't like being stuck here."

"But I can't see what's coming!"

"Nobody's coming, dammit. Except what we don't want coming at us. Just go!"

"Joan—"

"You were willing to steal a stupid stalactite! Why are you so law-abiding now? Just go."

"Okay," Miriam said dubiously. She gunned the engine again and turned left. The car only fishtailed a little as they found the correct lane. There were still no other cars.

"See? No hurt, no foul," said Joan.

"Okay," Miriam agreed with reluctance. "We shouldn't have left Cain behind—Yaaaaaaah!" She screamed again and slammed on the brakes, causing the Subaru to hydroplane.

"What is it?"

"The hillside! Look!"

As if in slow motion, boulders were bouncing down from the cut hillside to their left, into the road ahead.

"Landslide! Shit!" Joan looked wildly around. "Over there! There's an exit! To the right!"

Miriam turned the wheel, and the back of the Subaru slewed to the left. The car bounced over the first several rocks of the slide before catching, and Miriam managed to steer it straight across the road and onto the ramp.

Both Miriam and Joan let out loud sighs of relief as the off ramp wound down under the highway. The ramp ended at a crossroad. A sign at their right read, BUSINESS 24, MANITOU SPRINGS.

"Oh, good," said Joan. "We're not even lost. We can probably follow this right into Colorado Springs. It's only a few miles."

"Yeah. Good," Miriam agreed, sounding as if she hadn't quite recovered yet from her fright. "Which way?"

"Turn right."

Miriam did so, and even though Business 24 led into the main drag of Manitou Springs, there were still no other cars. *Oh, well,* Joan thought, *I guess anyone with any sense would be off the road by now. What does that say about us?*

The road sloped markedly downhill ahead of them, and Joan noticed water, lots of it, rushing ahead of them from under the car. The Subaru began to hydroplane again.

"Oh, shit," Joan said.

"Now what?"

"Flash flood. Get off this road. Get uphill, now!"

"Which way is uphill?"

"I dunno! Go left, now, soon as you can!"

"I don't see— Okay." Miriam managed to pilot the car to the left, where the wheels finally caught, and the narrow side road led, blessedly, steeply, uphill. Joan looked behind and saw through the rear windshield, by the glaring streetlights, a two-foot wall of water go down the road they had just left.

"Oh, man, that was close," Joan whispered.

"Good Sheila. Good girl," Miriam said, patting the dashboard.

Joan turned forward again. "Now, where are we?"

As if in answer to her question, the headlights shone on a large slab of sandstone, engraved on which were the words "Garden of the Gods."

"I don't know if that's a good omen or a bad one," said Joan, surprised to find herself believing in omens.

"Let's hope the gods are kind and that it's good," said Miriam. She slowed the car to a crawl again, Joan suspected not just because the speed limit signs read 15 mph. The rain had lessened a bit, allowing better visibility, but lightning flashes strobed across the sky.

"Isn't lightning usually heavier at the front of a storm?" asked Joan.

"Don't look at me. I'm no weatherman. And I don't think this is an ordinary storm."

"I'm inclined to agree with you," Joan said dryly. Staring out the window, she saw the Garden's enormous rock formations illuminated by each stroke of lightning. Joan had heard the names of some of the formations—the Kissing Camels, Cathedral Rock, the Three Graces. But now, under the strobelike glare of the lightning, she saw what seemed to be stern, scowling faces in the eroded spires and promontories—faces that did not approve of her presence.

"Can you drive a little faster?" Joan asked. "This place is creeping me out. Or maybe I'm just jumpy after what we've just been through."

"Well, this isn't exactly a safe park for women at night, I've heard," Miranda said. "Though I can't imagine even stalkers being out in this weather. What I'm afraid of isn't human. Oh, damn, now which way?"

They had come to a fork in the road. Joan said, "I remember the visitor center is on or near a main street. Go that way."

Miriam turned. A bolt of lightning came down very close, momentarily blinding them. A gust of wind rocked the car. "Fuck the speed limit," Miriam growled. "We're getting out of here." She peeled out, and Joan grabbed onto her seat and the car door to keep her balance.

They rounded a curve, and a huge, antlered buck leaped out of the bushes and stopped in the road, staring at them.

"Oh, God!" Miriam slammed on the brakes and the car slewed sideways. The buck jumped out of the way at the last possible moment. The car stopped, sitting sideways across the narrow road. Joan and Miriam sat in silence for some moments, catching their breath and their wits.

"Maybe . . . we should go . . . not quite so fast," Joan said when she could at last speak.

"Jeez," Miriam said. "Is Somebody Out There trying to tell us something?"

"You think?"

"But *what*? What are we supposed to do? Whom do

we have to appease? What did I do in a previous life to earn this?"

Joan put both her hands on the dashboard and took a couple of deep breaths. "Maybe, just maybe, we've just been through a bad rainstorm, in which things like flash floods and rockslides are common happenings, and deer jumping onto the road happens all the time in Colorado."

"And those things in the Cave of the Winds parking lot? Are those common in Colorado too?"

"Give me a minute. I'll think of something."

They sat in silence for a couple of minutes, and Joan tried to concentrate on calming her nerves and rounding up her stampeded wits. The rain eased up to a light sprinkle, though gusts of wind still now and then shook the car.

They heard a strange, wailing cry, like a wounded dog, not far away.

"Shit, *now* what?"

"Relax, Miriam, it's just a coyote. I'm pretty sure of that, at least."

"This close to the city?"

"Hey, where do you think they find the most food? Let's get going. At this rate, we'll jump out of our skins when a moth hits the windshield."

Miriam managed to straighten out the car and drove, somewhat more slowly. Joan braced herself for the next surprise, but her only surprise was that there were no more shocks before they finally reached a long, descending stretch of road and saw the visitor center in the distance. Joan's guess had been right—a major crossroad ran beside it, and to her immense relief, there were cars, several of them, driving down that road.

"Looks like we've reached civilization at last," she said. "Wanna stop in the Springs for some dinner?"

"No," Miriam said. "I want to get home. I'll take some of that jerky we bought back in Johnson Village, though."

Joan fished around down by her feet beneath the guitar case. She found a torn brown paper bag filled with torn and empty plastic wrappings. "Sorry. Looks like Cain ate all our road food."

"Oh, well. I wish we hadn't left him behind."

Joan felt the opposite but figured it would be rude to say so. "He wanted to leave, Miriam. I'm sure he's fine."

"This time I hope *your* intuition is right."

Joan hadn't thought herself to have much in the way of intuition, but didn't mention that either.

When they finally turned off I-25 into Dawson Butte, Joan had the feeling she often had whenever returning from a trip out of town—the place in some ways looked new and strange to her. This trip, she feared, there might be more reason for that. As Miriam turned into the parking lot of her condominium, Joan immediately looked for her truck—and gratefully saw it parked just where she had left it.

As soon as Miriam pulled the Subaru into a slot, Joan leaped out, guitar case in hand, and walked over to the truck. Still there, all in one piece. Joan ran her hand along the front fender, the door. Touching the metal and flaking paint eased something inside her. She was back to the Real World, her Real Life. If her arms had been long enough to encompass the truck, she would have hugged it.

Joan became aware of Miriam standing beside her. "I just wanted to be sure it was all right," Joan said.

"I understand," Miriam said. She didn't move. "Um, Joan?"

"Yeah?"

"I know this sounds childish and stupid. But ... could you stay here tonight? My couch folds out into a futon bed. I just ... I'd sleep better. I could set the alarm for you. And I'll fix you dinner. I'm just afraid ... I'm gonna have nightmares again. I'm still shaking from this drive. It'd really help me calm down to have someone else around."

Joan's first internal reaction was the urge to run away screaming. She wanted to flee Miriam's company, as if she were to blame for all the weirdness of the past few days. But Joan knew this was unkind, and besides, the thought of returning to her dark little den, while soothing, was also ... lonely. "Sure," she replied at last. "Shouldn't be a problem. Oh, wait. I don't have any clean clothes. I could go home and get some. And I should check for messages on my answering machine."

"You can borrow something of mine," Miriam offered quickly. "We're nearly the same size. You can return it whenever. And can't you call for your messages from my phone?"

Joan got the clear impression that Miriam did not wish to be left alone for any length of time at all. "Okay. You're right. Lemme get my suitcase out of your car, then."

"Great," Miriam said with a nervous smile.

They took their bags up to her apartment. Joan was pleased to see the place hadn't changed from the last time she had been there—she didn't know what she'd been expecting. As Miriam rummaged around in her bedroom closet for extra clothes, Joan picked up the phone and dialed her own number to pick up her messages.

The first two were from the clients she had had to cancel thanks to her trip to Summit Rock. One was understanding and forgiving, the other was politely snide in a way that made Joan wince. She figured she'd probably lost the snide one's business. The third message was from Gillian's landlady, plaintively asking if Joan had heard anything from Gillian and wondering whether to call the police. Joan grimaced at that one and made a mental note to visit the landlady to somehow dissuade her.

The fourth message began with silence. Just as Joan thought it might be a wrong number, she heard laughter. Deep, malevolent laughter, growing louder and louder.

Joan slammed down the handset.

"What's wrong?" Miriam asked, coming in from the bedroom.

"Oh, some idiot left a prank call on my machine. Probably some disgruntled client." Joan folded her arms to hide the way her hands were shaking.

"Oh. I'm sorry."

"S'okay," Joan grunted. "Not your fault."

"How about some dinner? I can make brown rice and veggies."

"Sounds good. Right now anything sounds good."

"Okay. Have a seat. I'll nuke it up."

Joan sat on the futon couch and idly turned on the little TV with its remote. She caught a late local news channel and watched for a while. The weathercaster finally came on and remarked about the evening's storms. Joan leaned forward to hear more. But after the brief mention of rain, the show went immediately to sports.

"What?" Joan said aloud. "What about the flooding? What about the rock slide?"

"What's up?" Miriam said, peeking out of the kitchenette.

"You get cable out of the Springs, right? There was tonight's news and they didn't even mention the flash flood in Manitou Springs or the rockfall on US 24!"

"Maybe they don't know about it yet."

"Oh, come on. Reporters today are like vultures. They can smell a disaster before it happens."

"Beats me, then," Miriam said with a weary smile and a shrug. The microwave chirped. "Whoops. Dinner's on."

Joan sighed and clicked off the TV. The brown rice and vegetables tasted surprisingly good. And the futon bed felt surprisingly comfortable and welcoming when she finally settled down to sleep. And her dreams were undisturbed except for a brief period when she was annoyed by the yipping and whining of somebody's damn dog down by the parking lot.

Chapter 8

Joan woke up suddenly, her shoulder being shaken.

"Hey, Joan. It's six o'clock. You wanted me to wake you. There's coffee."

Joan groaned, blinked, and sat up. "Oh. Yeah. Thanks." Miriam stood over her wearing a huge nightshirt. Outside the living-room window Joan could see a bright sun rising above the eastern hills. "Man, never thought I'd be so happy to see a morning."

"Me, too," said Miriam.

"How'd you sleep?" asked Joan, rubbing her face.

"Better. I had dreams, but . . . they were more wistful than horrible. Here, I found some stuff that might fit you." She set down some folded clothing on the coffee table.

"Thanks."

Miriam went to the kitchen and brought out steaming bowls of oatmeal and cups of coffee that she set out on her tiny dining table. "Um, Joan? You're not gonna need me to come along on your cleaning gigs today, are you?"

Joan was riveted by the smell of apples, cinnamon, and coffee. "No, I suppose not. Why?"

"I'd just . . . I'd like a day to stay home and recover.

I'm just not ready to face the real world again right now. I have to absorb what I've been through. You know?"

"Oh, sure. Take all the time you need." Joan joined her at the table and took a long sip of rejuvenating java, over which she surreptitiously studied Miriam's face. She seemed pensive and a little worried, but not nearly so pale and afraid as she had been the morning before. "You sure you're okay, then?"

"I will be. I just need a little time."

"Want me to call your folks?"

It was the wrong thing to say. Miriam slammed down her mug, spilling coffee on the table. "No, hell, please don't! They'll only insist I go back into therapy. No, don't tell them anything about this, please!"

"Okay, I'm sorry. Forget I mentioned it. I won't tell them a thing." *Therapy?* Joan decided it would be impolite to ask. She ate quickly and dressed quickly—the T-shirt and shorts Miriam was lending her were tighter than what she usually wore, but they would do at least to drive home in.

As she was leaving, Joan noticed Miriam had not moved from her seat at the dining table and was staring blankly out the window. "Hey, you're *sure* you're all right?"

"Huh?" Miriam blinked up at her. "Oh. Yeah. Just . . . meditating. Zoning out. I'll be fine."

"Okay. Thanks for dinner and breakfast and all."

"Sure. Thanks for staying. I think it really helped." Miriam reached up and squeezed Joan's arm.

"Good. I'm glad." Joan patted Miriam's hand. "Well, if you need anything, or just want to talk, call."

"Sure. Have a great day. Don't work too hard."

Joan grinned. "I never work harder than I have to. See you later."

"See you."

Joan felt uneasy somehow about leaving Miriam alone, but she didn't know what more she could do, and duty called.

Taking Gillian down to the truck with her, Joan wondered if she ought to talk to the guitar more often. It was too easy to think of her as an object, not a person stuck in an object. But it was so difficult to understand her, when she could say only one syllable per string pluck and if you strummed past when she was finished speaking she would get annoyed and complain. Still, as Joan placed the guitar carefully in front of the passenger side of the truck's bench seat, she resolved to sit down that evening and spend more time talking to Gillian.

It felt so good to be back in the truck again, Joan thought as she started it up and heard the familiar roar and rumble of the engine. To sit high above the road and have that much steel around her made her feel strong and secure. "Time to go home, old pal," she said. And then winced, realizing she'd never talked to her truck before. *Either I'm losing it or Miriam's style is rubbing off on me. Maybe soon I'll be needing therapy.*

It was pleasant to set her mind on automatic pilot and let the truck take her the couple of miles home. Her little house looked the same, though the small lawn needed watering and mowing. As Joan drove up her concrete driveway, she noticed that it was cracked, and that the siding on the house needed painting. She resolved that when she'd accumulated enough profit from the business she'd get the driveway resurfaced, and maybe later that summer she could touch up the paint herself. Wasn't good for a cleaning lady to have a shoddy-looking home, even if most of her clients never knew or cared where she lived.

Holding the guitar case in one hand with the overnight case stuffed under her arm, Joan awkwardly fished her keys out of her pocket and unlocked the front door. With a sigh, she stepped into the comforting, familiar gloom of her living room. And was struck by the unmistakable odor of urine, as if someone had let several unhousebroken pets stay there.

Joan flicked on a lamp switch. All the furniture seemed in order. She set Gillian down on the couch and walked cautiously around. She looked into the kitchen, and her stomach immediately sank. "Oh, my God . . ." The refrigerator door was wide open, and torn food packages covered the floor. The cupboards too had been raided, and cereal, rice, and spaghetti littered the counters. She froze in place, wondering if it was the work of vandals, or if—and the thought made the hair on the back of her neck rise—a bear had somehow gotten in. It was rare but not unknown in Colorado for them to come out of the mountains and into inhabited areas, even into a town the size of Dawson Butte. But that was usually in spring, just after they woke from hibernation, and here it was the beginning of summer—

"Hi!"

Joan shrieked and jumped at the voice behind her. She turned and saw Cain leaning casually against the wall, wearing only jeans and his loopy grin, a sliver of raw beefsteak hanging out of the corner of his mouth. "You!" she finally blurted out.

"Me!" he said. "'Bout time you got home." He sauntered over to the old recliner in her living room and sprawled in it.

Joan noticed that his upper arms and back were gouged with scratches and bruises. "Are . . . you all right?"

"Hmm? Oh. Yeah. Fine, now."

"How . . . did you get here?"

"Your window was open."

"Oh." *That'll teach me*, thought Joan. "I mean, how did you find my house?"

"Followed my nose," Cain said, tapping his handsome proboscis for emphasis.

"Uh . . . huh. Right. Okay. *Why* are you here?"

"Couldn't get into Miriam's place."

"Oh. So you decided to come here and trash my place instead."

"Trash?"

"This mess! You made this mess, didn't you?"

Cain looked around, blinking innocently. "Got hungry."

"And it smells like you pissed on the rug! Haven't you heard of toilets?"

Cain shrugged. "I don't use those."

"Agh!" Joan slapped her forehead in astonished frustration. "And that horrible laughing message! I'll bet you were the one who put that prank call on my answering machine!"

"What's an answering machine?" asked Cain.

"You know, attached to the telephone? Takes messages when you can't or don't want to?" Joan said as if speaking to a six-year-old.

"I don't use phones," Cain said. "Hey, wanna fuck?" He waggled his hips in the chair suggestively.

"What? Hell, no! I want you to leave. Now. Before I call the cops."

Cain pouted, looking genuinely hurt. "Leave? But who's gonna keep the elvesies away?"

"Oh, like *you* are?"

"Elvesies don't like me."

"Can't imagine why."

"Show you something?"

"What?"

"Catch." Cain reached under the recliner and tossed to Joan something long and narrow and yellow-green.

Joan awkwardly caught it in both hands. It was a forearm with a slender hand attached, a hand whose nails were long and purplish blue. Bits of bone and muscle hung out the torn end of the arm. The hand convulsively opened and closed as if clutching at her.

"Yah!" Joan dropped it on the rug and jumped back. The hand contracted once more, then subsided.

"See?" Cain said with a shit-eating grin. "I got 'em."

Joan fought down the urge to vomit, but it was hard. "Look, I don't know who or what you are or who sent you, but you're going to have to leave. Now." Joan strode to the front door and flung it open. "Out."

Cain whimpered and slunk ruefully to the door. Stopping in the doorway, he turned to her and asked hopefully, "Sure you don't wanna fuck?"

"*Out!*"

"Okay, okay . . ." Cain stepped out.

Joan slammed the door shut behind him and locked it. She ran into every room, checking every window and latching every one that wasn't latched. She stopped to catch her breath and her wits and then noticed the time. "Oh, no. I have to be at the McDougalls' in fifteen minutes!" She went into whirlwind mode, grabbing the carpet cleaner and spraying every part of the living-room rug that smelled. She gathered up the strewn garbage in the kitchen and threw it in a trash bag, resolving to go grocery shopping that evening. Then she looked at the yellow-green arm lying on the living-room floor.

What the hell do I do with that? she asked herself. Take it to some biologist for analysis? *I don't have the time to deal with this right now.* She grabbed a large Ziploc baggie and an old pair of barbecue tongs from the kitchen. As if it were some enormous insect, Joan approached the arm cautiously and grasped it with the tongs. The hand snapped at the tongs once, but Joan steeled herself and stuffed the arm into the baggie, zipped it shut, and ran to the kitchen, where she threw it in the freezer. Grabbing those cleaning supplies she could find quickly, she took them out to the truck, careful to lock the door behind her, and left.

Fortunately, the McDougalls were understanding folk who lived on small-town time themselves and didn't complain at all that she was ten minutes late. Mrs. McDougall was a potter and was building up her inventory for the summer craft shows, so she greatly appreciated the housework help. Sometimes, along with her check, Joan would get a mug that was only "slightly off," and she would treasure these gifts for being unique. It felt good to get back to cleaning off countertops and sweeping up floors. Such simple, worthwhile tasks gave Joan a sense of peace and control again. One could see the results of one's labors so quickly. Spray, wipe, wipe: the Formica sparkles. Sweep, sweep, vrooom: the floor is no longer crunchy.

Replace a bulb here, a room is filled with light. Fill a garbage bag there, a room no longer smells. It was so satisfying it almost restored Joan's faith in the ability of human will to overcome adversity.

I'll have to talk to Gillian's landlady, she thought as she wiped some dried clay slip off a lamp base. *Try to keep her from panicking. Maybe I can pay Gillian's rent for this month, at least. I can probably afford that. If we can't do anything about her shape in a month, then there's probably no hope. Maybe I can look over Gillian's notes again and find something more to go on.*

She had only one other client that morning, a harried new mother who could afford only an hour a week of Joan's time, but counted it a blessing nonetheless. Joan sometimes worked a little over an hour for her, for free, just because she could see how much she was needed and appreciated.

Finally, after a lunch at the local fast-food joint, where she worked on getting her story straight, Joan headed over to Gillian's apartment. Sighing and steeling herself to an uncomfortable bout of dishonesty, Joan got out of the truck, walked up to the landlady's ground-floor apartment, and rang the doorbell.

As the door opened, Joan began, "Hi, Agnes, I'm sorry I didn't return your call, but—"

"Joan, honey!" the landlady, dressed in T-shirt and sweatpants and reeking of cigarette smoke, interrupted her. "Come in, come in! You know, I was just going to call you again."

"Uh, thanks." Joan stepped into an apartment that she knew Miriam would declare to be bad *feng shui*—she didn't feel welcome to sit down anywhere, and the decor consisted of every bit of furniture that had ever been on sale at the local Wal-Mart. "But—"

"I've already called the police," Agnes went on in a semiconspiratorial tone, "and do you know what they told me? They told me I'd have to have some other proof that there was foul play for them to do anything and that students disappear and reappear all the time. They acted like I was wasting their time! And poor Gillian could be lying dead by the side of the road somewheres, and here I am owed a month's rent! I just don't know what it is about cops these days. I swear they've gone soft. It's no wonder they haven't solved that there Jon Benet case."

Something growled at Joan's feet, and she looked down to see an immaculately groomed white poodle baring its teeth at her.

"Oh, don't mind Porthos," Agnes went on. "He's that way about any stranger, especially if he smells another dog on you. You got a dog?"

"Um, no, I don't, but—"

"Anyway, they won't do nothin', not without evidence. So I was just about to call you again, to ask you if you ever found that nice Mr. Amadan."

"Yes, I have!" Joan jumped in before she could be interrupted again. "And I've talked to Gillian too!"

"You have?" Agnes said, looking hurt. "Well, why didn't you tell me all this time?"

"I'm sorry, Agnes. I've been out of town myself and I just got home this morning. Gillian's . . . fine, but she won't be home for a while. She had . . . a project with Mr. Amadan, but it isn't finished yet. And we're . . . she's not sure when it will be done. So . . . so she asked me to come over and apologize and to pay this month's rent for her. She's gonna pay me back, she says."

"You're gonna pay her rent?"

"Yep." Joan fished out her checkbook from her back pocket. "How much do I—does she owe?"

"Three hundred and fifty. Three seventy-five with the late fee."

Joan was startled but tried not to show it. *Three-fifty for that tiny place? Either Gillian's getting ripped or it's true what I heard—rents are rising all over.* She wrote out the check and handed it to the landlady.

"Well, all right," Agnes said dubiously, "if this is how she wants to handle it, I guess that's between you two." She looked sidelong at Joan. "Gillian *is* all right, isn't she?"

"She's fine," Joan said quickly. "She's just really wrapped up in this project right now and doesn't want to come home until it's finished."

"This must be something pretty big, isn't it?"

"It's . . . big," Joan could say in all honesty.

"Might make her career, huh?"

"Oh, she's seen some changes in her life already."

"Uh-huh. I knew it might be big. That Mr. Amadan is some flashy guy. Hollywood-type. Or New York?"

"Uh, more European, I think."

Agnes grinned. "Well, good for her. It's good to see young people make something of themselves and not piss their life away. I've got this nephew, you see, who—"

"Um, excuse me, but Gillian asked me to check on a couple of things in her apartment for her. Would it be okay for me to go up and . . . ?"

The landlady shrugged. "Sure. You paid her rent—go on up and do whatever you have to do."

"Thanks. Nice talking to you." Joan rapidly backed out, avoiding the growling Porthos, and dashed around the side of the house to the outside stairs.

Joan let herself in with her key and closed the door firmly behind her. Everything was the way she and Miriam had left it. She went over to the desk and saw the computer was still unplugged. Just to be safe, Joan disconnected the speakers from the computer before plugging the CPU back in and rebooting it. The monitor came back up to display the normal Windows desktop. She looked at the papers strewn beside it and decided that despite Gillian's warnings, a sorting of those would be a place to start. Then she could tackle what she could find in the computer files. She sighed, anticipating a long afternoon of work ahead of her.

Two hours later, in a fog of fatigue and cold anger, Joan dialed Miriam's number. After several rings, she began to despair, but at last Miriam answered, nearly breathless. "H-hello?"

"Miriam? It's Joan. Did I catch you running in the door?"

"No! Joan! You'll never guess who showed up at my place!"

Joan shut her eyes. "Cain."

"You . . . you guessed."

"He was at my place when I got home this morning. Didn't he tell you?"

"Uh, no. No, he's just been, um, hanging out and . . ." She giggled and said something away from the phone, clearly muffled by her hand. When she returned, she added, "And he's been, um . . . really nice. *Really* nice." And she laughed again.

"Uh-huh." *So you took him up on the offer I turned down, eh?* Joan wondered if he had pissed on Miriam's rug yet, but didn't ask.

"He's not like . . . anyone I've ever known before. He's so . . . wild and free, you know?"

"Wild and free. Yep. That describes him, all right. Listen, Miriam, I'm calling because I'm back at Gillian's and I've been reading her files. There's stuff we've got to talk about."

"But she told us not to—"

"Tough. She hasn't been completely straight with us, I think."

"We haven't talked to her much at all."

"Well, it's about time to. Can you meet me at my place? I'll make you dinner. It's my turn, after all."

"Can I—"

"Don't bring Cain!"

"But Joan!"

"He pissed on my rug and tore up my kitchen. He's not welcome. Got that?"

Miriam sighed heavily. "He just wants to protect us."

"Yeah, right, and eat up all our food and mess up our furniture. Don't bring him. So, see you at my place?"

Miriam sighed again. "Okay. How about giving me an hour so I can dress. And stuff."

"An hour it is. See you."

"Bye."

Joan gathered the papers into a file folder and went home. She thought about what Miriam might find acceptable in the way of a meal and opened the freezer door. The baggie that had held the faerie arm plopped out onto the kitchen floor. Only now it held a stir bubbling mass of black goo that might once have b arm-shaped.

Joan stepped back, wrinkling her nose in disgust. She wondered if there was still any point in delivering the mess to some biologist for testing. To her horror, the baggie began to roll around the floor, and the Ziploc's top puckered, letting air escape.

The kitchen filled with the smell of rotting vegetation, and the baggie collapsed, its contents seeming to flow away into the floor, or into nothing. In moments, the ugly mess was gone, leaving only its stench behind.

Dang. There goes my evidence. Then again, there goes my problem, thought Joan. She shut the freezer door and cautiously tossed the baggie into the garbage, then brought a floor fan into the kitchen and opened a window to get some of the smell out. Her appetite for some reason diminished, Joan decided on take-out food rather than cooking. She dashed the couple of blocks over to a mom-and-pop sandwich shop and got a veggie sandwich of tomatoes and bean sprouts for Miriam and pastrami and cheese for herself.

She hurried back to be home on time, but Miriam was late, as usual. When Joan opened the door for her, Miriam bustled in, frowning.

"Hi. You know, Cain is really upset with you for not inviting him."

"Tough. He can come over when he's housebroken." From Miriam's scowl and then embarrassed glance, Joan wondered just how Cain had expressed his displeasure.

"Is that what that smell is?"

"Some of it. Some of it is a certain elfy arm Cain gave

s a present that went past its sell-by date and rotinto oblivion."

"Ewww. So." Miriam plopped herself onto the sofa. What did you find out that's so important?"

My, aren't we snippy tonight? Okay, be that way, thought Joan. She brought out the file folder that held Gillian's papers and opened it on the coffee table. "You could say it's what I didn't find out. See this?" Joan pointed at the date on the first set of notes. "Gillian's been studying these sidhe people longer than we thought. She's got notes from research at least three years old. Here, on these sheets, she's noted the big UFO outbreak in Colorado back in the 1970s, which she suggests might be fairy lights. And she mentions some sightings of Bigfoot-like creatures that she suggests might be spriggans, boccans, or leshy, whatever they are."

"They're the less noble, more monstery, kind of sidhe," Miriam grumbled, "that supposedly live in mountains and forests. Go on."

"'Okay. And she's known about the Lay of the Amadan ever since she heard about it from some nowdead Irish uncle. Apparently he taught her little bits of it when she was a child, but never the whole thing. So when she was old enough, she did some digging and research and learned the parts she was missing. That's what the letter from the Irish monastery was about.

"So she tried the Lay of the Amadan a couple of years ago, as soon as she had the whole song—but thought it didn't work. See, here she writes, '. . . some presence of glamour but no manifestation.' I'll bet it did work, though. Just not the way she planned. She might have summoned Amadan or given him some way into this

150

world, but didn't see it. Didn't the folks in Sun
Rock say he'd been around for a couple of years?"

Miriam seemed, if anything, more angry. "Still tryin.
to pin the blame on Gillian, are you?"

"Miriam, I'm only saying Gillian's not entirely an
innocent bystander. She was trying to beg the faerie
powers for a . . . a gift or something—the way that her
ancestors had. So here's the deal—we're trying to pull
her nuts out of the fire when she didn't even know
what she was doing. That's why she can't tell us what
to do to make it right.

"She knows she made a mistake in the process.
Maybe only men are supposed to sing this—there are
hints of that in her notes. Or maybe she didn't do it in
the right sort of place. Or maybe, and this is what I
think, there's part of the puzzle missing. She knew
enough to summon Mr. Amadan, but instead of getting
a favor out of him, she pissed him off."

"I don't believe your attitude, Joan! What are you
really saying? That we should let her stay a guitar
as . . . as punishment for her stupidity or hubris or
something?"

"No, no, no!" Joan shook her head wildly. "I'm just
saying . . . we've got a bigger problem here than we
thought. My only gripe with Gillian is that she should
have told us right off the bat, before we went running
off to possibly get killed or worse, what she didn't
know."

"Well, maybe she didn't know what she didn't
know! Or maybe she's been so scared and upset she
couldn't get her thoughts straight," Miriam snapped.
"Did you think of that?"

"Yeah, sure, but—"

Yeah but nothing. Why don't we ask her? I'm sure e's heard us through the thin walls of her guitar case." Miriam jumped up, got Gillian out of her case, and sat back down with the guitar on her lap. "So, Gilly, you must have heard us. What do you say?"

> *its true   its true   so sor ry*
> *I can't think right like this*
> *I'm scared I'm sad*
> *Don't know what to do*
> *so sor ry sor ry*

Miriam glared at Joan with a "See?" expression.

Joan said to the guitar. "So what really happened, Gilly?"

> *When the first time failed*
> *I pro grammed the MI DI to sound like*
> *male voi ces add more rich ness to*
> *the song more re so nance*
>
> *It worked and sum moned Am a dan but*
> *did not bind not bind him and*
> *I wished an y way I asked him for*
> *the know ledge of the pow er of*
> *mus ic I wan ted to com pose*
> *to write great mu sic*
>
> *He laughed at me and said few mor tals*
> *are giv en such a gift and I was not*
> *wor thy when I de man ded it he*
> *said he would let me see mu sic*
> *from the in side and then he*
> *touched me and I be came*

*as you see me now and he laughed and
then he left he left he left
that's all I have to say
don't know why it went wrong
I'm sor ry sor ry sor ry.*

Miriam stopped playing and Joan favored her with a "See?" glare of her own. "It's okay, Gilly," Miriam said. "*I* forgive you. You just rest now, and we'll think of something." Miriam put the guitar back in the case and closed it.

"Miriam . . ." Joan said, tossing her hands in a helpless gesture. "It's nice that you're . . . sympathetic to her condition, but we really need more information before we make stupid mistakes too."

Miriam stood up and scowled down at her. "What *we* need is a little less judging and a little more heart. I think you're just trying to find an excuse to give up on her, and I*'ve* gotten burned worse than you. Sure. I'll go off and look some more at my sourcebooks. But I suggest *you* do some examining of *yourself!*" She grabbed her purse and stomped out the door, slamming it behind her.

Joan sighed and buried her face in her hands. Conflicting thoughts spun round in her head, like demons circling her, shouting advice.

One said, *Screw her! Who wants to work with such a flake? She'd only mess things up even more.* But righteous anger made Joan feel a little queasy.

Another went, *Poor Miriam! She's been so traumatized by Mr. Amadan and Cain that she can't think straight either.* But patronizing pity didn't feel very good either.

A third muttered, *What if she's right? What if I've really*

ost sight of the pain this has caused Gillian and I'm just
being a stone-cold, unfeeling bitch? And that felt the worst
of all.

Joan stood up and looked down at the guitar case.
"Sorry, Gillian. I'll try to be more . . . understanding. I
just want to do what's best for everybody." She picked
up the sandwiches and took them into the kitchen,
where she took a couple more bites of the pastrami and
cheese before losing her appetite again.

Joan wondered how long she should wait before calling Miriam to apologize. *Probably I should wait until tomorrow. She might need some time to cool off.*

Darker thoughts drifted in as well. *What if this tiff is
their doing? What if the fairies are trying to split up our team
to weaken us? Just like they've been trying to scare us off. Just
because you're paranoid doesn't mean they aren't out to
getcha. And if they are, paranoia can be healthy. Am I really a
coward? And isn't being a coward sometimes healthy?*

Just as she decided this, there came a knock at the
door.

Joan froze. As she gathered her jangling nerves, she
thought, *With my luck, it's Cain, come to demand an
apology. But maybe it's just the local Avon lady. Or Jeho-
vah's Witnesses. Or a neighbor. Or Agnes. Or the cops.*

The knock came again. "Hell with it," Joan muttered,
and she got up and went to the door.

It was Miriam, standing there sheepishly, holding a
large white candle with twigs stuck onto it. "Hi," she
said with a wan smile.

"Um, hi." Joan stepped back and let her in. "What's
that?" she said, nodding at the candle.

"A peace offering?" Miriam placed it on top of Joan's
bookcase. "Burning a white candle is supposed to bless

a place, and the sage branches—there's some embedded in the wax too—they're supposed to cleanse a place of evil spirits and negative energy. Good thing the Angel's Wing stays open late in the summer. Okay if I light it?"

"Um, sure. At least the scent might cover up the rug odors in here."

Miriam took out a book of matches in nervous-shaking hands and managed to get the candle lit. The flame lent a bit of golden glow to the room, and Joan discovered its scent of sage-with-a-touch-of-vanilla or whatever was pleasant. Stepping back with a preparatory breath, Miriam said, "I'm sorry I snapped at you. I was out of line."

"Hey, it's okay. We're both under a little stress these days, aren't we? Um, I could bring out the sandwiches again, if you're still hungry."

"Thanks," said Miriam with a grateful smile. "I'd like that. And I think . . . I think I have a plan."

"A plan?" asked Joan. "For what?"

"For getting Gillian changed back, silly. It's all in the music. We have to use it again. It'll be tricky. And maybe kinda dangerous. But Gillian's got all the equipment we need at her place. And we won't have to leave Dawson Butte."

"That last point is almost enough to sell me by itself," said Joan. "Tell me more."

Chapter 9

It was about ten o'clock when Joan at last saw Miriam out the door, and as Joan shut it she realized she was exhausted. Miriam's "plan," in the glow of late-night bravado, had sounded almost feasible, and at least it would make her feel like they were doing something. *Every little effort helps,* Joan remembered her mother used to say. *And we need all the help we can get.*

Joan cleaned up the kitchen to a level of tolerable clutter and decided that was enough. She saw that the sage candle was starting to leave drippings on the bookshelf, and so she put a plate under it. But its light and scent were soothing, so rather than extinguish it, Joan brought the candle into the bedroom and put it atop the dresser.

What is it about candlelight? she wondered. She had seen candles in churches often enough that perhaps they were a symbol to her of spirituality. Candlelight also made her think of philosophers of old, writing their profound thoughts by its dim flame with quill and parchment. And a candle flame in darkness, of course, had always been a symbol of hope.

She checked all the windows and doors to make sure they were closed and locked—an annoying task, since one thing she had always liked about Dawson Butte was that you didn't have to live paranoid like folks in Denver. At last satisfied that no ghoulies or ghosties or long-leggety beasties were going to get in, Joan finally went to bed.

She fell into a sound sleep nearly right away. But some time later, she awoke feeling thirsty. The candle on the dresser had burned down about halfway, the flame drowning in a pool of paraffin. Joan got up and blew it out and staggered out into the living room with intentions of getting water from the kitchen. She stopped in the doorway to the living room, aware that she wasn't alone.

Someone was sitting in the armchair, a man with skin so dark he blended in with the shadows. Only where highlights from the streetlights outside glinted on his arms, knees, and cheekbones could Joan see his shape. Light glistened on his woolly hair. A strong animal scent, like cattle only muskier, was noticeable in the room.

He stood up, and by his silhouette she could see he had powerful, broad shoulders and narrow waist and hips. She was surprised that she didn't feel afraid, only confused and annoyed. "Who are you?" she asked.

"You could say I am a friend of the one you call Cain," the man began. By the rhythm and accent of his voice, Joan could tell he was not from Denver, possibly not even American. "Although you should not, for it is said Cain truly has no friends."

"Why are you here?"

"To speak with you."

Joan scratched her head. "In the middle of the night?"

"We do not like you," he said, ignoring her question. "But you are the enemy of our enemy, and you have opened a way, and therefore I have come."

The streetlights glinted in his eyes, a strange golden-brown light. Joan decided that she must be dreaming and that was why she was unafraid and that naturally things wouldn't be making any sense. "Come to do what?"

"The faerie lord must not succeed."

"We agree on that," said Joan. "But why talk to me? Why not Miriam? She has Talent."

"She has been tainted," he replied, and Joan could hear the disdaining curl of his lip as he said it. "*He* has touched her. Come with me."

As if it were no more than crossing the room, Joan followed him from night into day, from the interior of the house to the outdoors—the ridge of Hunt Mountain overlooking the valley in which the town of Dawson Butte . . . should have been. It wasn't there. Just an open meadow down which an unimpeded Plum Creek flowed, flanked by pine-robed buttes. Farther west rose the Rampart Range, foothills of the Rockies. Again, she did not feel afraid, merely full of wonder.

She turned and, to the east, could see the high plains fall away, flatter and flatter in the distance. She remembered coming to this ridge as a child of twelve or so, just to sit and wonder what it looked like before there were people here. Now she knew. A raven circled overhead and seemed to be observing her. In the far distance to the east, on the plains, she saw a brown smudge that at first she took to be smoke. Then she saw it was a herd of bison, many, many thousand of them.

"We will ally with you," said the dark-skinned man,

"because you know. You have eaten this dust and you know this land. It sings in your blood. It is part of you. For a time, you will have our assistance."

Joan wondered what assistance was being offered. To trample the elves? "Do you know what Mr. Amadan is?" Joan heard herself asking.

"This world was not made for his kind. Yet they wish to take it for themselves. They must not succeed."

Joan thought about this. "One could say that about humankind too."

"Humankind are unruly children. You take too much. You destroy what you take. Yet the sea is in your blood and the earth in your bones. You are of it. They are not. They twist nature out of its purpose, for theirs."

Joan wanted to ask what nature's purpose was, but that was not what came out of her mouth. Instead, she asked, "What is crystal sage?"

"You seek in the wrong direction," said the dark man, starting to walk away, to the east.

"Then what is it?" Joan called after him.

"It is a banding together, a place, but in the heart," the dark man said, dropping to all fours and growing in size. Then he galloped away to rejoin his herd.

The scene faded around her, and Joan was again standing in her dark living room. "I hate dreams like this," Joan muttered. "Even if I write this down, it will all look like nonsense in the morning." Joan got herself a drink of water and staggered back to bed.

The next thing she knew, bright sunlight was streaming through the bedroom window. Joan sat up in bed and yawned. In mild panic, she glanced at the alarm clock, but no, she hadn't overslept. She thought she could still smell the pines and prairie grasses—probably from the sage candle. But the feel of the dream had stayed with her, as sometimes happens with the most vivid of dreams.

Joan swung her feet over the bed and stood up. She noticed the rug felt gritty on her bare soles and chastised herself for not vacuuming often enough. She wondered if Cain was to blame for the dirt and decided it was no good trying to blame him for everything, tempting though it might be.

There was only one job that day, but a long one. A wealthy couple's large house up in the hills. Joan sighed and wandered out to the kitchen to make some coffee. As she passed the armchair, she noticed some fluff on the headrest. She idly picked it off. It was coarse woolly fur or hair, dark brown . . . nearly black. "No," Joan groaned, and she tossed it into the nearest wastebasket.

After a long, hard day, Joan showed up at Gillian's apartment that evening, tired and sore. The rich folk in the hills were pleasant in a superficial way, but clueless. They always seemed slightly disappointed after Joan put in her six hours of work, as if they had been expecting her to get more done in that enormous house. They paid well, the money was nice, but Joan kept wondering if she could think of an excuse someday to turn down that job, or get fired from it. Maybe she could bring Miriam along sometime and encourage her to comment loudly on the bad *feng shui*.

Miriam was supposed to meet her here, to start work on "the plan." But she hadn't arrived yet, so Joan slogged alone up the stairs into Gillian's apartment. She hoped the landlady wouldn't come up to visit and ask questions. Joan expected she would only have to come to the place a couple more times to get what they needed for the last, best attempt at saving Gillian. She wished she could be more certain that this would work.

Joan opened the door and turned on the lights. No goblins jumped out at her, and things were pretty much the way she had left them. She turned the computer on and then crossed the room to examine Gillian's stereo equipment. It was clearly of good quality and had more levers and knobs than Joan felt comfortable dealing with. She had had more than one former boyfriend shriek at her for messing up his stereo settings, so they tended to make her twitchy.

As she was studying the control panel, the phone rang, making her jump. Probably Miriam, apologizing for being late, Joan guessed, although she wondered what to say if it were a friend of Gillian's. Joan had forwarded her phone here, since small-town folk never paid much attention to business hours and she wanted to catch any client calls. She couldn't afford to turn any away if she could help it. She picked up the handset and said, "Hello?"

"Hi, doll! How you doing, sweetie?"

"Dad!"

"Hey, listen, your mom and I finally got to see Mount Rushmore today. Whoo-ee! Even more impressive than it looks in pictures. Remember that picture book you used to love that had all those photos of national parks?"

"Yes, Dad . . ." Joan said, reverting to an adolescent whine.

"Well, I think we're gonna manage to see all of 'em. And hey, the Black Hills are really beautiful, ya know? I swear they're nicer than the Rockies. Your mom and I went for a hike yesterday and—"

"Um, Dad? I kinda don't have a lot of time to chat right now. I'm trying to help a friend who's in a real bind." Joan knew if she let him go on he'd describe every bird they'd seen, and every kind of rock, and tree, and what the clouds looked like and what new people they'd met that day. It was as though her parents had become children again—everything new and bright. Joan found it both cute and annoying.

"Oh, all right. But you know, you really oughta come out and see this too, honey. Why don't you just hop on a plane to Rapid City and come on out and join us? We'll pay for the tickets and everything. Whaddaya say?"

Her dad made a similar offer every nice place her parents stopped at—it had become almost a ritual with each phone call. But this once, just for once, Joan felt an awful desire to take him up on it. To drop everything, her troublesome clients and her impossible task with Gillian and Mr. Amadan, and just go. She ached so bad for it she felt a tear well up in her eye.

"Hello? Joan? You've gone quiet there, honey," her dad prompted.

Joan swiftly wiped the tear away. "Sorry, Dad. I'd love to join you, I really would, but I can't afford to give myself a vacation just yet. I have to keep up with my clients or I'll lose them. I'm not the only cleaning service in town, you know."

"Joan, Joan," her dad sighed. She could almost see him shaking his head with that peculiar grin of his. "You gotta take some of the weight off those pretty shoulders of yours and live a little. Lord knows, your mom and I could have used that advice years ago.

We're doing the best we can with what little time we have left on God's green earth, but you've got your whole life ahead of you."

Joan felt an old, familiar tight anger welling up inside her. "I won't have much of a life if I can't make a living for myself. You and Mom taught me that hard work is the only honest way to get ahead. You wouldn't be having so much fun now if you hadn't put so much sweat into the ranch to make it worth so much."

Her father chuckled, a sad, ironic sound. "Honey, I think you're old enough to understand this—but it wasn't our work at all that got us that windfall. It was just the land itself. We happened to be sitting on the right parcel at the right time when a developer wanted it real bad. It never was that much good as rangeland, you know. I hear John Sanderson is thinking of putting up a factory outlet mall there. That should give you a nice place to shop. Sorta shop-at-home, heh heh. Yep, I figure all the work we did, as far as the land's value is concerned, didn't amount to a hill of beans."

"Don't say that!" Joan yelled into the phone before she caught herself. "I mean . . . I'm sorry, Dad, I shouldn't have yelled at you like that. I'm just really stressed right now. I gotta go. Give my love to Mom—"

"You wanna talk to her? She's right here. I can put her on—"

"No, Dad, really, I gotta go. Talk to you later. Love to both of you. G'bye." Joan hung up and clutched her stomach, hoping that the ache there would fade soon. "Factory outlet mall," she grumbled, and sat down heavily in Gillian's desk chair. She imagined a tacky western clothing goods store falling down from the sky onto the corral in which she used to ride Misty, the way the wicked witch's house had fallen onto the yellow brick road in Oz.

The phone rang again. Joan jumped and swore at it. On the second ring, she picked it up. "Hello?"

"Miss Dark, I presume?" The male voice was low, musical, with harmonics of amusement, arrogance, and threat.

"Mr. Amadan."

"Very good. I'm so glad you remember me. How are you and your charming friend doing?"

"We're fine," Joan snarled. "What do you want?"

Mr. Amadan clicked his tongue. "Dear me, they really should be teaching young people better telephone manners these days. Truly, I called to learn how your search was faring."

"It's . . . going," Joan said as she frantically tried to figure out what he really was asking.

"Ah, then you have found crystal sage, have you?"

"We're . . . getting there."

"Are you?" There was speculation and, perhaps, concern in his tone.

"If that bothers you, why don't you just tell us and be done with it?"

"But where would be the fun in that?"

"What makes you think this is fun?"

"Isn't it? My dear, you really should take a lighter view of life."

"Look, I've already had one lecture on life. I don't need another."

"In my experience, mortals need all such lectures they can get. You spend such a brief time in your world. Why not enjoy it?"

"Because a friend of mine, because of a certain spiteful . . . creature, can't enjoy hers. I am sure Gillian has suffered enough and learned whatever lesson you intended for her. Why don't you stop playing games and do the honorable thing and change Gillian back?"

"Ah, honor. Now there is a virtue debased in these times. One could speak volumes about honor. And you have no real idea of my intent for your friend. But, sensing your impatience, I will address the purpose of my call. It has come to my attention that you have gathered . . . allies to your side. This is not, as your English say, cricket. Not part of the game. It changes the entire dynamics of the situation."

Allies? Joan could only think he meant Cain, unless there was more to her last night's dream than she thought. "Well, we needed a little help, didn't we, against those green-skinned things you sent to harass us the other night? And that storm?"

"My dear, I have no idea what you are talking about."

"Yeah, right. Plausible deniability. I get it."

"Just a word of friendly advice: Those who offer you aid are not powers you can control. They will very likely do you more harm than good. I suggest you turn them away, or else things will go less smoothly for you. I would find their interference . . . most annoying, and it would not help your friend's cause in the least."

"Oh, wouldn't it?"

"You would do well to heed me."

"Yeah, well, we'll see who needs to heed whom when the time comes." She slammed the phone down. It occurred to her that being rude might not have been the wisest way to treat such a powerful person, and her counterthreat had been a little . . . weak. Nothing to do about that now.

Allies, eh? Perhaps Cain had gone to wherever Mr. Amadan was and peed on *his* carpet. The thought made Joan chuckle aloud. *Oh, I could only wish that were true.*

She heard someone come clumping up the outside stairs and a tentative knock on the door. "It isn't locked, Miriam."

Miriam opened the door and peered in sheepishly. "Sorry I'm late." She bustled in, reeking of sandalwood, and bent down to put a plastic bag on the rug.

"Been hitting the incense kinda hard lately, haven't you? Or is that a new perfume you're wearing?"

She shrugged one-shouldered. "I needed to meditate a long time to clear my thoughts. That's why I'm late."

"S'okay. You just missed a call from our favorite fairy."

Miriam stood up, wide-eyed. "The Amadan called you? Here?"

"Unlike some of our friends, Mr. Amadan uses phones. Anyway, he wanted to see how we were doing. To him, this is all some sort of game."

Miriam nodded. "That's the way they are. I did some reading earlier today on elf lore. Playing games with mortals is a big sport of theirs."

"Learn anything we can use?"

Miriam gestured weakly with her arms and rolled her eyes. "So much of this stuff was written by Christians that they mostly recommend crosses, prayers, holy water, the sound of church bells, that sort of thing."

"We tried the God line on him, remember? It didn't work. Unless . . . are you a believer?"

"I'm a pagan, if anything."

"What do pagans suggest to keep the fey away?"

"Oh, various herbs like wolfbane, Saint-John's-wort—wolfbane is also called monkshood, and it grows in these mountains, you know."

"That's worth keeping in mind, I guess. Anything else?"

"Wearing your clothes inside out."

"What?"

"So they can't recognize you."

Joan rubbed her face. "I cannot believe that Mr. Amadan would be that stupid."

"No, you're right. They're just folktales, after all. Who knows which of them are true?"

"Well, it would be good to find out before we use any of them in the big showdown."

"You . . . didn't tell the Amadan what we were planning to do, did you?"

"Miriam! How stupid do you think I am?"

"Sorry. I thought maybe he might have called to find out what we were up to. But he just wanted to needle us, huh?"

"I suppose. But there was one other thing." Joan felt oddly hesitant to tell her, even though Miriam was probably the last person on earth who would laugh at her. "He's somehow aware that we've got . . . allies on our side. And he doesn't like it."

"Allies? You mean like Cain?"

"I guess."

"But you sent Cain away," Miriam said with just a hint of reproach.

"I'm not certain he's gone. And there's something else. I had . . . I guess it was a dream, last night."

"You guess?"

"Well, I thought it was, but then . . . well, let me tell you what happened." And Joan described her encounter with the buffalo man and the bit of fur she'd found afterward. She omitted, however, her question of why Miriam hadn't been chosen and the man's reply of her being "tainted."

Miriam sat cross-legged on the floor. "Wow," she said in genuine admiration. "You had a real visitation from an animal spirit. I'm envious."

"Don't be. He said he didn't like me, remember? And he said he knew Cain, so perhaps our filthy boytoy is more than he seems, too."

"I already knew *that*," said Miriam.

"Yeah, okay, you win. Anyway, I don't even know what kind of help we were being offered. I only know now that Mr. Amadan doesn't like it, and I figure that's a good thing. It's funny—the buffalo man said that the world wasn't made for the elf types. I wonder what he meant by that."

"Well, there are lots of ideas in the folklore about where the sidhe come from. Some of the books I read said they were fallen angels—"

"Like Lucifer?"

"I suppose."

"That describes Mr. Amadan pretty well. Go on."

"Well, or that they're the gods of a conquered people. Or spirits of the dead."

Joan sighed. "If they existed long before we even evolved, they couldn't be those, could they?"

"Or aliens," Miriam added helpfully.

"Stop, my head hurts already," groaned Joan. "I suppose if I'd known what they were, I wouldn't have had to ask the buffalo man. Or I'd have known how he could help us."

"He's already helped. He told you something about crystal sage."

"Yeah, but it's just another riddle instead of a clue. I looked in my Colorado atlas in case he meant 'place' literally, and there is no river, town, mountain, or what-have-you called that. Still, Mr. Amadan seemed worried that we're closer to the answer."

"You told him the clue?" Miriam said, aghast.

"No! Just that we were making progress."

"Whew. For a moment there I thought you were getting as sloppy as I am!"

Joan felt stung. "Well, I wasn't thinking too clearly. I had just got off the phone with my dad. And he told me— Never mind."

"So you were letting your issues get in the way of your common sense," Miriam said.

"You could put it that way. If you wanted to rub it in."

"Sorry. S'okay. I've been there. Done that. Maybe we should get on with tonight's project before we chicken out. Ready to do some recording?"

"Yeah. If we can figure out that stereo setup."

Miriam turned around and looked at the stereo control panel. "Good system. No sweat. I can work with this."

"You can?"

Miriam gave her a pained glare over her shoulder. "Just because I have a spiritual nature doesn't mean I'm not a technophile. I adjust my stereo a lot listening to what you'd call New Age music. When you use music for meditation, you want the levels to be just right. You want the perfect balance between bass and treble, and that can vary from piece to piece."

"Okay, I get the picture. Can we record straight from the computer without using the speakers?"

Miriam followed the electrical cords that ran from the stereo to the keyboard to the computer, muttering, "Line in, line out, line in, line out. Yeah. Looks like she's got it set up just for that. Are the speakers still disconnected?"

"Yep."

"Then we're ready to rock and roll." Miriam pulled a package of new tapes out of the plastic bag and began to tear off the wrapping.

Joan hadn't wanted to bring it up, but some part of her soul was going to eat at her for days, she knew, unless she asked. "Miriam . . . is your dad really gonna build a factory outlet mall on my family's ranch?"

Miriam froze and glanced away. "That was the plan last I heard. I . . . I wasn't going to say anything to you about it. Why? Who told you?"

"My dad told me. How could . . . Never mind. It's not your fault. It's just . . . making me cranky."

"I understand," Miriam said softly, as she continued to open the tape package. "You really are tied to that land. No wonder the buffalo man appeared to you."

"Yeah, yeah, I've got the land in my blood," Joan grumbled. "I feel as bad about it as you do about your dreams for some faraway fairyland you'll never see. It's an ache that just won't go away."

"I hear you."

"If there was some pill I could take to forget all about the ranch—"

"You'd take it?"

Joan paused. "No."

Miriam popped a tape into the tape deck. "Didn't think so. Wanna start that program running so I can check the levels before we record?"

"Sure." Joan brought up the music program and clicked on the file "Amalast." Just before clicking on "run," Joan paused. "You know, if this is a magical, mystical thing, might invoking the program cause as much trouble as actually playing it?"

Miriam thought a moment before responding. "I don't think so. I mean, by that logic, it couldn't be written down either, and Gillian had found a music manuscript of it. I think it's the actual sound that's important. That's why Gillian had to futz with so many versions to make it work. I think we'll be safe."

"We could put one of Gillian's sweaters on inside out just in case."

Miriam laughed. "I don't think that will be necessary. Are you ready?"

Joan positioned the cursor over the run button. "All set."

Miriam punched the record button and said, "Tape's running. Hit it."

Joan clicked. The next minute they spent in silence as Miriam watched the level gauges. Nothing untoward happened. The piece was short, only three minutes, so the recording was done quickly.

"That's that," Miriam said, pushing the eject button.

"Great. We'd better make several copies. On separate tapes."

"Good idea," said Miriam. "You been watching lots of cop suspense shows, I can tell."

"It just seems practical."

"Okay. How many? I bought a pack of five."

"Let's do all five. If that's okay with you."

Miriam shrugged. "Sure. No problem."

It took less than twenty more minutes, which they passed mostly in silence, to make the four additional tapes.

"Done!" Miriam announced as the last one finished.

"Wait," said Joan. "Shouldn't we play just a little bit to make sure it recorded?"

"Less than an hour ago you were worried that just running the program might trigger something, and here you are wanting to tempt fate by playing the actual tape."

"I just don't want to be ready to do the deed and then find out there's nothing there."

"So the worst that would happen is . . . nothing."

"We don't know yet the circumstances in which we're going to use it. If we have to go to a lot of trouble to set up the Amadan trap, it's going to really set us back if the tape doesn't work. We can't keep coming back here without the landlady getting suspicious, and I'm not going to keep paying rent on this place for Gillian. I can't afford it."

"Look," said Miriam, "if we trust the technology, sound is getting onto the tape. Why should we assume it isn't working?"

"Just a millisecond," Joan suggested. "Just the barest hint that the right piece has gotten recorded. That can't possibly . . . summon anything, can it? According to Gillian's notes, the whole song was needed by her ancestors."

Miriam sighed and put the tape back in. She hit the rewind button, saying, "If you say so. Let's hope you're right." She waited a minute for the rewind to finish, then forwarded it to the exact point sound began to show on the indicators. "Here we are. One second. Ready?"

"Wait! Turn the volume way low," said Joan.

"I doubt that will make any difference," Miriam muttered, but she turned the volume dial down. "*Now* ready?"

"Okay. Now."

They waited. A beautiful, faint chord emanated as if forming in the air around them, as if wafted to them on the most exquisite of warm summer evenings. It wasn't until the synthesized male voice began to sing that Joan yelled, "Stop it! Stop the tape!"

Miriam did. "I was afraid of that. That we might get caught up in the music. It went four seconds, not one." She quickly rewound the tape.

"We're probably still okay. The magic is in the words, isn't it? And the first word of the song hadn't finished. But let's get out of here, just in case." Joan turned off the computer as Miriam shut down the stereo and gathered up the tapes.

Miriam handed two of the tapes to Joan. "Two for you, two for me. What do we do with the odd one?"

"Leave it someplace else. Let's leave one here. Just in case."

"Okay." Miriam tossed it on top of the stereo.

They shut off the lights and left, Joan locking the door behind them. A stiff breeze was blowing, whistling through the leaves and pine needles of the trees around them. The moon was bright and nearly full.

"When shall we two meet again?" Miriam asked.

"After I grill Gillian some more about where and how we should use the song. We need to plan it carefully. I'll call you when I know something."

"Okay. Good night." Miriam dashed to her car, her long skirt swirling around her.

Joan jumped into her truck and stuck one of the tape copies in the glove compartment. The other she put into her jeans pocket. She started up the truck, and its familiar rumble deeply reassured her. She hadn't realized how wary and nervous she had been during the recording session. Taking a long breath, she willed herself to relax, and then headed home.

Chapter 10

As Joan was pulling into her driveway, however, she saw perhaps the last thing she had wanted to see. Cain was leaning nonchalantly in her doorway, holding Gillian the guitar in his arms.

Joan herself was surprised at what a hot rage she could suddenly summon despite how tired she was. She jerked on the parking brake, yanked the key out of the ignition, and jumped out of the truck, slamming the door. She stalked over to Cain, fists clenched. "I thought I told you never to come back here."

Cain attempted to look down his nose at her with a smug sneer. Had Joan not been furious she would have laughed.

" 'Bout time you showed up," he said.

Through gritted teeth, Joan growled, "Put . . . Gillian . . . down. Now."

"You abandoned her!" Cain said with disappointed anger. "You left her by herself, unprotected. Elvesies almost got her!"

It was then that Joan looked past Cain and saw that her front door had been smashed in. "Did you do that?"

"Nope. Elvesies did. I stopped 'em."

Joan glared back at Cain, hoping he wasn't going to toss any more body parts at her. He didn't. "Give her back now." Joan lunged for Gillian.

"No!" Cain held the guitar up high over his head—he was enough taller than Joan that she couldn't possibly reach it. "You're stupid. You won't protect her. I'm taking her because I can keep her safe." Cain danced away, capering across the front yard.

Joan tried to run after him. "Stop! Cain! Bring her back!"

"No! You can't have her. Not until . . . not until . . ." He seemed to think a moment. "Until we meet near the pool table!" he finished with an I'm-so-clever grin. Then he turned and ran, flat out, down the sidewalk.

Joan ran to her truck and jumped in. She had a hard time getting the key back in the ignition, her hand was shaking so bad. Finally she got the truck started and peeled rubber backing into the street. She was glad it was a quiet night with no traffic.

Breaking the local speed limit by a lot, Joan roared down Pine Street, but saw no sign of Cain. She went around the block. She expanded her circuit to two blocks, then three. He had vanished. Stopped at one of Dawson Butte's three stoplights, Joan tapped the steering wheel and tried to engage her brain. On an inspiration, she drove over to Miriam's place and pounded on her door.

Miriam opened it, wearing only a long nightshirt, toothbrush in hand. "Joan?"

"Is Cain here?"

"No. Haven't seen him since yesterday."

"Damn."

"What's wrong?"

Joan walked in past Miriam, shuting the door behind her. "He's stolen Gillian."

"What?"

"He said the 'elvesies' tried to get her and I obviously couldn't protect her, so he's gone and taken her God knows where. He said something about meeting him at a pool table. I was so hoping he would come here."

"Well, shit." Miriam sagged and sat on the couch. "Now what do we do?"

"Damned if I know. I'm going to call the cops, okay?"

"If you gotta. What are you going to tell them?"

"One of my high school buddies works the night desk there. Maybe I can talk to him." Joan found the number at the front of Miriam's phone book and dialed. "Hi, can I speak to Bernie, please?" she said when the police station answered.

"Officer Buell."

"Hey, Bernie. This is Joan . . . Joan Dark."

"Hey, Joan! How ya doin'?"

"Well—"

"It's been ages since I heard from you. How are your folks? I hear they retired and skipped town in a souped-up Winnebago."

"Bernie, I'd love to chat, but this isn't a social call. I have to report a robbery."

"Oh. Sorry. Lemme grab a form here. Okay." His voice became more businesslike. "You still living on Pine Street?"

"Yeah."

"Okay, what time did this happen?"

"Just . . . now, fifteen minutes ago."

"Describe as clearly as possible what occurred."

Joan paused to collect her thoughts. "I came home

from a friend's place. A guy I sorta know was standing in my front doorway holding my guitar. The front door was broken open. Then he ran off with the guitar."

"Did you check the house to see if anything else was missing?"

"Um. No. But I'm pretty sure all he wanted was the guitar—he really liked it. I tried to chase him but lost him. Now I'm over at another friend's place."

"Okay. Describe this guy."

Joan did.

"You know his name?"

"He calls himself Cain. Cain Eslatranz, though I don't think it's his real name."

"Okay. Describe the guitar. What make is it?"

"Um. It's handmade. One of a kind. Six-string, blond wood."

"No pick guard," Miriam called softly to her. "Brass tuning pegs."

"Oh, um, no pick guard and brass tuning pegs," Joan added.

"Estimated value?"

"Priceless," Joan said.

"Yeah, to you, I'm sure, but I have to note something here."

"God, I dunno. Five hundred bucks? A thousand?"

Bernie whistled. "Okay. That'll help. We can pass word to the music and pawn shops in town to keep an eye out for it."

"Uh, Bernie, I'm pretty sure he's not going to sell it. Can't you put out an all-points bulletin to find this guy? He said I might find him at some pool table."

"Hah. You been watching too many cop shows. And there are several bars around with pool tables. A couple of which a nice girl like you shouldn't go walking into alone, if you know what I mean."

"We have bad bars in Dawson Butte?"

"You'd be surprised what goes on around here. I learned a lot just working here that I never knew growing up in this town. Anyway, uh, do you have reason to believe this Cain guy is dangerous?"

"Um . . . he's destructive of property. But . . ." Then Joan remembered the severed fairy arm. "Yeah, he could hurt someone if he felt like it."

"Okay, look. I'll get word to the squad cars we got out tonight to keep an eye out for him. But remember we're not like *NYPD Blue*. We've only got two cars and— Hang on a moment."

Joan heard the mouthpiece being covered and a muffled conversation.

Bernie came back on. "Oh, hell. Sorry, Joan. An emergency came up and I gotta go. Bad timing. Call me back tomorrow, okay? Bye."

Joan sighed as she hung up. *Emergency? What sort of emergencies happen in Dawson Butte?* She heard a siren go by in the distance, from the hospital she figured, from its direction.

"What's up?" Miriam asked.

"Oh, he got distracted by some emergency. I'll bet there's been a big accident on I-25 or something. He wants me to call back tomorrow."

"Are they going to pick up Cain?"

"I'll bet not. I'll bet that boy's long gone, and Gillian too. I don't suppose you want to go barhopping to look at pool tables, do you?"

Miriam winced but said, "If you think that's what we ought to do."

"No. Never mind." Joan could feel the adrenaline rush draining away, and she really craved the comfort of her bed. "Let's just sleep on it. Maybe somebody nice and helpful will appear in our dreams and give us advice. Maybe we'll be lucky and Cain will be like those kids or dogs who like to play Chase Me. If you don't chase them, they come whining back to find out why not."

"Yeah. Hope so. Wanna stay here tonight?"

"No, I gotta go home and see if he's done any more damage. My front door was broken open, and by now the local hoods could have made off with all the rest of my possessions."

"Dawson Butte doesn't have local hoods."

"I think Bernie could tell us otherwise. I'll call you tomorrow, okay?"

" 'Kay. Take care, Joan." Miriam came up and hugged her.

"You, too." Joan broke off the hug, fearing that she was about to break into a crying jag, which Miriam would want to soothe for the next hour. Instead, Joan left and hurried down to her truck, where she let the tears leak out all the way home.

She managed to get her front door braced with a chair so it wouldn't hang open. Joan was grateful it was summer; the drafts coming through wouldn't be too cold. Nothing else in the house had been disturbed, and no "local hoods" had taken advantage of her open door, reassuring her somewhat on the character of Dawson Butte.

Finally confident that nothing more could be done, Joan flung off her clothes and crawled into bed and pulled the covers over her head.

She dreamed, but not of buffalo man. Just the normal surreal collage of the day's events. Joan pushed open a broken door leading into a smoky bar, knocking over Agnes the landlady, who was trying to leave. Joan stepped over Agnes as Porthos the poodle growled and barked reproachfully at her. Joan saw her dad was the bartender, and he was smiling and handing out beer. He waved at her and she smiled back. Then a man in a gray suit sitting at the bar turned—it was Mr. Amadan, of course, and he nodded at her. Joan turned and left the bar area, entering a gaming room, where she saw a brightly lit pool table. Cain stood there, grinning, using Gillian as a cue stick. He winked at Joan, then knocked a tape into the center of a perfect circle of billiard balls. "Hole in one!" he said triumphantly.

"Now what?" Joan said, walking up to him.

"That," he said, leaning toward her conspiratorially, "is up to you."

"You spirit types are *so* helpful."

"Didn't wanna ruin your dream."

"And *so* clever."

Cain rapped on his head. "Thick as adobe bricks."

"What am I going to do about you?"

He thought a moment. "Exhibit me at the State Fair in Pueblo?"

"Sounds about right."

A cold wind blew into the game room, and an avalanche broke through the ceiling in slow motion. Cain turned to look at it. "Whups. Emergency's come up. Gotta go." He vanished, taking Gillian with him.

Joan got up at seven the next morning. It was earlier than she needed to, since she only had an afternoon client that day, but she hadn't been able to fall back to sleep. She staggered out toward the living room, chanting, "Show me it didn't happen. Show me it didn't happen." But no, the front door was still propped with a chair, daylight streaming past its splintered edges. "Shit."

Not bothering to dress, she made herself coffee and oatmeal and ate breakfast in front of the TV. She thought maybe she'd see something about a crash on I-25 on one of the Colorado Springs morning news-casts. But there was nothing. There was the usual fluff piece on the beauties of Rocky Mountain National Park, the "in-depth" piece on a suburb that was dealing with growth, a list of the "most uncrowded campgrounds in Colorado" (which would doubtless ensure they would become crowded shortly), and a brief, superficial look at NORAD under Cheyenne Mountain.

"Slow news day," Joan grumbled. Whatever Bernie's emergency had been, it must have been of local interest only.

Joan channel-surfed awhile, trying to hold off the lead weight of guilt pressing down on her. It would be so easy to just give up. To let Cain have Gillian and not bother to track him down. *Who knows, maybe she'd like being a guitar for the rest of her . . . existence. But given how destructive Cain is, how long will it be before he damages her?* The other half of her mind argued, *Sometimes there are forces just too big to fight. Heck, I wouldn't even contest a traffic ticket . . . even if I knew I was innocent.* Joan liked to think that unlike her namesake, she picked her battles carefully. *Saint Joan may have succeeded at liberating Or-léans, but then she went on to tackle Paris and got burned. Literally.*

In the midst of such morose thoughts, the phone rang. Joan answered it on the third ring, just before the answering machine cut in. "Hello?"

"Joan! It's Bernie. I'm glad I caught you in."

Her spirits lifted at once. "Hey, Bernie. Did you find my guy, or the guitar?"

"Oh, um, no, this call isn't about that at all, actually. It's about the emergency I had to cut you off for. It turns out you may have information on the case. Did you know an Agnes Linswotter who lives on Columbine?"

Joan's stomach rocketed to the basement. "Yeah. Yes, I do. Is she . . . is she all right?"

"Well . . . no. She's alive, but mostly paralyzed. The doctors at the hospital said she had a massive stroke. What happened was, her downstairs tenant heard an awful ruckus and some shouting in the upstairs apartment. When the tenant went up to see what was going on, she found the door open and Ms. Linswotter lying on the floor. The place had been trashed . . . computer smashed, stereo melted down as if struck by lightning. It was ugly. The tenant said Ms. Linswotter hadn't been too happy about the tenant in that apartment, a Ms. McKeagh. The tenant said that you had talked to Ms. Linswotter recently. I was wondering if she might have said anything to you that seemed like . . . irrational anger. I'm wondering if her brain might have been snapping leading up to the stroke, but the docs say strokes don't work that way."

And now it all unravels, Joan thought, numb with shock. *Dear God, is this my fault? Did the elvesies come searching for us because of those four seconds of tape we played, only they found Agnes instead?*

"Joan?"

"Oh, God, Bernie, I'm sorry. I'm . . . I'm just so sad that this happened. Yeah, I talked to Agnes a couple of days ago, but she wasn't particularly angry."

"Lessee, the downstairs tenant said you cleaned the apartment for Ms. McKeagh now and then, right?"

"Yeah, twice a week."

"Did you notice if there was friction between her and the landlady before?"

"Um, no. Gillian was late on her rent this month, but that's all." *Damn, how much should I lie to him?*

"Okay. We've been trying to reach Ms. McKeagh to inform her of the incident and see if she wants to press charges. We've reached her folks, but they say they haven't heard from her in a while. Do you have any idea where she might be? Got a current phone number or anything?"

A part of Joan wanted to fling herself on his mercy, crying, "I'm guilty! Snap the cuffs on and lock me away!" But instead she heard herself say, "Gillian's been on the road, working on one of her music projects, Bernie. Sometimes she calls in and asks me to check on something for her, but I don't know where she is right now." At least that last was true.

"Huh. All right. Do you know anyone we can reach who could tell us how to find her?"

"Gosh, I don't know, Bernie. Maybe one of her professors up in Boulder, I don't know. God, poor Agnes. Is she still at the hospital?"

"I suspect she's gonna be there a long time, Joan. She can't even talk to tell us what happened."

"Yeah. Damn. I'll go visit her this afternoon. I feel so sorry about this."

"Sorry I couldn't give you better news. I'll be in

touch, okay? There are some odd angles to this that I might want to follow up on. And don't be surprised if Fred Winter from the local paper drops by. He was nosing around here this morning and heard somebody mention you."

"Ah. Okay." *Just what I need.*

"Talk to you later. Bye."

Joan hung up and wondered if she should just go slash her wrists now or wait until something worse happened. She'd heard of the samurai warriors who would do the Death by Seven Cuts on themselves when dishonored. *Bet I wouldn't have the guts to do that,* she thought glumly. *I'm not just useless. I'm dangerous to others. I was unkind to whatever-Cain-is, so he ran off with Gillian. I insisted on hearing the tape, which summoned something to Gillian's place, and that something hurt Agnes. I'm not Joan of Arc, I'm Typhoid Mary.*

Not knowing what else to do, Joan called Miriam, but only got the answering machine. After the beep, she said, "It's Joan. God, Miriam, we . . ." Her voice caught and she took a deep breath before speaking again. "Gillian's place got trashed last night after we left. Agnes, the landlady, is in the hospital. I'm going over to visit her now. I'm . . . I'm so sorry I asked for those four seconds. Watch your back. Bye."

Joan dressed, her arms and legs feeling heavy as lead. She ran a brush over her hair and her teeth and went off to the local hospital.

Though it was a small building, the hospital was still mazelike and disorienting, and Joan had to ask directions a couple of times to find Agnes's room. Someone else was coming out just as Joan entered—a life-worn, dark-haired woman who introduced herself as Agnes's younger sister.

"She ain't able to talk yet," the woman said in a husky voice, "so don't be expecting much. Poor thing. I told her she oughta stop smokin', if not for herself then for the dog. But she always was a stubborn girl. You one of her tenants?"

Joan forced out a smile. "No, just . . . a friend of one."

The woman grunted and nodded. "I'm gonna go hassle a doctor. She doesn't look too comfortable in there. Go on in, but like I said, don't expect much."

"Okay. Thanks." Joan walked in and saw Agnes lying ashen-faced on the hospital bed, hooked up with sensors and IV so that she seemed like an abandoned unpainted clay marionette. Joan stood staring, a lump growing in her throat.

A black-haired nurse standing beside the bed turned and smiled at Joan. Her nameplate read Rodriguez. "It is good that she has visitors," the nurse said with a slight Hispanic accent. "This is a very frightening time for her. Please, go on and speak to her and let her know you are here and that you care."

Joan nodded and asked, "Will she be . . . all right?"

The nurse paused before replying. "We are doing all we can."

Joan walked up to the bed, her heart heavier with guilt with each step. Agnes seemed to be sleeping. Joan became hyperaware of the sounds around her, the quiet whirring of the monitor equipment, the nurse's footsteps. An orderly came in holding a tray and asked softly in Spanish where she should put it.

"*Sobre la mesa verde,*" the nurse replied. On the green table.

Joan leaned forward and gently grasped Agnes's arm above the IV tube. "Agnes? It's Joan. I . . . I came to see how you were doing. Can you hear me? It's Joan, the cleaning lady. Remember me?"

Agnes's eyes fluttered and then opened wide. She turned her head to look at Joan. "Juh . . . guh . . ."

"Yes, Joan." Joan squeezed Agnes's arm and tried to smile, but it was difficult while holding tears back.

Agnes's eyes seemed to be pleading with her, trying to tell a horrific, Poe-like tale of pain, fear, and betrayal. "Ah . . . ah . . . ahm . . . ahm . . ."

"Amadan?" Joan whispered.

A keening sound arose in Agnes's throat, and her back arched. Alarm noises came from the monitors, and the nurse rushed to the bed. She told the orderly to get the doctor and said to Joan, "I am sorry, you must go now!"

Joan backed away, held by Agnes's pleading gaze, until she was nearly knocked over by the doctor rushing in. She turned and left the room and sank down into the hard plastic chair beside the door. She sighed and tilted her head back against the wall, trying not to listen to the urgent sounds coming from the room. She felt worse than the day her parents told her they were selling the ranch. Then she could be angry and blame others. Now she could only blame herself.

"Joan?"

Joan looked up and saw Miriam coming down the hall. Joan jumped up from the chair, ran to her, and hugged her, letting the tears flow.

"I got your message," Miriam said. "How is she?"

Gasping, Joan said, "Not good. She tried to tell me . . . that Amadan did it. It's our fault, Miriam. My fault."

"What happened to her?"

"The doctors say she had a stroke."

"Oh, shit. Of course. One of the names for Amadan is Stroke Lad."

"Stroke Lad? That's kind of a strange name."

"Not really. I've been doing research on this stuff. Our word for the condition, for stroke, is from fairy folklore. They used to think all stroke paralysis was caused by the touch, or stroke, of elves. And Amadan is the king of the Bad Touch. Especially in June."

"And we summoned him. With those four seconds. And he was pissed. And Agnes just happened to be there—"

"Shhhh." Miriam patted her back. "We didn't ask him to hurt her. He's just a bad guy."

"We should have known better." Looking over Miriam's shoulder, Joan saw at the far end of the corridor the reporter Fred Winter, whom she recognized from his picture in the paper. "Let's get out of here," Joan said, and she turned and walked swiftly to the nearest hospital exit, Miriam following.

When they were outside the building, Miriam said, "This just proves we have to stop him!"

"Oh, right," Joan snarled back. "With a weapon we don't know how to use so it goes off in other people's faces. How are we going to use *that* to stop a guy who can do *that?*" She pointed back toward the hospital. More softly, she added, "How am I going to live with myself?"

Miriam took her arm. "My car is right over here. Wanna sit and talk for a while?"

Joan let herself be guided to Miriam's car. She sat in it, surrounded by summer warmth and the smell of hot vinyl. Miriam got into the driver's seat and left the door open to air out the car. "I've gotta get a shade for my windshield," she muttered.

Joan closed her eyes and rubbed her forehead. "Is that all you can think about right now?"

"Has it occurred to you," Miriam replied, "that demoralizing you is part of Amadan's plan? Look at what happened. He calls you . . . just to see how we're doing. Uh-huh. And he gets some inkling that we're making headway. He's bothered because we've got help. He thinks just maybe we might win. He's been trying to scare us off the game all along. First with those fairies at the cave. And those illusions of the flood and rockfall."

"Seemed damned real to me," Joan muttered.

"Yeah, well, I checked with Colorado Road Information. They never happened. Joan, if it was just those four seconds that could summon him, why didn't he show up immediately? Why didn't he trash stuff while we were still there?"

"Or give *us* strokes?"

"I think, by the nature of the game, he won't do that. It would be cheating."

"Oh, so he'll just hurt innocent bystanders?"

"Yeah. 'Fraid so."

"Wonderful."

"But don't you see? He *wants* to make us give up."

"Damn near succeeding."

"What if by catching him we can make him cure Agnes too?"

Joan had to think about that. "You think it's possible?"

"For someone who can turn a human into a guitar? Why not? Worth a try, isn't it?"

Joan sighed heavily. "The only person who could tell

us how is now in the hands of a maniac who wants us to catch him at a pool table."

"Cain wants us to find him. I had a dream about him last night."

"So did I," said Joan, feeling the cognitive dissonance of wanting to believe it Meant Something and reminding herself it was probably just coincidence. "What did he say to you?"

Miriam shook her head. "Stuff about the past being dead. And he told me why I've been having such trouble since we met Amadan. It's so stupid."

"What?"

"I ate their *food*, Joan. Remember that mint I ate in the Amadan's office? That was fairy food. In disguise. It makes you long for the world Under the Hill for the rest of your whole life. And that's what I've been going through. The feeling only went away while Cain was around. He soothed me in the dream, but . . . that's all he could do."

Joan grasped Miriam's arm and gently squeezed it. "You didn't know when you ate the mint. Don't kick yourself."

"Yeah." Miriam's face scrunched up as if she were about to either laugh or cry. "It's just . . . one thing on top of another. So. What did Cain say to you in your dream?"

"Oh, just strange, surrealistic stuff. He was playing pool with Gillian. Maybe we should have gone bar-hopping last night."

"Well, you know, dreams aren't always supposed to be taken literally," said Miriam. "Maybe you have to look at the symbols in it. Or maybe it's a riddle. What is a pool table? Something green and flat with pockets."

"Like the orderly's scrub shirt . . ." Joan murmured, letting her mind free-associate. The brief exchange with the nurse ran again in her head. Put it on the green table. ". . . *sobre la mesa verde*," Joan said.

"What? What did you say?"

"*Mes . . . mesa verde.* It means 'green table' in Spanish."

"That's it!" Miriam said, pounding the steering wheel. "That has to be it! Cain wants us to find him at Mesa Verde!"

"Aw, Miriam, that's clear across the state! That's a long way to go to check out a hunch. Think of the time we'd lose if we're wrong. Besides, what would he be doing in a bunch of old Indian ruins?"

Didn't want to ruin your dream, Cain had said. . . .

"Oh, shit. Oh, shit, of course!" Miriam slapped her forehead. "I'm so stupid! That's who he is! Oh, man, wow."

"Cain is a who?"

"To some Native American peoples, a very important who. Kind of like your buffalo man. In which case Mesa Verde is the perfect place for him to go. And where better to hide from the sidhe than in an area really inhospitable to them?"

"Are you going to tell me who he is?"

"No. You'd only argue, and I'm tired of arguing with you. Are we going to Mesa Verde?"

"I need to think about this."

"Amadan may not give us time. The longer we delay, the more damage he'll do."

"In case you've forgotten, I have a business to run. Think of the damage being done to that if I skip out on my clients."

"Oh, of course," Miriam said with mock contrition. "Surely your cleaning business is worth another stroke victim or two."

Joan stared at her. "Really know how to twist the knife, don't you? Oh, hell. Life is so weird already. And I don't have any other ideas. Okay. I'll go home and pack a bag."

"There's the brave Joan I know," said Miriam, and she started up the car.

Chapter 11

They drove around the hospital building to the area where Joan had parked her truck. It wasn't there.

"My truck!" Joan yelled. "Where is my truck? I parked it right here! I swear!"

"Calm down. You're upset. Maybe you got confused about where you parked it," Miriam said. "Let's drive around a little and maybe you'll see it."

"Miriam, I'm telling you, this was where I parked it. Right by this tree."

Miriam slowed the car near the spot. "Well, it isn't illegal to park here. I can't imagine you got towed. Did you lock it?"

"I don't remember. Damn!" Joan pounded the dashboard with her fist. "Who would want a funky old truck? With my logo on it, even."

"Kids wanting a joyride, if it was an easy target."

"Oh, God, I don't need this." Joan slumped down in the seat and covered her face with her hands. "Not now. That truck is half my business!"

"Let me drive you home. You can call your cop friend Bernie and tell him your car's been taken too."

"Yeah, great. I'd say Cain stole it, except I'm sure he doesn't drive."

"Just because our life has gotten really weird doesn't mean everything that happens to us can be blamed on the weirdness. It might be just a coincidence that some kids ran off with your truck. Chaos attracts more chaos."

"Must be our magnetic personalities. We're attracting so much we must be the beauty queens of chaos by now," Joan grumbled.

Miriam drove the few blocks to Joan's house, but slowed down at Pine where she would have turned. It was blocked by a fire truck and a cop car. Joan turned and looked down the street. There was her truck—or the back end of it, sticking out of the front window of her house. Smoke was billowing out the other windows and the door. The firemen were rapidly unreeling the hose and running toward it.

"Oh . . . my . . . God," Joan said.

Miriam accelerated past the street.

"Wait! Stop! Didn't you see it? They rammed the truck into my house! I've gotta go back—"

"I saw it. I've changed my mind," Miriam said grimly. "This is part of the weirdness. Think about it. Why would kids on a joyride smash into your house? This is the work of someone who has it in for you."

The sudden icy flow of fear and anger helped to calm Joan quite a bit. "Not for me, but my possessions. Things I care about. Damn, that truck was half my business. And one of the tapes was in its glove compartment, too."

"The tape? Shit, maybe that's it—that's the connection. Amadan discovered the tape at Gillian's place, realized what we'd done, and trashed it along with the equipment we used to make it. Somehow he figured out you had another, and he had to smash that. Where's your second copy?"

Joan thought a moment, then shut her eyes. "In the pocket of the jeans I wore yesterday. Which I left beside my bed this morning."

"So . . . you've lost both your copies."

"Yeah. Guess so. And we've lost the one we left at Gillian's." Joan looked at Miriam. "You still got both of yours, right?"

"So far."

"Where are they?"

Miriam looked in her rearview mirror anxiously as if someone might be close enough behind them to overhear. "One's at home. The other one . . ." She tugged on a chain around her neck just enough to let Joan know that Miriam wore it on her person.

"That's either really smart or really dumb."

"Yeah, I know. But I figured it was worth the chance. Remember, Amadan won't harm us physically while we're playing the game. Matter of honor and all that."

"You're counting a lot on his sense of fair play."

"Yeah. Guess so. Anyway, we've got to keep moving. Let's go to my place."

"Right. And what makes you think he hasn't smashed up your place too?"

"We'll just have to find out." Miriam hit the gas and, daring the local law establishment, drove at high speed toward her condo.

Joan huddled in the passenger seat, her shock disconnecting her more and more from the mind-set of her comfortable routine of life, back into the mode that reality had become unstuck and anything could happen.

As Miriam stopped at a stop sign just before she would have turned onto the street that led to her condo, Joan looked up. Standing in the cross street to her right was a tall black policeman, directing traffic. He looked directly at her, pointed straight ahead with his right arm, and made a circle with his left arm, indicating they should proceed that way. It was the buffalo man from her dream.

Miriam turned the wheel and began to turn right.

"No!" Joan said, grabbing her arm. "You'll hit him!"

Miriam slammed on the brakes and looked wildly around. "Hit who?"

"The cop! Don't you see him?"

"What cop?"

"Shit. It's the buffalo man, Miriam. He's standing right there, telling us to go straight on. He's shaking his head at us. Can't you see him?"

"No," Miriam said regretfully. "You're sure?"

"I can see him plain as day!"

A sport utility truck honked behind them, then pulled around and zoomed past them—right through the buffalo man. Who made no sign of noticing it.

Miriam sighed. "I'm going to take your word for it. There's another way into the complex. Let's see if he'll let us in that way." She pulled the steering wheel to the left and continued on. At the next intersection, she asked, "Is he there?"

"No," Joan said softly. "God, I hope I'm not going crazy."

"For what it's worth, I don't think you're crazy."

"Thank you."

Miriam turned right and drove two blocks, then turned right again. As she neared the side entrance to the condo complex, she slowed. "The driveway's coming up. Tell me if it's blocked."

Joan peered out the window. As they passed a large aspen tree, Joan saw the buffalo man again, standing in the driveway, shaking his head and directing them onward. "There he is again! He doesn't want us to go in."

Miriam slowly cruised past the driveway, craning her head to look down it. "I can almost see my place from here. I don't see any smoke or obvious damage to the building."

"If you're carrying that tape, they may be waiting for you to arrive. To ambush us or something. That may be why buffalo man is warning us away."

"I just wish I could understand the pattern to this," Miriam said. "There's got to be one. If we knew, we could at least use it to protect ourselves." She pulled ahead at faster speed.

Joan sighed and sank back into the seat. "My place is toast. Gillian's is toast. Yours might be toast. Where do we go now?"

"I say we head on out to Mesa Verde. Might as well."

"With just the clothes on our backs?"

"There are stores on the way. Have credit card, will travel. Speaking of stores, I think we'd better make one stop first."

Joan assumed Miriam was headed for a convenience store, or maybe the King Soopers grocery store. So she was surprised when they pulled up in front of the Angel's Wing. "Why here?"

"Protection," Miriam said as she hopped out of the car.

Joan followed her into the store, not sure if she should be annoyed or hopeful. As she stepped inside,

Joan felt an easing of the tension between her shoulders. The soft music and incense seemed to surround and soothe her. She no longer felt she had to watch her back. She looked over at the counter and saw that old beaky-nose Frank was there, perusing a magazine.

He looked up at them both, narrowing his eyes at Miriam. "Didn't listen to me, didja?"

Miriam looked away from him, embarrassed, and began to examine a rack of amulet bags hanging on the wall.

Joan walked up to the counter. "Where's Ted?"

"I fired his ass. I can't have an assistant who breaks the rules behind my back."

"I hope you don't mean his showing us the flyer."

"Sure as hell do, that and other things. Got you in trouble, didn't he?"

"It wasn't his fault."

"When the hell does that matter? Kids come in to work here, thinking this is all silly woo-woo, and a lot of it is, but that's how we make our money. I don't mind the stupid ones so much, but the ones who think they're gonna be some sort of sorcerer's apprentice, that they're gonna learn the inside dope and get the power and all. They're the dangerous ones. Don't know enough to keep out of what they don't know anything about. Had to fire the asswipe before he got somebody killed, probably himself."

Miriam shyly approached the counter, a satin bag in each hand. "We'll take these."

"Don't buy that garbage!" Frank snarled. "Those wouldn't keep away a prairie dog. Wait here a minute. *Wait* here," he said pointedly at Miriam, then stalked off behind the curtain to the stockroom.

"Do we need to stay here and take this?" Joan asked.

Miriam was staring at the curtain. "He must be a white wizard."

"You can tell by his foul temper?"

"No, did you see how he looked at me? He *knew*."

"Yeah, he knew he had a couple of suckers he could make feel rotten."

"I trusted you on Mr. Buffalo. Trust me on this."

Joan opened her mouth to protest, but caught herself. "Okay," she finally said.

They waited in awkward silence a few minutes before Frank returned through the curtain. He plunked down onto the counter a couple of fist-sized satchels made of sackcloth. They reeked of skunk, sage, and something burned. "This'll do the stuff," he growled.

"Yeah, it'd sure keep me away," Joan murmured.

"How much?" Miriam asked.

"Fifty bucks a pop," he said. To Miriam, he added, "If you wear it, it'll itch your skin something fierce, especially at night."

"Thanks for the warning," she said with a rueful smile as she handed him her Visa card.

"Since you seem to know some things we don't," Joan said, "can you give us a clue what we're up against?"

"Wouldn't help," Frank said, as he ran the card through the credit check.

Miriam said, "We learned that the Amadan wants people to buy land and plant it with elf-friendly stuff, to make the Rockies the way they were millions of years ago."

"Yep. They're not from around here."

"So we heard," Joan said.

"Where are they from?" Miriam asked. "Are they fallen angels? Or aliens? Or ghosts? Or . . . something else?"

"How the hell should I know?" he grumped.

"Since you think these satchels will keep them at bay," Joan said, "just maybe you have a theory as to what the sidhe are."

"My personal theory," Frank expounded, "is that they're like a virus or a parasite, those Shay. Found that people were stupid and willing hosts. Willing to make them out to be whatever people wanted. That stuff," he said, pointing at the satin amulet bags, "those are herbs that maybe used to work hundreds of years ago, maybe. But just like bugs, them Shay are developing an immunity. They'd laugh at you if you wore those. We've got monkshood all up and down these mountains probably don't give your Mr. Amadan more'n a sneeze. They don't care for local flora much, though. That stuff"—he pointed at the sackcloth satchels—"will at least give 'em a moment's pause. Sign here, please."

As Miriam dealt with the receipt, Joan poked at one of the satchels and noticed something handwritten on the bottom. She picked it up and read it: Made at Crystal Sage.

"Where is this place?" she nearly yelled at the store owner.

"Don't know. Somewhere out on the Ute rez. They just write that so I know it's genuine."

"The Utes make these?" Miriam asked.

"They make 'em for white folks, not for themselves. They got their own ways of keeping the bogies away.

They're smarter than some people," he said, glancing sidelong at Miriam.

"Look, I don't care what you think of us, but we have to find this place," Joan said. "We were told it has to do with changing . . . helping our friend."

"Who told you that?"

Joan and Miriam looked at each other. Miriam finally said, "The Amadan himself told us, in the name of fairness. I suppose he might have been kidding us, huh?"

Frank shrugged. "Might've been. Might've been challenging himself. Never can tell with them."

Joan muttered, "Buffalo man said they're not from around here. Guess there's no reason they should follow our rules of fairness."

The shop owner glanced at her sharply, then seemed to stop and think a moment. He bent down and got something from under the counter—a business card. He wrote on the back of it and handed it to Joan. "This here's a store, on Highway 160 just east of Cortez, past Mesa Verde Loop Road. Don't call—go in person. Talk to Jake. Use my name if you gotta. Can't guarantee nothin', though."

Despite his scowl, Joan almost wanted to hug him. "Thanks! Other things are sending us that way anyway."

"Then you'd better be goin', hadn't you?" With no word of farewell, Frank went back through the curtain.

Joan and Miriam nodded to one another and headed out to the car.

"Guess we ought to just zoom on out of here," Miriam said as she got behind the wheel.

"Don't you want to stop for some road food and maybe a change of clothes?" Joan asked. She was traveling lighter than felt comfortable.

"Plenty of places for that farther on," Miriam said. She frowned up at the rearview mirror. "Now how'd that get out of whack?" As she adjusted it, Joan looked at the reflection and her heart froze.

A dark shape was rising out of the backseat.

Joan screamed and tossed her satchel in the back like a grenade.

The back doors flew open and ... things skittered out, screeching and gibbering. Joan couldn't see what they were, only a blur of their movement, and then they vanished.

For a moment, Joan and Miriam both sat with mouths open, trying to get heart rates down to near normal.

Miriam swallowed and said, "Shit. They almost got us. Thank ... God you saw them in time."

Joan got out, retrieved her stinking satchel from the backseat, and shut the rear doors. Getting back into the front seat, she said, "They were just trying to scare us again, I'll bet. They could get us anytime they wanted. They're just playing, the way a cat plays with a mouse. Or maybe they're testing our defenses, learning what weapons we have against them. These stink bombs old beaky gave us may not work for long."

"Yeah." Miriam gripped the steering wheel as if it were a lifeline. "Shall we go?"

"Let's get outta here."

Miriam peeled away from the curb, and out they went down I-25 to US 24 again. This time there was no stopping to admire scenery, no picking up hitchhikers, or even much discussion of philosophy. Joan kept an anxious watch on the road for more illusions of disasters, but saw none. They did not stop except for gas and bathroom breaks, and even took early dinner as drive-through food to go.

Even so, the last fifty miles they drove in the dark over the winding mountain roads. Again, the car felt like a little traveling island of light and warmth and humanity, surrounded by invisible wilderness. Their only link to the outside was the radio station that kept fading in and out of static. Hurtling through the darkness, it seemed important to play the radio rather than a tape, to remind themselves that civilization did indeed still exist, out there, somewhere.

At last they reached the reassuring lights of Johnson Village, and then Poncha Springs. Rather than attempt the high and treacherous Monarch Pass in the dark, Joan and Miriam headed into Salida.

They checked into the Wagon Wheel Motel, and then, out in the parking lot, Joan happened to look up. Three circles of light, flying in perfect V formation, zoomed silently overhead, flying north to south faster than any aircraft would go. Then they separated and bounced around in no discernible pattern before vanishing. From elsewhere in the town, she heard whoops and cheers.

"Goddam," Joan muttered. "I've just seen UFOs."

"Fairy lights," Miriam said, behind her. "Welcome to the San Luis Valley."

"Fairy lights, huh? So that's what Gillian meant. Not alien spacecraft?"

"Think about it. We know the Amadan has been operating in this valley. And there are lots of reasons the debunkers say alien spacecraft aren't the most likely explanation. Fairy lights have been mentioned in folklore for centuries. Like the guy at the Angel's Wing said, people make of the sidhe what they want. Now that we're more into technology than magic, we decide that the fairy lights are spacecraft."

"And those stories of abductions . . . ?"

"Well, tales of fairy abductions have popped up for centuries too. People just see what they want to see. I'm bushed. Don't know about you, but I'm heading to a shower and bed."

Joan stared at Miriam, blue-limned by the lights of the parking lot. "How can you, of all people, be so blasé about what we just saw?"

"You don't know what I see in my dreams." Miriam walked away, leaving Joan wondering and yet glad that she didn't know.

Joan had a hard time getting to sleep that night. She kept having the nagging feeling there were shadows at the windows. A part of her wondered if she should take the tape from around Miriam's neck. Joan wasn't sure she could trust Miriam to keep it safe. The following morning, Joan had a vague memory of approaching Miriam's bed with the intent of taking the tape. But Miriam woke up and threw the stinky satchel at her and Joan went back to bed.

For breakfast, they went back to the Front Porch Flapjacks place, a.k.a. the UFO café. They weren't disappointed; the place was buzzing with talk of the lights in the sky the night before.

"Should we tell them?" Joan asked Miriam as they perused the menus.

Miriam shook her head. "They wouldn't believe us."

"Heh. Nuts calling us nuts."

"We all live in different universes, given the way we perceive things, and what we want to see," Miriam said softly. "Only in small ways do these worlds intersect. It's amazing one human can communicate to another at all."

Joan put her menu down and looked at Miriam, concerned. "Are you okay? How are you feeling?"

She shrugged and shook her head. "Just coming out of the dream world. You know how sometimes dreams can hang on to you for hours later?"

"Yeah."

"How are *you* doing?"

"Still feeling shell-shocked. Like I don't quite believe what's been happening to me. Like when I get home, everything will be fine and my house and truck will be okay, and Agnes will be okay, and none of this will have happened."

Miriam reached out and squeezed her arm. "Maybe everything *will* be okay, once this is over. If we do it right."

"Yeah. Sure. And I'm Marie of Rumania."

"I know how you feel," Miriam went on. "I felt the same after . . . well, I've felt the same."

Joan wondered if it was true-confessions time or if Miriam didn't want to be prodded. Joan did, anyway. "After what? You mean, like, when you went into therapy?"

Miriam took a deep breath and let it out in a long sigh. "I was a . . . what they call a sensitive kid. Ever since I can remember, I could walk into a room and know something about who lived there and what they were like. There were places, like my great-uncle's house, where my parents had to carry me in kicking and screaming because I just didn't want to go in. I still don't know why.

"But I was a pretty optimistic kid, I guess. I wanted the world to be this wonderful place, because I was sure it was. My mom still tells stories of having to turn off the news whenever I came into the TV room because if I heard of any disaster or crime I'd run out crying. Still, I was able to keep the bad vibes at a distance until . . ."

Joan did the appropriate prod. "Until?"

Doodling curves in the water droplets on the table, Miriam said, very softly, "My brother raped my best friend in high school."

"Jeez. I'm sorry."

Miriam shrugged. "My folks have just about disowned him. But it was hard for me. I'd . . . idolized him. The crazy thing is, I'd gone into his room, I dunno, countless times. And I never felt it. I never guessed, never knew that he could do a thing like that."

"Well, since he's family," Joan suggested, "maybe part of you did see it but denied it. Maybe it was something you just didn't want to see."

"I've wondered that. But that's why I've really gotten into the divination stuff. I was so . . . surprised. I don't want to be surprised like that *ever* again."

"I understand," Joan said, trying to be soothing.

"To make the whole thing worse, afterward, when word got around at school, everyone picked on my best friend. Calling her a slut and saying she deserved it. I was the only one who stuck by her, and people called me a traitor to my family. Even though I tried to help my friend, she got so depressed she tried to kill herself. Her family had to move just to get away from . . . everything."

"God, I'm sorry, Miriam."

"It was then I had to face it, Joan. In reality, it's an ugly world. Just . . . ugly."

"Not all of it. There's goodness and beauty too."

"But the fact that the ugliness exists, even where you don't suspect it, even in someone you trust . . . somehow makes the beautiful part . . . irrelevant? I dunno. So, anyway, we moved and I went into therapy for depression, but I wouldn't let them put me on Prozac. I took Saint-John's-wort for a while, and that sort of helped."

Joan wondered if this could be the same cheerful Miriam she used to know, or if she'd ever known her at all.

"That's part of why I couldn't hold a regular job, you know?" Miriam went on. "I tried temping, but I hated the corporate world, all the petty politics, all the stupid rules. I couldn't handle it. So I thought maybe I could learn to be self-employed, independent, like you, doing something simple that people really appreciate. Now I'm not sure I could even handle that."

Joan didn't know what to say to reassure her. "Is there a reason you're bringing all this up now? Has the . . . fairy touch made it worse?"

"Oh, like horrible memories ever go away."

"I'm sorry. That was thoughtless of me."

Miriam shook her head. "It's okay. It's just that . . . my dreams have shown me this whole other beautiful world."

"Yeah, but it's got its own ugliness—"

Miriam held up her hand to silence her. "It's not what you think. I keep feeling like if I could be there, in sidhe country, long enough, and if I could learn enough of what they know, then even the ugliness would make sense. That's the problem with this world. The ugliness doesn't make sense."

"It probably would if we knew enough about psychology. Heck, I've seen cattle do the stupidest blind-dumb dangerous things. Our problem is, we keep thinking we're better than animals, when we *are* animals."

"We're animals who should know better," Miriam said with quiet firmness as their food arrived.

As they paid up at the counter, Miriam asked about Monarch Pass. The counter clerk told her that the weather had been clear and dry, and the pass was almost never a problem this time of year. "But be sure to yell 'Yo, ghost!' when you pass the yellow bed-and-breakfast place."

Miriam and Joan had looked at each other. "Yo, ghost"?

"The place is haunted, or so they say. It's tradition. It's supposed to bring you good luck if you let the ghost know you know it's there."

"Well, we can use all the good luck we can get," said Joan grudgingly.

So Joan and Miriam had yelled "Yo, ghost!" when they passed the yellow bed-and-breakfast just before they got into the steep and winding turns. Gripping the dashboard and noting the way the slope dropped away steeply just across the road, Joan hoped the ghost would make good on the luck bit real soon. Fortunately, Sheila the Subaru took it in stride, and they made it up to the summit of Monarch Pass in good time.

They stopped for a bathroom break and coffee at the gift shop at the summit. Joan noticed a gondola went from there to higher peaks nearby. Despite her dislike and distrust of mountains, she felt an urge to someday return and take that ride, knowing the view from the top must surely be spectacular.

I don't think that view would be wasted even on me, Joan decided. *I hope I survive to see it.*

Chapter 12

Joan and Miriam descended from Monarch Pass with the car radio blaring Alanis Morrisette's "You Learn" on radio station KBUT. Miriam heartily sang along, slapping the steering wheel in time to the music. Joan held on to her seat, as Miriam took some turns a bit too fast for her comfort, but they made it down all right.

At Sargents, a crossroads with the temerity to call itself a town, US 50 entered a canyon that widened more and more until it became a broad valley. Joan noted that unlike the juniper and piñon woodland on the Salida side of the pass, here the pines gave way to sage scrubland. On one side of the highway, where a river flowed, the valley seemed to have prosperous ranches. The other side was barren brown hills leading to higher mountains in the distance. An hour later, Joan saw they were approaching another town.

"This must be Gunnison," Miriam said.

"Whoever Gunnison was, he was a popular guy," Joan said. "There are lots of things in Colorado named after him."

"Looks like a nice town. Kind of remote, though." Miriam slowed down as they passed the usual outskirt motels and eateries. Off to the right they passed Western State College. Across the highway from it was a old steam locomotive and a water tower, part of a Pioneer Museum. Miriam slowed still further as they approached a stoplight where Colorado 135 branched off to the north.

"Oh, damn," Miriam said. "Detour."

"Where?"

"What do you mean, where? Right in front of us. Don't you see the sign? The whole road is blocked."

Joan peered through the windshield. She saw an old building of yellow stone to their left, and a gift shop kitty-corner to that, and a more modern, towered building with a travel agency across the street from that. "Miriam," Joan said carefully, "I see no detour sign, and the road isn't blocked. If it is, a van and a big old RV just went through it. Didn't you see them?"

"I don't see any other cars," Miriam said, becoming more agitated.

"That clinches it. It's an illusion. Drive on through."

"No!"

A car behind them honked and swerved around them.

"What about *that* car?" Joan asked.

"He . . . he vanished when he got to the sawhorse with the sign on it."

"See?"

Miriam took a deep breath. "I'm going to do what the sign says and turn here." And she did, turning right onto what turned out to be the main street of Gunnison.

"Miriam!"

"Look, I trusted you when you saw the buffalo man and it turned out there was good reason, right? My gut says I should turn here."

"Yeah, but—" Joan caught herself to make sure she

as being diplomatic. "But you were . . . touched by
the Amadan. Maybe you can be tricked—"

Miriam stomped on the brake, hard. Joan was jerked
forward, but caught by her seat belt.

"Are you saying," Miriam cried, "that you don't
trust me anymore? Why? Was it because I told you I'd
been depressed and in therapy? Because if you don't
feel you can trust me, you might as well get out of this
car right now!"

"No! No! It isn't like that," Joan protested. "I'm
sorry! I really am. I didn't mean . . . Oh, Christ, Miriam,
I'm just worried, that's all. This is taking us out of our
way."

"Are you sure? Maybe there's some trouble down on
50. Maybe we're being shown a better way."

"Okay, okay, I'll check the map. Maybe there's another reasonable way from here. I'm sorry, Miriam. I
shouldn't have said what I did."

Miriam sniffed and began driving again. Joan
flipped open the glove compartment and pulled out
the road map. She studied it for several long minutes
and then sighed. "Oh, shit, Miriam, this road doesn't
get us anywhere. It just goes up to Crested Butte, a little
beyond, and then stops."

"Are you sure?"

"Well . . . there is a small graded road that goes northwest from Crested Butte over Kebler Pass—that sounds
familiar. I wonder where I've heard of it. Oh yeah, it's
an area that's great for viewing fall color . . . the papers
always mention it. Too bad we're too early. But the road
loops around to Paonia and Hotchkiss, and doesn't join
US 50 again until it's nearly at Grand Junction. Miriam,
this is taking us way out of our way."

"Maybe there's a reason," Miriam said thro ted teeth.

Maybe the sidhe are trying to get us lost, Joan tho feeling a knot of fear growing in her stomach.

Past Gunnison, the road wound uphill along a wi creek, past a tiny resort called Almont. The scenery became more and more spectacular as they ascended into a high valley cupped close by tall mountains. Odd little ranches beside the road had llamas, bison, even yak grazing in them. Wildflowers of riotous color lined the valley and hillsides—Wyoming paintbrush, daisies, lupines, monkshood, columbines. Had she been a mere tourist, Joan would have been pleased that they'd taken this route. As it was, she had to fight down her rising dread. Even the sign of one place they passed, ROARING JUDY FISH HATCHERIES, seemed ominous.

"Isn't this beautiful?" Miriam asked.

"Lots of beautiful things are deadly." Farther on, to their right, angular mountains of red stone came into view. Joan recognized them from photos she'd seen; they were part of the Maroon Bells Wilderness, and the map confirmed she was right. The mountain she could most prominently see was called Mount Teocalli. It reminded her of the name of an ancient Aztec pyramid. Which reminded her that human sacrifices were offered on Aztec pyramids. Which did nothing to reassure her.

Filling the north end of the valley was an isolated mountain with steep sides and a pointed crest.

"That must be Crested Butte Mountain itself," Miriam said.

"Where the ski resort is? They ski down that?" Joan

▬ting the near-vertical sloped etched with nar-
▬ky defiles.

▬ell, this is supposed to be the capital of extreme
▬ng."

'That's more extreme than I want to think about."

They came over a rise and the little town of Crested
Butte stretched out before them. New construction at
the town fringe showed it was a thriving place.

Miriam slowed way down, as the road signs demanded, and then suddenly turned left at the sign that
said CRESTED BUTTE HISTORIC DISTRICT.

"What are you doing?"

"Didn't you see— Never mind. I have to go this
way."

Joan knew better than to ask this time, but she was
truly beginning to fear the sidhe were successfully
messing up their plans. *What would I have to do if I have to
abandon Miriam? How would I get the tape from her? Oh,
please, God, let her regain her senses so we can get back on
track!*

They were on Elk Avenue, clearly the main drag of
town. A couple blocks down, Miriam abruptly pulled
over and parked.

Joan tried to keep her voice neutral. "Why are we
stopping?"

"Because it doesn't look like there are any parking spots farther on." Miriam opened her door and
hopped out.

"Oh." Joan unbuckled herself and tied her stinky
satchel to a belt loop on her jeans. By the time she got
out, she saw Miriam nearly skipping down the sidewalk some distance away. With a sigh, Joan ran to catch
up to her.

"This is where we were meant to come, Joan. ⬛
it!" She was smiling and gazing around in wonde⬛

It's a tourist trap. Joan wanted to shout it at her. B⬛
in a historical district, the buildings had clearly be⬛
coded to maintain a turn-of-the-century look. *But ho⬛
many buildings were painted pink and purple in 1910?*
Joan wondered. The overall effect was rather twee—
Colorado as interpreted by Walt Disney. But still, when
she glimpsed an old church steeple with magnificent
mountains as a backdrop, saw the roaring creek rushing through the center of town under wooden bridges,
saw wildflowers and gardens everywhere, smelled the
fresh, brisk air, Joan understood how one could come to
like the place.

The town seemed young—clusters of teens and
twenty-somethings gathered at the corners, near the
bars and coffee places. Most of them seemed to have bi-
cycles and dogs of the large variety: black Labs, mala-
mute breeds, rottweiler mixes, or just plain mutts.

"It almost looks like bikes and dogs are required in
this town," Joan muttered to Miriam. "When you move
here, does the welcome wagon show up and say, 'Welcome to Crested Butte—here's your bike and your
dog'?"

Miriam laughed. "I'd like to live here."

"Hah. As if you could afford it. Oh, that's right—you
probably could." Unable to hold back any longer, Joan
said, "So, okay. We're here. What are we here for?"

"We'll find out eventually. C'mon, let's have lunch."

"Eventually," Joan grumbled. She followed Miriam
into a place called the Idle Spur. The tiny patio section was full, so they were seated beside a huge rock

e. On its mantel a stuffed mountain lion snarled at them.

athletic-looking young woman with a pierced e handed them menus, and Joan stared into hers. Hmm, I wonder how the buffalo burgers are here."

From the depths of her menu, Miriam said, "I think it would be sacrilegious of you to have one."

"Heh. Oh, look, they serve microbrews here."

"May I commend unto you the Red Lady Ale?" said an unfamiliar but mellow and musical voice.

Joan peered over her menu and saw they had been joined at their table by a slender young man with long, golden-brown hair. The extraordinary green-gold shade of his eyes told Joan right away that he was Other. She immediately ripped the stinky satchel from her belt loop and threw it on the table.

"I cry you mercy!" the fellow said, holding his arms up. "I swear I mean you no harm."

Uh-huh. Slowly Joan drew the satchel back toward herself and dropped it into her lap, not letting her gaze leave their visitor.

"Are you the one who guided us here?" Miriam asked.

He put his arms down with a relieved sigh. "Among others. Only I am sent to speak with you."

"Why?" Joan demanded. "Did you mean to drag us off course?"

"Nay—well, yes, but for a moment."

"Why?" Joan asked again, even harsher.

"I pray you, if you will but hear me you will understand. We are not all servants of the Amadan, and some of us do yet oppose him."

"How can we believe you?"

"By this. I will give you a phrase by which you may better bind and command him, for we know that is what you intend."

"You do?"

"Word is as breath and wind among us," he said.

Joan assumed that meant the same as word travels fast.

"The song you bear has more magic than you know," he went on, "for Lord Amadan himself was the composer. He made it long ago, a gift for one family whose sons and daughters were charming and fair."

"Why would he write a song that would compel him to grant a wish?" asked Miriam.

"Ah, the compelling came after, in the hands of one of the blessed clan with too much skill in sorcery. The merest change of word and tune and what once was a boon freely offered became a tithe demanded. Chance came for Lord Amadan to see the music safely lost, or so he thought. Until your friend chose to seek it out and, with clever artifice, wrought it so that it doth not only compel, but bring exquisite pain."

"I'm . . . sure she didn't mean to," said Joan.

"The meaning matters not," said their visitor. "But surely you can compass the source of Lord Amadan's ire."

"Even so," Joan grumbled, "your Lord Amadan has gone a bit overboard."

"Were I you I would agree."

"And so," Miriam asked, "you will tell us what to say to correct this injustice?"

"If you would think it so, though 'twas not my aim."

"What *is* your aim?" Joan asked suspiciously.

"E'en this. That you use what you have and what I give only to redress those wrongs done 'gainst you and yours. Do not curse us all, or attempt to deny us passage to your world, or condemn us with sweeping punishment. For we are not all of evil mien, and there are places in your world that we protect and embellish with our glamour."

"This is one such place, isn't it?" asked Miriam. "That's why you detoured us here . . . to make sure we saw it."

The sidhe nodded once in confirmation. "Think what might become of it should you banish us."

Joan was dubious. Yet it gave her hope that here was proof that their plan would work and that, if they pulled it off, perhaps Joan could reverse the damage done, both to Gillian and to Agnes. And even more.

"Does this mean you ask us not to punish your Lord Amadan?"

The sidhe did a one-shoulder shrug. "Do with him what you will, but beware. He has allies more powerful than he, who would take it amiss if the justice you exact o'ersteps the bounds."

"We'll remember that," Miriam said. "What is the magical phrase we must use?"

"First swear, by that which is dearest to you, that you shall forbear as I have asked." He stared Joan right in the eyes, and she knew he would know if she was lying.

"All right. I so swear." Joan held up her right hand a little as if she were a witness in a courtroom.

"What is't you most hold dear?"

Joan felt very reluctant to say, for fear of seeming foolish and also because it was so intimate a question. "My . . . my family's ranch," she admitted softly.

He acknowledged this with another nod and turned to Miriam. "And you."

"I . . . also . . . swear," said Miriam, her voice a little shaky.

"And by what?"

"By . . . by my dreams," Miriam said so softly Joan almost did not hear her.

"Very well." The sidhe pulled out of his shorts pocket two slips of folded paper. He slid them simultaneously across the table, one to Joan, one to Miriam. Then he stood.

"Wait," said Miriam. "Can't you give us more help—like tell us how to use this and where?"

Joan glanced at Miriam, alarmed, and hoped she hadn't given too much away about what they didn't know.

"I fear I may, even now, have done too much." He turned and walked into the small crowd milling at the bar in the back of the room.

Joan watched him disappear. She turned her attention to the folded paper he had given her and cautiously opened it. She noticed Miriam doing the same thing.

But the writing on the paper seemed to writhe and blur as Joan squinted at it. It didn't even seem to be English or a normal alphabet. "We've been tricked, Miriam. I can't read this."

"I can," Miriam said. With a sigh, she refolded her paper and tucked it into her bra.

Joan was once again acutely aware of how much she would have to trust Miriam. "What's it say?"

"I'm not going to say it *now,* here. That's like making the same mistake we did with the four seconds of tape."

Joan sighed. "Okay."

They ordered Red Lady Ales (discovering they lived up to the sidhe's recommendation) and ate lunch, mostly in silence. Miriam seemed thoughtful, and Joan didn't wish to distract her, in part because she didn't really want to know.

After the waitress delivered the check, Miriam said, "You've been quiet."

"Do I hear the pot calling the kettle black?"

"Okay, I haven't held up my end of the conversation either. But I'm surprised you aren't more, you know, optimistic. We just got a big boost to our plans. I have to confess, I wasn't sure before, but now I think it's really going to work out."

Because I don't know if I can trust what you know? Joan didn't say this. "You know, maybe I'm just feeling . . . unnecessary. I mean, you have the tape. You know the words to say. You get along better with Cain than I do. You know more about the sidhe than I do. A part of me is just kinda wondering why the hell I'm here."

"Oh, don't say that." Miriam reached over and clasped Joan's arm. "You're vital. We're a team. There has to be two of us."

"Oh, that's right. The I Ching said so."

Miriam made a face. "Yeah, it did, but that's not what I meant. Remember how I pulled the plug when we first ran Gillian's music program? Remember how you snapped me out of it when the Amadan was trying to turn me to his side of the Force? We have to look out for each other. One of us alone is too easily defeated."

Joan sighed. "Yeah, okay. You're right. One for all and all for one."

"Even Jean d'Arc needed an army."

"Sometimes I hate that my parents named me after

her. Does living up to my name mean I have to get burned at the stake eventually, too?"

"No, no! Your advantage is that you can pick just the good parts. History doesn't *have* to repeat itself."

Miriam did not see a detour sign when they returned to US 50 at Gunnison, so they turned right and continued driving west. The highway took them past Blue Mesa Reservoir, a man-made lake that was one of the largest in Colorado. Motorboats, kayaks, and even Windsurfers scooted across its surface. Joan and Miriam both laughed when they passed the sign marking BAY OF CHICKENS, and Joan wondered if it had been the site of an even more embarrassing fiasco than the Bay of Pigs.

"Maybe it's where windsurfers go when they look at conditions out on the lake and change their minds," Miriam suggested.

US 50 wound on down through a tight canyon just south of the famed Black Canyon of the Gunnison and into a beautiful area with hillsides so green, and so dotted with grazing sheep, they could have been transported from Ireland. Joan wondered if the "good" elves might have settled in the Cimarron area too.

They descended into Montrose, down on the Western Slope. The tilt of the Uncompahgre Plateau to the west made it appear as though the whole valley were tilted at a thirty-degree angle, and Joan felt a little vertigo looking at it.

They turned left at Montrose onto US 550 south, and here Joan got her first look at the range known as the San Juans. The mountains were jagged, but not in a regular shark's-tooth pattern. They seemed more like odd-shaped polygonal blocks that some giant child had tossed onto the earth, with angles unexpected and disconcerting in a mountain range.

"The trouble with Colorado," Joan said to Miriam, "is that the scenery here keeps breaking the rules. Strange tilted valleys, mountains that look like a mad modern-art sculptor got loose in them—"

"And I've heard of a valley southwest of here," Miriam put in, "called Paradox Valley, where a river runs across it rather than down it like in all other valleys."

"Maybe the Amadan or other critters have been playing here longer than we thought."

"Or maybe the land just has a mind of its own."

"Don't know if that's reassuring or a lot worse."

They ate dinner in a town called Ridgway, at a café that had been favored by John Wayne when he was doing a movie in the area—signed photos of him covered the walls. Joan and Miriam entertained themselves discussing how the "e" in the middle of the town's name might have gone missing.

"It ran screaming from the scenery," Joan suggested.

"It tried to rob the local bank and got run outta town," Miriam offered.

"It was a typo the city fathers were too embarrassed to correct."

"There was some other town named Ridgeway and they had to change this town's name or get sued."

They both laughed for no good reason, punchy from the long drive. But Joan noticed the sadness in Miriam's eyes and wondered if she or Miriam would ever be innocently happy again.

Joan and Miriam stayed overnight in Ridgway at a

nondescript motel and headed out again early the next morning. Though the view had been interesting from the valley below, the scenery was positively amazing as they passed Ouray. A sign declared the area "the Switzerland of America," and Joan could well believe it. The rugged, snow-clad peaks were as alpine as any she had seen, and as the road they drove on rose higher and higher, Joan could see rank upon rank of mountain range marching away in the distance, an army of peaks assembled, unassailable. She felt overwhelmed.

Near the top of Molas Pass, Miriam insisted on stopping the car and getting out to look at the view. Here, even in early summer, the snowpack was thick enough to make a wall on the right side of the road. But to her left, to the east, was a small glacial valley containing a lake. Clouds hovered there, partly obscuring the sun, and mists rose from the lake and surrounding snow, and Joan could not tell where they joined. It was a breathtaking sight, otherworldly, and Joan had a hard time imagining she was still in the world she knew, yet it was not the world of faerie either.

"Incredible, isn't it?" asked Miriam, shivering beside her.

"I . . . don't know what to say. I've never seen anything like this."

"I expect an arm to rise out of that lake bearing a sword," Miriam said.

"If one did, would you take it?"

"Would you?"

"I'm named after Joan, not Arthur."

"Saint Joan had a sword, didn't she?"

"Not a special one."

"What a rip. No special horse or sword. As heroes go, I think she got gypped."

"I like to think that gave her an advantage," Joan said. "The power came from her, not a magic sword or horse. Better tug me back to the car before I freeze in place here."

"Are you that cold?"

"No, I'm just finding it hard to tear my gaze from that view."

"Maybe Colorado isn't wasted on you after all," Miriam said with an odd little smile.

They wound down the valley of the Animas River until they reached Durango. The air was much warmer here and starting to have the feel of true high desert. They changed drivers at a gas station in town, then turned right onto US 160 going west.

A few miles outside of Durango, Miriam looked up in the rearview mirror. "Hmm," she said.

"Hmm?"

"We've had the same car behind us for a while."

"For how long?"

"I don't know. Since Durango at least."

"Well, it may just be someone going our way."

"It may."

"Just keep an eye on him for now, okay?"

"Okay."

The land opened up before them in the afternoon sunlight, looking more like the scenery Joan associated with the word "southwest," the hillsides covered with juniper, piñon, and sage. A brown sign indicated their approach to Mesa Verde.

"Do you think we should go into the park?" Miriam

asked. "Do you think we'll find Cain and Gillian there?"

"Maybe, but actually I think we should talk to this Jake guy that your friend at the Angel's Wing suggested. Like you, I don't want to go in blind. The more we know, the better."

"I think the sooner we get it over with, the better."

"I'd agree," said Joan, "except getting it over with could mean a lot of things, some of them no fun."

"I hear you."

They drove past the entrance to Mesa Verde Loop Road and continued west toward Cortez. Along the roadsides, billboards began to pop up. INDIAN CURIOS! FRIENDLY NATIVES! YOU GOT WAMPUM, WE GOT BARGAINS!

"Ugh. How embarrassing," Miriam said.

"I guess it brings in the tourists," Joan said.

"Who would want the tourists those signs would bring?"

"Those who want to separate them from their money."

The gift shop turned out to be the one they had been told to look for, but Joan was not heartened by the fake teepee and totem pole in the parking lot. "Isn't a totem pole a northwest tribe kinda thing?"

"I don't know," Miriam said, as she pulled into the lot. "I think they just wanted symbols out front that screamed 'Indian.' "

"If I didn't know better, I'd say Frank sent us here just to shame and embarrass us."

"I doubt Frank knew or cared whether it would shame or embarrass us." Miriam parked in front of the main window, through which they could see shelves crammed with southwestern bric-a-brac. There was only one other car in the lot, some yards away, in which some guy appeared to be sleeping.

Joan and Miriam went into the shop and found themselves in a long, narrow building. To the right were shelves loaded with pottery in every style that screamed "southwest!"—some genuinely indigenous, but Joan would bet that some of them were stamped "Made in Japan" on the bottom.

To the left was a larger room containing kachina dolls, Navajo blankets, bottles of painted desert sand layered to create scenes, moccasins, a children's section with rubber tomahawks and drums (no doubt to delight white parents on long drives, Joan thought evilly), paintings of big-eyed Indian children, candles on pueblo-shaped pedestals, ashtrays shaped like an Indian head with an open mouth, not to mention the ubiquitous T-shirts, mugs, and gimme caps.

A glass counter/display case filled with silver and turquoise jewelry and with a cash register atop it stood directly in front of them. A tired-looking middle-aged Indian with a weather-beaten face leaned on the counter, reading a book. He looked up at them and said, "Can I help you? We'll be closing shortly."

"S'okay, we're not here to shop," Joan said. "We're looking for a guy named Jake."

"Frank sent us," Miriam added.

Joan gave her a brief scowl, remembering that they weren't supposed to use Frank's name unless they had to.

The man at the counter stood up and squinted past them out the front window. "That your car?" he asked, pointed at it.

Joan heard a car start outside, and she and Miriam whipped around. The Subaru was pulling out of its parking slot. The young man behind the wheel glanced up at them once before peeling out of the lot. It was the receptionist from Mr. Amadan's office.

Chapter 13

"My car!" Miriam shrieked, and she ran out of the store, Joan following right behind her. Miriam stopped in the space where the Subaru had been parked and watched it drive away down the road, back the way they had come.

"My car!" She clenched her fists and stamped her foot. "Dad will kill me!"

"Come on," Joan said, grasping her elbow. "Let's go back inside and call the sheriff."

"My car," Miriam wailed softly as Joan pulled her back toward the store.

"You didn't leave the tape in the car, did you?"

Miriam felt around her neck. "No, I still have it on me."

"Good. Mr. Amadan probably didn't know that."

As they reentered the curio shop, the Indian salesman was lowering the blinds on the windows and turned around a sign to read CLOSED.

"Can we use your phone?" Joan asked.

"No." He peered out through the blinds at the parking lot.

"But our car just got stolen!"

"You'd better come with me."

"What?" Joan said, wondering if she was facing another of Mr. Amadan's minions.

"I'm Jake. Frank told me you were coming. We have to leave. Now. Come this way." He led them around the counter and through a back storage area into a graveled area behind the shop. Parked there was an ancient brown Ford station wagon that Joan figured was older than she was.

"Where are you taking us?" Miriam asked.

"Crystal Sage," he replied.

"Oh, thank God!" Joan said as she settled into the front bench seat of the dusty station wagon. "We were wondering how we were ever gonna find it."

Miriam sat in the backseat and moaned, "Shouldn't we follow my car?"

"It's probably in a ditch by now," said Jake. He started up the wagon and spun the wheels in the dust, backing out in a hurry.

"Oh, that's an optimistic thought."

"You just lost a car. I'm gonna lose a store. And maybe my livelihood."

Joan paused. *Have I just brought trouble on another innocent person?* "Gosh, I'm . . . I'm sorry. I didn't know."

"Nope. You didn't."

"How could you work in a place like that, anyway?" Miriam whined from the back.

"Ever hear of hiding in plain sight?" Jake said enigmatically.

"Hiding from what?" Miriam went on.

"What's chasing you."

Joan wasn't sure if what he said was a statement or a question, so she just said, "Oh." If Jake was one of the people who made the stink-bomb satchels that seemed so effective against the faeries, he might have reason to be worried.

Jake turned west on US 160 and headed down to Cortez. The afternoon sun was lowering in the sky, and Joan had to pull down the visor to keep from being blinded. Beyond Cortez lay Sleeping Ute Mountain, which really did resemble a giant lying on his back under a blanket. Joan thought about asking if there were any local myths about the giant rising and walking, but she didn't.

"So what did you want to find us for?" Jake asked.

"Mr. Amadan . . . um, he's—"

"I know who he is. Go on."

"Well, you're going to think this is weird, but he turned my friend into a guitar, and we tried to get him to change her back, but he wouldn't unless we told him what Crystal Sage was and brought him proof."

"Figures. Mr. Amadan's been after us for months. See, we sent some people up to his seminars. Armed with stuff, you know. He didn't like that much."

"I'll bet not," Joan said, imagining what having a few audience members lobbing stinky satchels would have done to the seminar she and Miriam had seen. "But you weren't at Summit Rock."

"He has too many friends there."

"Yeah . . . I guess. His receptionist was the guy who stole the car. I recognized him. He's a Ute, I think. He said that Mr. Amadan and he shared values. How come he's on Mr. Amadan's side and you're not?"

Jake gave her a sidewise glare. "Do you"—he jerked a thumb at her and back at Miriam—"all speak with the same mouth and think with the same heart?"

"Uh . . . no. Sorry. I just said something really racist, didn't I?"

"Ten points for the white girl!"

Joan didn't know if she should laugh or melt into the car seat in embarrassment. She curled up with her knees to her chin and stared out the window. She didn't hear any reaction from Miriam and wondered what she might be thinking.

At Cortez, they turned south on US 666. Joan recalled that was the Number of the Beast and considered it might be a bad omen and wished she could stop thinking of things as omens.

A road sign declared the next town was Towaoc, and another sign declared they were entering the Ute Mountain Indian Reservation. Joan had the unsettled feeling of being a foreigner in her own country, or in a place she clearly didn't belong.

"So what were you going to do when you found Crystal Sage?" Jake asked.

"Oh. We have a tape recording of the music that our friend, who is now a guitar, used to summon Mr. Amadan, to ask him to grant a wish. We also have a magic phrase that's supposed to twist his arm and make sure he grants what we ask. Although we gave a promise not to ask for too much. But what we don't know is where to play the tape. For that matter, a guy named Cain ran off with the guitar and told us to meet him out here near Mesa Verde."

"Cain?"

"Yeah. Cain Eslatranz—at least that's what he says. Cute guy but really crude and rude. You know him?"

Jake muttered the name to himself a couple of times,

then snorted what might have been a laugh. "Okay. I think I know what's going on."

"Okay. Can you tell us?"

"Nope. But I think I know where you can find this guy. I'll take you there."

"Well, that at least will be a big help. Thank you."

"Might be a place where you can use that tape, too."

"Great." Then Joan smacked her forehead. "Shit, I forgot! The boom box we were gonna use to play the tape! It was in Miriam's car. God, *now* what do we do?"

"Eh, don't worry about it," Jake said. "I think I've got an idea."

"Okay. Thanks for helping us."

"I don't like this guy Amadan any more than you do."

"Has he done anything to you?"

"He's tried." Jake didn't elaborate, and Joan decided not to press him on it.

Another road sign announced the turnoff for Towaoc up ahead, but Jake suddenly turned right onto a dirt road before then. The wagon bounced and jostled as the road took them a short way up the foothills of Sleeping Ute Mountain. To the south, Joan could see the cluster of buildings, a few large and modern houses surrounded by many much smaller ones, that was Towaoc. Jake pulled up to a group of three single-wide mobile homes perched on the hillside crest. A little hand-painted sign next to the door of the nearest trailer said, CRYSTAL SAGE HANDICRAFTS, INC. Somewhere behind the trailer, someone was loudly playing country-western music.

Jake got out and said, "Wait here."

"So. This is the place," Miriam said, sitting forward.

"You've been awfully quiet."

"Just . . . thinking."

" 'Bout what?"

" 'Bout stuff."

"Still bummed about your car?"

"Yeah."

"Maybe we can ask Mr. Amadan to give it back to you."

Miriam snorted. "We can't ask for too much, remember?"

"Oh. Yeah. I guess we'd better think about exactly what we *are* going to ask him."

"To change Gillian back," Miriam began.

"Uh-huh, and to heal Agnes," Joan added.

"To fix your house and truck."

"And whatever they did to your place. And tell Mr. Amadan to get the hell out of Colorado. I think I see we have a problem." Joan could faintly hear what sounded like two men having an argument, but she couldn't understand what they were saying.

"Well," said Miriam, "we could sum it up by asking him to make everything the way it was before Gillian got changed."

"That's such a general wish he'd be bound to twist it somehow, like make the past two weeks run all over again, like in that book by Vonnegut."

"Mmm. You're right, he might. Oh. Someone's here."

Joan looked around to her right. A woman had appeared in the doorway of the trailer they were parked next to. She had short gray hair, wore a plain brown sweater and skirt, and glasses.

She smiled at them and said, "Would you like to come in for some tea and fry bread?"

"Um, thank you," Joan said, "but I don't think we'll be staying long."

"Oh, well," the woman said. She walked up to the car and handed each of them a sprig of sage tied to a feather, with a little quartz crystal dangling from it. "Good luck to you," she said and walked back inside the trailer.

"How sweet," Miriam said.

"Probably just what they use instead of business cards."

"Oh, you cynic." Miriam bopped Joan on the head with her sage sprig.

"En garde!" Joan said, holding hers out like a dagger.

But their little mock sword battle was interrupted by the loud roar of an engine, and a truck pulled around from behind the trailer. Jake was at the wheel of a big-tired truck not much newer than Joan's truck, but it had clearly been lovingly cared for.

Jake grinned at them. "My son's truck. Best car stereo system in the Four Corners! Hop in."

As Joan got out of the station wagon, she saw a young man hanging back beside the trailer scowling at the truck. She smiled at him apologetically and ran over to the passenger side. She and Miriam had to squeeze into the front seat, Joan trying to keep her legs out of the way of the gearshift. Jake thrust the lever into first and they roared off with a jerk. Joan could understand why the son was kinda upset at letting his dad drive his precious machine.

They roared and bounced back down to Highway 666 and turned north. Jake drove only about three miles before he pulled off again, to the right, onto a barely visible dirt track that climbed up a rise. Hanging on to

Miriam, the seat, or sometimes Jake's shoulder, Joan tried to keep her head from smashing into the roof as they crashed through brush and over rocks on what was clearly not meant to be a road. Joan felt truly sorry for Jake's son, given the damage being done to the truck's suspension and paint job.

Something furry leaped out of the bushes and trotted ahead of them, tongue hanging out of its mouth.

"Look, a coyote!" Miriam said.

" 'Course it is. It's his mesa," Jake said. He leaned out the window and shouted something in Ute, Joan supposed, at the animal. Then, chuckling, he pulled his head and arm back in and followed the coyote a way.

The animal suddenly ducked to the left into the bushes, but Jake drove on ahead.

"We're not going to follow him?" Miriam asked.

"We'll catch up to him," Jake said.

Joan wondered what the heck was going on but decided this time just to wait and see.

The track switched back up the side of a steep slope, but shortly it leveled out and Joan saw that they were driving atop a high mesa. Jake slowed down gradually and then stopped at a group of large rocks and turned off the ignition. Joan thought she could hear a guitar being played, and she nearly pushed Miriam out of the cab ahead of her.

Ahead of the truck was a bowl-shaped depression in the mesa, its edge surrounded by standing stones. Some of them were as tall as Joan, and one or two had spirals inscribed in them.

"Oh my God," Miriam said. "Of course. Fairy rings. Standing stones. Just like the Celts and Druids used. Of course this is where we'll summon him!"

"Well, this isn't exactly Stonehenge—" Joan began.

Then Cain walked out from behind one of the stones, playing on Gillian. He abruptly stopped, grinned, and said, " 'Bout time you got here."

"Sorry we're late," Joan growled.

"Cain!" Miriam ran to him and hugged him.

"Hey!" Cain flung one arm around her. "Wanna fuck?"

"Not *now,* silly!" Miriam bopped him with her sage sprig.

He flinched. "Ooooh, I am chastised!"

Joan took Gillian out from under his arm and looked her over. There was no damage to the wood that she could see. "Gillian, are you all right?" She plucked a few strings.

> *hi Joan hi Joan hi*
> *yes yes yes yes*
> *fine fine fine*

Joan found a soft, sandy spot between two of the standing stones and set Gillian down. "We're going to summon the Amadan, okay? You just sit tight and we'll have you back in no time."

On the wind humming through the strings, Joan heard her say softly:

> *care ful be care ful be care ful*

Joan heard Jake chuckle behind her, and she turned. He was pulling out the large speakers that had been hanging in the back of the truck cab and setting them carefully on the hood.

"Can I help?" Joan asked.

"Nope." As he positioned the second one, Jake said, "We should wait a few minutes for sundown. I'll be right back." He went off into the bushes.

Ignoring Cain and Miriam's silly flirtation, Joan walked around the truck to where she had a good view to the east. It was breathtaking. Rows of mesas curved away to the southeast, turned copper-gold by the setting sun, under a cloudless cobalt sky. The shadowed canyons between them were sharp knife slashes in the earth. Here and there, Joan could dimly see ancient pueblos sheltering under grottos in the cliffs. The air was hot and very dry, but with hints of a cold night to come.

The land felt . . . old. It had been old when the first people to arrive there built their huts and their houses and their kivas and begged a living from the land. The land suffered their existence for a time and then, it seemed, shrugged them off, uncaring. Unlike the vaguely malevolent mountains, Joan felt, the mesas held no love or hate for mankind or anyone else. They simply *were* and would remain so until the rains wore them away eons from now.

Miriam came up beside her and leaned against the truck, staring out at the view.

"Cain couldn't talk you into it?"

"We've got other things to think about."

"Glad you remembered. Beautiful, isn't it?" Joan said, nodding at the vista.

"I guess," Miriam said, frowning. "I know a year ago I would have said this was beautiful. Now it just feels . . . empty and dead."

Joan turned and stared at Miriam a moment. "You mean to tell me we've actually switched sides on this?"

Miriam looked back with a fleeting, sheepish grin. "Maybe. But the landscapes I dream about now aren't the earthly sort."

"Oh." Joan didn't think now would be a good time to get Miriam dwelling on her dreams, so she didn't pursue it.

The sun set quickly, as it seems to in the desert, and even with twilight on the land, the stars came out like eager children leaving school. A cold wind blew, and Joan rubbed her shoulders, wishing she had not left her jacket in Miriam's car.

"Okay." Jake came around the truck. "Time to get the show going. You got the tape?"

"Right here." Miriam took the chain from around her neck and unclasped it and pulled it out of the tape cartridge hole.

Joan walked over to the standing stones.

"Don't go into the circle," Jake warned as he got into the truck and popped the tape into the deck.

Joan was about to ask him why not when she realized the stones must serve as some sort of protection or containment. Joan stood just in back of a gap between two of the larger ones. "Gillian's . . . um, the guitar is in the circle. Is that okay?"

"Beats me," said Jake. "Guess if you want him to change her, that's an okay place."

Joan sighed and faced the circle again. Miriam walked up silently beside her. There was no sign of Cain. "Where'd Cain go?"

"He said the fun was over here so he's off looking for fun somewhere else."

"Didn't even say good-bye?"

"Politeness isn't his sort of thing, remember?"

"Just as everything else civilized isn't."

"You got it," said Miriam with a sigh.

"Ready?" Jake called from the truck.

"Let her rip," Joan said.

The music swelled from the car speakers, so loud it felt like a physical thing, a rush of water flowing over and around her, holding her in place, spilling into the stone circle, where it echoed against the stones and seemed to pool in the middle. A light glowed there, in the center of the circle, and a shriek joined the swelling of the music.

Twisting and grimacing, Amadan appeared, his eyes alit with a yellow-green glow, his face sharper, more pointed, his long-fingered hands bearing nails like claws. "Who summons me?" he howled.

"I do!" Joan yelled over the music, trying to sound braver than she felt. "I, Joan Dark, summon you."

"Foolish bitch! This was not part of the agreement! You've no right to this song. It is not for those of your birth nor blood."

"Nonetheless," Joan said, "we could not trust you would keep your part of the agreement. Or that we could ever find you in order to keep ours. We felt we needed the song to compel you. And I can't say I'm sorry, after all you've done to damage everything around us."

" 'Twas for *this*," Amadan shouted, enraged, "that I changed your greed-ridden friend into her musical but mute form. Oh, for the age when only the most skilled at string and song could form a tune. But here, *now*, you have machines that can warp sound all out of shape or

239

slice it with a precision gem-cutters would envy. Worse yet, such sounds can be reproduced in numbers to rival the hare and the serpent. If all could compel their will from me and other sidhe, would chaos not fall upon mortalkind? Can you not see why I would wish to stop your friend's efforts and destroy all your copies of the song?"

Joan swallowed, feeling a moment of self-doubt. *He's right. Give everyone a genie in the lamp and who knows what could happen to the "thread of causality," as Miriam calls it. But what about his efforts to change Colorado?* "Oh, and I suppose getting people to plant all sorts of strange things to bring your folk more into the world isn't adding chaos to the pattern of the world?"

"Do not speak of that which you know naught. I tire. This circle saps my strength. Have you found what I asked of you?"

"We have," said Joan. "The crystal sage you're looking for isn't a plant, or a stone. Or any one person. It's a company. An idea. A joining together of people in a shared goal. The goal of stopping you and your kind from taking over Colorado. Crystal Sage helped us set up this little trap for you. The fact that it worked is proof of its existence and power. If you want more proof, I have a sample of Crystal Sage's wares right here." She held up the stink-bomb satchel as if to throw it.

"No! I accept your proof," said the Amadan, cringing behind his clawed hands.

"Then by our agreement, you must change Gillian back."

"Done and done. Now let me go!" He twisted and writhed within the pillar of light. A flash of green phosphorus appeared between his hands. Joan looked at where she had left Gillian and saw her huddled there, now in flesh, naked, her long strawberry-blond hair shining in the magical light, staring fearfully at Amadan.

"There is more," said Joan, hoping she might push her advantage. "You must restore Agnes, whom you gave a stroke, to health. And undo the damage you have done to my house, my truck and Miriam's apartment and car."

"Does it appear to you that I am Father Yule?" Amadan shrieked. "With a bagful of boons to give away? We have made our bargain. Let me go!"

"You must undo the damage you have done!"

"One gift and one gift only do I grant! Like so many other mortals before you, you risk your life with your greed!"

Then Miriam shouted out a phrase in a language Joan did not know, and Joan presumed it was the one given them at the Idle Spur. Amadan grabbed his ears and fell to his knees. "Aaagh! Unkind woman! Where learned you such a phase? What traitor gave it you?"

"I've no reason to tell you," Miriam said firmly. "Now fulfill our demands."

"Had you not tasted of our food and felt our touch, such words would burn your mouth," growled the Amadan.

"How nice to know," said Miriam. "Must I say it again?"

"No! Very well!" he shouted. "Your homes shall be restored!"

"What about Agnes?" Miriam persisted.

And then the song faded and ended. Silence fell upon the standing stones. The magical light vanished, leaving only the truck headlights as illumination.

Amadan stood up straight, again looking like a mortal man, but powerful and sure of himself, a triumphant smile upon his lips. "Your greed has sealed your doom. You should have dismissed me while the song was played." He began walking slowly toward Joan.

Miriam tried shouting the phrase again, but Amadan merely waved it away.

"That works but while the song plays," he said. "Whatever traitor gave it should have told you that."

Joan stepped away from the stones and wondered if it would do any good to run. "Rewind the tape, Jake!" she shouted, but Jake wasn't in the truck. He was walking along the perimeter of the standing stones, softly humming or chanting something under his breath and lightly scattering some powder on the ground. He walked in front of her and Miriam, then straightened up and said, simply, "Finished."

A strong breeze swirled around Joan's feet, lifting the dust, twigs, and leaves. The darkness surrounding them seemed to loom nearer, pressing toward the stones, blotting out the stars. Joan's hair stood on end and her skin shivered, as she felt herself in the presence of powers greater than she had ever known, as if the sleeping mountain and mesas had walked over and were now watching, waiting.

"Aren't you fortunate to have friends?" Amadan sneered at her. "I shall play no more games with you. Farewell."

"Wait!" Miriam shouted. "What about Agnes?"

"I have said I am done. I shall give no more boons. Further goods delivered must be paid for."

What could we possibly give him, Joan desperately thought, *that would be worth Agnes's life?*

"Then, for your payment, take me," said Miriam.

"What?" said Joan, unable to believe what she heard.

Miriam ignored her. "I will accept the position you offered back in Summit Rock. I will go willingly with you Under the Hill. Is this sufficient payment?"

The Amadan paused and stroked his chin. "Hmmm. A life for a life. There is balance in this. And your Talents do suit us. You would have to render us . . . service, for a time, of course. And you realize you could never return to mortal existence. Even your visits to this world would be closely bound."

"I know," Miriam replied softly.

"Miriam, have you gone *nuts*?"

Balling her fists at her side, Miriam growled, "I don't really belong in this world, Joan. I've known that as long as I can remember. I never fit in. No one understands me. The horror of the world hurts me."

"You're just sensitive, Miriam," Joan argued. "Lots of people are sensitive. They get over it. Or get therapy or take Prozac or something."

"You don't understand either. You've never felt the pain. And . . . I couldn't tell you this earlier, but as soon as I saw the Amadan's world, I knew that's where I belonged. I *knew* it. Maybe I've been a changeling all along. Swapped at birth or something. Besides, do you want Agnes to die, or be a vegetable all her life? This is her only chance." Miriam stepped over the line of powder Jake had scattered, walked between the stones, and entered the circle.

"Miriam!" Joan shouted. "No!" She started in after Miriam, but Jake grabbed her upper arms from behind.

"Don't go in," Jake said in her ear. "Or he'll be able to take you too."

Miriam said, as she approached Amadan, "I give myself and my mortal existence as payment for Agnes's health and well-being."

"I accept." Amadan pulled a gray glove from his jacket pocket and put it on. And he held out his hand to her.

"Miriam!" Joan yelled. "Don't! Come back!"

Miriam turned and said, "I'm sorry, Joan. Take care of Gillian and yourself. I'll do what I can for you from the Other Side." She took the Amadan's hand, and he began to walk backward. As if they were walking into a fog, he gradually vanished, and after him so did she.

Jake let go of Joan's arms, and she rushed into the circle. There was no sign that Miriam or the Amadan had ever stood there. Joan peered hard at the standing stones at the spot where Amadan and Miriam had disappeared, hoping maybe to see a door, some way she might follow to rescue her. She waved her arms through the air, but found nothing.

Gillian still crouched beside one of the standing stones, her eyes wide and fearful. Joan knelt down beside her and put an arm across her shoulders. "Gillian, are you all right?"

Gillian held out her hands and flexed them. Then she touched her face, her hair, her breasts, her legs. Slowly, she nodded. "Yes . . . yes. I'm all right. I'm all here." She choked back what might have been a sob or a giggle. Then she glanced guiltily at the center of the circle. "That poor girl," Gillian said softly. Joan found it strange to hear Gillian's real voice again, her words no longer in a singsong melody. "She actually went with him. Doesn't she know where she's going?"

"She knows," Joan said, with a sad wince. "She knows."

Chapter 14

Jake approached them, holding a blanket he must have gotten out of the truck. "She okay?"

"Yeah," said Joan. "Just a bit scared." She took the blanket from Jake and wrapped it around Gillian. Fortunately, the blanket was long enough to reach from Gillian's shoulders to her knees.

"We'd better go," said Jake. "This is a sacred place."

"Right. Of course," said Joan. She helped Gillian to stand. "Can you walk all right?"

Gillian nodded, a little too quickly. "I'm fine."

Joan took one arm and Jake took the other and they helped Gillian back to the truck. As they stepped out of the stone circle, Joan glanced back once more at where Miriam had disappeared. *She'll never be coming back,* thought Joan. *Not ever. Dear God, what will I tell her folks? What more could I have done?*

As if echoing her thoughts, Gillian murmured, "It's all my fault. I'm so sorry. I didn't know . . . didn't know all this would happen."

"It's okay," Joan said, squeezing her shoulder. Yet Joan felt she was lying. It was not okay, and it had been partly Gillian's fault. Joan didn't know if she could forgive her. And yet, if not for Gillian's silly scheme, the

Amadan's plot might not have been discovered, and far worse things might have happened, later down the road.

"My wife will lend you some clothes," Jake said, as he helped Gillian up into the truck.

"Thank you," she whispered.

Joan slid in beside her and shut the door. "Yeah, thank you for all your help, Jake. Sorry we, um, polluted your sacred place."

Jake shrugged as he started up the engine. "Coyote led you here," was all he said, as if it were explanation enough.

After a pause, Gillian asked, "But why did Coyote look like a white guy?"

"Is that how he looked to you?" Jake replied as the truck leaped into reverse and scrabbled back out of the hollow.

They returned to Towaoc, where Jake returned the truck to his less than pleased son, Gillian received the offered clothes—an old sweater and a pair of jeans that were too short for her—and they were fed herbal tea and fry bread. They ate mostly in silence.

"So," Joan finally asked Gillian, "do you think he'll be back? The Amadan, I mean?"

"Why are you asking me?" she replied, petulantly staring at her tea mug.

"I figure you're the resident expert. After all this."

"You probably know more than I do, now. I've been a guitar, remember?"

"What did it feel like?"

Gillian shrugged. "Like being paralyzed. Helpless. Not being able to move or talk without someone else's help. Frustrating and scary. Except when Cain played me. That felt . . . nice."

Joan nodded, not wanting any elaboration. "So . . . will Mr. Amadan be back?"

Gillian shrugged one shoulder. "Probably."

"If not him," Jake put in, "then some other of his folk. They'll always be trying, if not here, then somewhere."

"Always seeking more power," Joan said. "More territory. Never satisfied with what they have."

"Doesn't that sound familiar?" said Jake, the irony in his voice unmistakable this time.

Joan felt an inner sting of truth. "Yeah. Guess we have more in common with the sidhe than I like to think."

Jake drove Joan and Gillian all the way back to Dawson Butte that very night, claiming he had to make some deliveries to the Front Range anyway. Joan pitched in for gas with what little money she had left on her. Joan and Gillian slept much of the way in the back of the station wagon. Drifting in and out of dreams, Joan imagined seeing Miriam floating among the stars. She wanted to shout up questions to her, but Miriam couldn't hear her.

They did not get home until about five the next morning.

Joan walked Gillian up the steps to her apartment and opened the door with her copy of the key. She went in with Gillian to make sure everything was all right.

Gillian turned on the light. From what Joan could see, the apartment was just the way it had been before it had been trashed. Only much, much tidier. The computer hummed on the desk, showing a screen saver of a starry night sky. The stereo system was intact. Everything was clean, and there was the scent of night-blooming flowers in the air.

"Hey, good cleanup job," Gillian said. "I'm glad I hired you."

"Um, thanks, but I can't take credit. I think you'd better put out milk and cookies tonight."

"Yeah? Okay, but anyway . . ." She turned and faced Joan, tears starting to run down her guilt-ridden face. "I owe you so much . . . everything."

"You owe me three hundred and seventy-five bucks. I paid your rent for last month. Other than that, forget about it. What are friends for?"

"Usually not for chasing down high sidhe wizards."

"Think I should add it to my advertising? Houses cleaned, spells revoked, wizards chastised?"

Gillian laughed, covering her mouth. "Better not. You don't know what kind of business you'd get. But your friend Miriam, she's—"

"She's probably happier wherever she is. Don't fret about it. Get some rest. And, uh, maybe you should choose a different subject for your thesis, huh?"

Gillian nodded. "Yeah. Damn, it's way too late to change direction. Maybe I'll take a year off, do something else. I'll always love music. But I won't be able to think about it the same way. I don't think I'll ever pick up a guitar again."

"Hey, I could use a new assistant in my cleaning biz."

Gillian grinned sadly. "No thanks. I'm allergic to dust."

A faint beep of a horn outside reminded Joan that Jake was still waiting. "Guess I'd better go. Stay in touch, okay?"

"Yeah." Gillian hugged her. "Thanks again."

"Sure," said Joan, pulling away quickly. "You're welcome. Good night." Joan gave Gillian her copy of the apartment key and ran back down to Jake's station wagon.

"Everything okay?" Jake asked.

"Yeah, I guess. Ever try to do your best to be helpful and kind to someone you're not sure deserves it?"

"All the time," said Jake. "All the time."

When they at last pulled up to Joan's place, she thought she'd never been so happy to see her somber little hovel, in all her life. But the sight that most brought joy to her heart was that of her old white truck parked neatly on the driveway pad, in as good shape as ever.

"Looks like they kept their end of the bargain," Jake said.

"Yeah. It does. Um, Jake, I don't know how to thank you—"

"Then don't. But the schools on the rez could use a donation."

"They'll get one," Joan said, smiling. She didn't know what sort of farewell gesture would be proper, so she simply shook his hand and got out of the car. She waved as Jake pulled away from the curb and sped off into the night.

Joan strolled up the driveway in a state of tired relief. She ran her fingers along the side of the truck, noting that it seemed to have been repainted. In the bright starlight and predawn glow, it was hard to tell, but it seemed that the driveway was no longer cracked and the paint on the house was no longer peeling. *When they keep a bargain, they really keep it*, Joan thought.

She walked to the front door and found it intact. Joan opened it, found it swung open easily, and went inside. The first thing she noticed was that the smell of dog urine was gone, replaced by the scent of wildflowers. A lone white taper candle was lit on her dining table, its faint light showing that her house had also been tidied, just like Gillian's place. The answering machine's red light was blinking furiously.

Joan closed the door behind her and went to the table. The candle had no drippings on it, as if it had been lit the moment Joan had come in. On the table beside it were a folded piece of heavy paper, perhaps parchment, and a delicate columbine blossom that appeared to be made of silver. Joan opened up the paper and read what was written on it:

> Praise and prize of battle go
> to her who is the honored foe
> But he who fought and got away
> shall fight again another day. . . .
>
> A

"Of course," Joan muttered. "But people will notice, now, when you do." She blew out the candle and staggered off to bed.

Joan got up late the next morning and didn't even bother to check her answering machine. Instead, she went down to the hospital. She hadn't really believed it could be true, but when she walked into Agnes's room, Agnes was sitting up in bed with only an oxygen tube to her nose.

Agnes grinned and said in her raspy voice, "Well, howdy, Joan! I heard you'd been to visit me while I was out. Bet I wasn't looking my best then."

"Hey, who would be?" Joan said, unable to keep from smiling. "I'm just glad to see you're better again. What does the doctor say?"

"Says it's a miracle. Calls it a, what, a spontaneous remission, or what-have-you. Doctors don't like it 'cause it's rare and can't be explained. I just figure the right people musta been prayin' for me. Anyways, he wants me to stay one more day for observation and if everything checks out I can go home tomorrow."

Joan grasped her hand. "I'm so glad, Agnes. I'm just . . . I'm so glad."

She left the hospital in a strange, happy daze, feeling as though she had gotten away with something amazing. All the damage undone. *Is this how my namesake felt after winning her first big battle?* Joan wondered. *Or did she just always know she would win?*

She went home again and finally faced the answering machine. Two messages were from clients returning her requests to reschedule. Then Miriam's voice came on, sounding far away.

"Hi, Joan? Can't talk long. I think I've done it! Anyway, there should be a big surprise awaiting you. Hope you won't be mad. Bye!"

The time stamp on the machine wasn't working, so Joan didn't know when the call had been made. *It must have been before Miriam met me at the hospital, before we made our long and final dash to Mesa Verde. But what had she done that was a surprise she hoped I wouldn't be mad at? Getting that information about Amadan?* Joan had an intense wish to call Miriam back, to tell her that Agnes was all right, and that her house was all right, and to tell Miriam about Amadan's note—and remembered that, of course, she couldn't. Miriam might as well be dead, as far as this world was concerned. She would never see Miriam again. Or hear her latest strange divination, or her laughter.

Tears began to leak out of Joan's eyes, and she put her hands over her face.

The phone rang, preternaturally loud, right beside her, startling Joan out of her doldrums. For a moment she had the impossible thought that it might be Miriam again. Or Amadan calling to gloat. He had used the phone before, although it was while he had been in this world. The phone rang a second time before she picked it up. "Hello?" she said, her voice cracking.

"Joan? Is that you? This is Bernie down at the police station."

"Oh. Bernie. Hi. Just a sec." Joan grabbed for some nearby tissues and wiped the tears from her face and blew her nose.

"You okay, Joan?"

"Yeah, yeah. Just . . . some allergy or other."

"Yeah, I hear the pollen count's high this season. Listen, I'm calling to check back on whether you've heard anything new about your stolen guitar. Our guys haven't seen the perp you described anywhere in town."

"Oh, I'm sorry, Bernie. I shoulda called sooner. I've been out of town. I just got back in late last night. I ran into the guy out in Cortez. Everything's okay."

"So you got the guitar back?"

"Yeah, yeah. Turns out it was all just a practical joke."

"Heh. A lot of that going around lately. Things have been pretty weird around here the last couple days. Lotta false alarms and stuff. Weird. I'm not allowed to talk about it, but let's just say some of us are gonna be needin' vacations real soon."

"I . . . understand. Sort of. Hey, did you hear the good news? Agnes, who had the stroke? She's fully recovered and will probably go home tomorrow."

"Hey," said Bernie, "that is good news. How often do you get a total recovery like that?"

"Not very often," said Joan. "She figures it's a miracle."

"Yeah, well, we could use a few of them. Oh, say, that reminds me, did you ever hear from her tenant, Gillian McKeagh?"

"Oh, God, I should have called you about that too. I saw her late last night, when I was coming in. She'd just gotten back from a long trip herself."

"So she's back in town? We can talk to her?"

"Sure, you can call her, but I'd be a little easy on her right now. She's just been through a real tough time."

"Okay, I'll pass that along. Well, thanks again. Glad your missing guitar turned up. Hey, call me sometime when I'm not on duty. We can catch up on stuff."

"Sure, Bernie. Thanks for all your trouble. Bye." Joan wondered whether she should call Gillian and warn her that the police would be calling and help her decide what to say. Then she wondered if her phone was tapped or the police checked phone records and if such a call would look suspicious. Joan decided she was being paranoid but didn't call anyway, figuring Gillian could manage her own alibis.

Instead, Joan began to call her regular clients, trying to reestablish her business, and her life. Trying to ground herself in reality once more. Though she wondered, now, if she had ever known what reality was.

* * *

The next day, Joan returned from her last client to find the message on her answering machine she'd been dreading:

"Hello, Joan Dark?" said a male voice, "This is John Sanderson—you know, Miriam's father? Listen, something rather strange has come up, and I wonder if you could meet me at my office tomorrow in the Larkspur Building downtown. I've something to discuss with you, but I'd rather not do it over the phone. I'll be in from noon till four, so if you could come in during that time, I'd appreciate it. Thank you. G'bye."

Oh, God, Joan thought, *he's going to ask me where Miriam is. We should have asked the Amadan— No. There's no way one wish could have solved this problem. I'll have to think of something. Too bad he wants face time. It would have been easier to lie over the phone. Maybe that's why he wants to see me in person.*

Joan wolfed down a TV dinner and spent a long, restless night trying to think of what to tell him.

She went to Mr. Sanderson's office at one o'clock the next day, dressed a little better than usual, in a skirt and blouse. The Larkspur Building was one of the first edifices built in Dawson Butte, in 1880, and had first housed railroad offices, then a bank, then a hotel. Now it was a historic landmark, but the upstairs was back to being offices again, of a pricey sort.

Joan found Mr. Sanderson's office a bit sooner than her jumpy nerves would have liked. But she swallowed her fear and went in.

To her surprise, as soon as she was through the door, she found the place soothing and pleasant. Tall windows let in lots of air and light. Plants were everywhere, in colorful Mexican pots large and small. Corkboards hung on the walls with architectural drawings pinned to them, representing projects under development. A large desk of wood stained golden brown stood off to the side, surrounded by comfortable-looking office chairs. Joan noticed the computer on the desk sat in what Miriam would have called the "money spot," and then she also saw the chunk of amethyst geode by the door. Joan smiled. Miriam had clearly advised her father on good *feng shui.*

Mr. Sanderson looked up from his computer terminal, smiled, and came around his desk to greet her. He had sandy brown hair, graying at the temples and crown, and was wearing a casual polo shirt and chinos. He stuck out his hand and shook hers warmly, and his expression was pleasant, open, though a little worried. Joan found to her dismay that she could not hate him, despite the fact that he was going to put a mall on what had been her family's ranch. And she began to think perhaps Miriam's sensitive nature had come from her dad.

"Thanks for stopping by," Mr. Sanderson said, starting to pace the office as Joan sat down on one of the office chairs. With one hand on his waist, the other rubbing through his hair, he continued, "I'm afraid this is kinda awkward, and really I should be dealing with your father, but I can't seem to locate him."

My dad? Oh, God, am I going to have to deal with some picky legal detail about the sale of the ranch? Can Fate twist the knife any harder? "Yeah, he and Mom are on the road a lot these days. The last I heard, they were going through the Dakotas. They call me about once a week, though, if there's something you'd like me to pass on to them."

"Well, I'm afraid I have to deal with this quickly, and you dad had left word that I could run matters through you if I had to."

"What sort of matters?" Joan asked, resigned, trying to remember the name of the family lawyer, only she couldn't recall any lawyer involved in the sale.

"About your ranch. See, I got a disturbing tip yesterday. Seems the appraisers happened to overlook a little something before the sale. A little matter of . . ." He cleared his throat. ". . . of mine tailings."

"Mine tailings?" Joan asked, astonished. "There were never any mines on that land!"

"Well, now, that turns out not to be the case. Although it's clear your folks didn't know about it, so I don't think it would be right to sue them, although legally I could. After I got the rumor I sent an inspector over right away. Here's what he found."

Mr. Sanderson took some papers off the desk. The top sheet was a crude map of the land that had been the Dark ranch. He pointed at some symbols at the southeast corner. "Here, on the land near Hunt Mountain, is where he located a small tunnel and shaft. It was probably just recently revealed by a landslide, maybe triggered by a little earthquake, maybe too small for anyone to feel. Anyway, the mine looks to be about 1890s work, he figured. Somebody was trying to dig for gold there."

"Gold?" asked Joan. "That's ridiculous. You find gold up in places like Cripple Creek, not down here."

"Well, there were a lot of desperate men back in those days, and they tried their luck anywhere. Maybe this miner didn't know enough or got cheated. There's no record of a claim in the quick check I did of local records, but that's not too surprising. Claim-jumping and illegal mines weren't unknown back then. When it proved unproductive, either the guy covered it up or a handy rockslide hid it."

"Huh." Joan remembered hiking there sometimes, as a kid, especially when she needed to get away from the folks for a while, but she couldn't remember any rock-falls in the area.

"The inspector did a few tests on the tailings—you know, the dirt that's piled outside the tunnel. Sure enough, he found arsenic, lead, and copper. Not enough to declare it a Superfund site, but the EPA might get just a tad concerned. And any buyer for the properties we were thinking of building there might end up socked with a whopping cleanup fee. Which might make said prospective buyer a tad skittish. And if I tried to sell it without telling buyers, lawsuits would fall on me. Just for starters. You see that we have a little problem here."

Joan felt her stomach sink to her feet. "I assure you my folks and I had no idea about that mine!"

"Yeah. Well, I believe you. I don't know how it happened, but this is a cutthroat business, and word has already somehow leaked out."

"Do you have enemies in the business?"

"Don't need enemies when your friends are all vying for the same buyers."

"Ranchers are sometimes the same way. Competitive. Maybe my folks have enemies they haven't told me about. Who was it who gave you the bad news about the mine?"

"Gave his name as Buck Jones. I've never heard of him, and he's not in the phone book in town. Could be an alias, I guess."

A creepy feeling came over Joan, like a hundred spiders crawling up her back. "Buck Jones? He, uh, didn't have a deep, gravelly voice, did he?"

"Yeah, guess you could describe it that way. Someone you know?"

"I met a guy by that name once, recently, but I can't imagine what he'd have to do with this." *Unless the Amadan is trying to get really strange revenge . . . but Jones said he'd never had anything to do with the Amadan.*

Mr. Sanderson shrugged. "Or it might be a coincidence. Now my current buyer—"

"The one who wants to put up a factory outlet mall?"

"The very same. Naturally now he wants out of the deal. He can't afford to clean it up to EPA standards. So you could say I'm stuck holding the bag."

"I'm . . . I'm really sorry." Joan was having decidedly mixed feelings. A part of her was pleased there would be no mall, but she knew it was a lot of money for Mr. Sanderson to lose, and this bad news might backfire on her family.

Mr. Sanderson sat down again at his desk and leaned forward on his elbows. "Now here's what I'd like to suggest we do. I hope you don't take this the wrong way, but I did a little investigation on your family's finances. I have a friend who works in management at the Butte Bank. And he told me about your little trust fund."

"Trust fund," Joan repeated. *But I don't have a trust fund.*

"Yeah, the one your parents set up for you five years ago?"

This is crazy, Joan thought. *They never told me about*

any trust fund. Why would Dad set it up and not tell me?
"Um," was all she said in reply.

"Anyway, apparently they stuck much of what I paid them for the ranch into that fund, as well as a good chunk of savings. So, here's what I'd like to do. I know I'm about to take a bath on that land anyway, and Miriam has told me that you kinda miss your old homestead."

Miriam? When did she tell you that? thought Joan.

"Rather than go through all the legal mess of trying to find fault and fix blame, here's what I'll do. I'd be willing to sell this portion of the property, the part possibly affected by the mine tailings, back to you for the money you got in your fund. As you can see, that's nearly half the ranch. That price is more than competitive by market standards, and I could develop and sell the northern half, so at least I wouldn't be losing everything. Would you be willing to consider such a deal?"

Joan's mouth dropped open. *The ranch. He's telling me I can have the ranch back. For money I never even knew I had. A miracle! Or part of the Amadan's bargain to make things the way they were? Or the work of grateful elves of a different sort?* She recalled Miriam's message on the answering machine, and how Miriam had said she'd try to take care of things from the Other Side. Was this her work, her parting gift? Joan felt a warm glow growing inside her. "Why, yes, Mr. Sanderson. I think it would only be right for you to get some compensation, after this terrible surprise. I will be happy to take our ranch back off your hands."

"Phew. I can't tell you what a relief that is. Now, I gotta be honest with you. If you buy it back, given that pollution and stuff, you'll have a devil of a time ever selling it again to anyone else until those tailings get cleaned up, and that can be mighty costly."

Joan smiled. "I think I can deal with that somehow."

She filled out some forms and got the process rolling, and as she stood to leave, Mr. Sanderson said, "By the way, Miriam says hi."

Joan nearly dropped her purse. "She does? You've heard from her? I mean, I hadn't . . . um . . . how is she?"

He made a dismissive wave. "Oh, you know how that kid is. Flighty. She dropped by the other night to say she was going off to some island or other to study some woo-woo philosophy or something and that we should terminate the lease on her apartment and sell her stuff. She looked happy, but I do worry about that girl. Hope she hasn't joined some cult. Wonder if she'll ever settle down."

"I got the feeling she'd been pretty busy lately," Joan said. "But as long as she's happy . . ."

"I know. She's a legal adult. She can make her own choices. What else can we do?"

Joan shook his hand, they made an appointment to arrange the next step of the land transfer, and Joan left his office feeling so light it was as though she were borne on fairy wings.

Epilogue

As evening was falling, Joan took one of the boarded horses out for a short ride. It had been a year since she had gotten the ranch back, and she was almost making a profit, though she expected to be in the red for a few more months. She still had to take the occasional cleaning job to make ends meet, but they were getting fewer and fewer. Maybe by next year she could see about getting a horse of her own. She'd been talking to some breeders down by Pueblo who had some reasonable Arab/quarter mixes.

She'd gotten the land back too late to get the house—it had been razed already. But the barn had still been intact. So she had moved a single-wide trailer beside it and figured someday, when money rolled in, she'd build a new house. Prefabs were coming down in price, she's noticed, but her real dream was to put up a log house. Someday.

The cool early-summer breeze blew around her, swaying the bushes beside the trail. It had been a wet spring, and so the land was green and blossoming. She rounded a little hill and noticed a ring of mushrooms had grown up out of nowhere.

Hasn't been that wet, Joan thought.

The air within the ring of mushrooms shimmered, and Miriam appeared, sitting on the ground, in a beautiful pale green dress. Her long, curly brown hair flowed over her shoulders like the figure in a Raphael painting. She looked radiant. Serene. Beautiful.

The horse whinnied in surprise and took a step back.

"Hey," Miriam said.

"Um, hey there," Joan said, when she got her wits back. "Looks like living in fairyland agrees with you."

Miriam smiled. "It has its good points."

"Um, how . . . why . . ."

Miriam shrugged. "It's Midsummer Eve. I can be anywhere I want tonight. No special dispensations necessary. I thought I'd stop by and see how you were doing."

"I'm . . . wow, I'm . . . great. I'm doing good. You know, I can never thank you enough for giving me . . . this." Joan swept her arm around to indicate the ranch.

"You're welcome. I felt I owed it to you."

"You didn't owe me anything. It's Gillian who owes us."

"How is she? I stopped by her place, but someone else lives there now."

"Last I heard, she had gone to Egypt on some ethnomusicology study program. She hasn't talked with me much since getting back from Mesa Verde. I only got the rent money she owed me just before she left for Cairo."

"Maybe she felt guilty," said Miriam, "and that made it hard for her to deal with you. Anyway, if she gets herself turned into a mummy over there, it'll be someone else's problem."

Joan chuckled. "I guess. Um . . . about that trust

fund that suddenly appeared at my bank. Did you set that up?"

With a sly grin, Miriam said, "You'd be surprised how easy it is to alter electronic records from the Other Side. Almost as good as fairy gold."

"Wait—so you bilked your own father to give me this land back?"

"No, not exactly. Don't worry, it will all balance out."

"Balance—"

"You don't want to know."

"I'm beginning to get a bad feeling about this," said Joan.

"All fairy gifts have their price," said Miriam. "But don't worry—I'm the one doing the paying."

"Miriam—"

"It's all right. I'm where I belong, just as you are now. A lot of . . . service is expected of me these first few years. What's a little more to make my friends happy?"

"Service? Miriam, what did you get yourself into?"

"Oh, it's not what you think. Not . . . all of it, that is. Since Lord Amadan had to lose Colorado for the time being, he's set his sights on California—which I know pretty well. I console myself with the knowledge that they will hardly notice our meddling there."

"Are you saying people from California are gullible and oblivious?"

"You think?" asked Miriam, coyly chewing on a fingernail.

"Working for the enemy," Joan said softly.

Miriam stared at the ground. "The sidhe aren't always the enemy."

"They aren't our friends . . . humanity's friends."

"They have gifts to offer."

"With high prices."

"Well . . . yeah," Miriam conceded.

"But you're happy?"

"Mostly. Oh, the music get monotonous sometimes. I wish somebody Over There would learn some hip-hop or salsa. And some of Lord Amadan's friends are pompous jerks. But I'm . . . fitting in. I can't imagine living anywhere else now."

Joan found herself at a loss for words, not knowing whether she should shrug off the heavy blanket of guilt descending on her.

"But, hey, enough about me." Miriam went on, in a perky tone. "Found any good cowboys yet?"

Joan smiled. "I've got my eyes on a likely prospect."

"Well, you'd better round that steer up, girl, and brand 'im. Time's a-wastin'."

"There's no sense in spooking a bull so's he runs away. I'll handle my own love life, thank you, and you handle yours. Um, do sidhe have a love life?"

"Love life! Hah! You wouldn't believe it. It's amazing! They—" Then she paused and seemed to think better of it. "Um . . . it's complicated."

"I'll take your word for it."

"Do. Well, I gotta flit. I wanna see how my folks are doing."

"Okay. Thanks for stopping by. Feel free to sit among my toadstools whenever. Just watch out for the horse flops."

"Thanks. I can visit once a year, at least. If you need me for anything any other time . . . ask Frank at the Angel's Wing. He'll know how to reach me."

"Sure. Right. Of course. You take care now."

Miriam stood and dusted off her dress. "You too. A

last word of advice—don't go boarding any phookas. They'll only give you trouble."

"Boarding any *what?*"

Miriam smiled, shimmered, and vanished in a cloud of sparkling motes.

The horse whinnied again and shook its head.

"I'm with you, buckaroo," Joan said, and with a nudge in its ribs, they moved out down the trail.

Author's Note

Two of the locations used in this work, Dawson Butte and Summit Rock, are fictional although based upon a blending of features of genuine towns in the area in which they are placed. This was done for authorial whim and the freedom to have the buildings and locations be as I needed them. The rest of the cities, towns, and features mentioned in the book, with one or two minor exceptions, are real.